This book is a work of fiction. References to real people,events, establishments, organisations, places or locales are intended only to provide a sense of authenticity and are used fictitiously.
All other characters and all incidents and dialogue are drawn from the author's imagination and are not to be construed as real.

For My Beautiful Girls
Heather & Bella

CONTENTS

1. Prologue
#FamousForAllTheWrongReasons

Having taken a taxi directly from John Lennon International Airport, Terror now found himself waiting in the impressive Reception Area of the newly redeveloped Majestic Hotel, Liverpool. If his intelligence was correct, the man he was here to meet was a creature of habit who had opulent tastes and the need for discretion, so this location would be a natural choice for him.

The man, Owen Grant was a Belfast-born TV and Radio presenter, who after achieving success in his home Province, was now plying his trade UK-wide to a high degree of success. As he sat watching the comings and goings of the beautifully designed, yet understated Reception Area, Terror allowed himself to relish in the thoughts of a murder that he had so meticulously planned. His experience of Grant was that of a second-rate journalist who enjoyed the fame and reputation of taking on the Political and Celebrity heavyweights, and winning. The general public and even many of his opponents, seemed to be charmed by the man of the people persona that he presented. The thirty something, working class hero, whose self-mocking references to his gangly figure and his reluctance to truly leave the nest of his now elderly parents endeared him to them. Terror was not fooled.

The movement of an approaching taxi outside snapped Terror back to reality. He watched as Grant struggled out of the taxi with his luggage and paid the driver. As he entered the hotel and moved toward the Reception desk, Terror nodded subtly and smiled at him. He knew that Grant was very publicly guarded about his sexuality. He also, as a journalist himself knew that there were a number of injunctions in place, preventing any media outlet from 'outing' him.

Terror was aware that his chiselled features and the way his tailored suit moulded itself around his athletic frame, may catch the attention of Grant and it looked like he was right. As Grant picked up his room key, Terror moved quickly toward him.

'Excuse Me Sir, I hope you don't mind me asking but are you Owen Grant'? his dialect betraying his own Belfast roots

'Yes, I am' replied Grant somewhat shyly.

'I'm a huge fan of your work,' gushed Terror, 'would you mind giving a short interview for the folk back home?'

Mr Grant was about to become part of a Media sensation that would elevate his fame much more than he could ever have hoped.

2.

Bemoaning the fact that yet again she had caught the graveyard shift, the Majestic Hotel's newest recruit, Junior Receptionist, Jessica Miller began to update the social profile of the hotel. Just as she had logged on to the Majestic's Twitter account, a new post came in from the account of Owen Grant. She gasped in horror as her eyes locked on the picture of the naked and dead body of Owen Grant, posed upon the bed of the room that her colleague had checked him into earlier. Around the body were strewn a number of cards advertising male escort agencies and on the left thigh, in what looked like black sharpie pen, was scrawled, #FamousForAllTheWrongReasons.

Beside the picture, the post read:

#TheRiseofTerror #TheMajesticHotel

#TheOwenGrant #FamousForAllTheWrongReasons.

From his clearly less lavishly appointed room in the budget city centre hotel, Terror delighted himself in watching the 24 hour television news coverage reporting on his handiwork.

Outwardly he appeared relaxed, nursing a heavy tumbler containing equal quantities of vodka and coke over ice, whilst sprawled across the luridly patterned and dated bed clothing. Inside however, he was buzzing. Having had his fill of indulging in the televised media frenzy surrounding the death of Owen Grant, he was now consumed in thoughts of his own genius in executing his plan so efficiently, right down to

using Grants smartphone to publicise the murder via the media personality's Facebook and Twitter accounts. These thoughts gave way to his replaying the killing in his mind.
He relished in the fear in Grant's eyes as he realised that what he had thought would be a casual dalliance was to be something much more sinister. Relish progressed to sheer elation as the fear in Grant turned to despair, then finally acceptance, before Terror released his stranglehold of the now lifeless body.
Drifting back to consciousness of the room around him, Terror began to feel weary from the night's events. He drained his glass before turning off the TV and setting the alarm on his iPhone. All too soon he would be flying back to Northern Ireland to his cubicle at the Belfast Chronicle, to fill pages of saccharine laced copy on the, 'tragic murder' of Ulster's own Owen Grant. At least he had a headline in mind already. THE RISE OF TERROR.

3.
Part One- Farset Investigations

The first gulp of my third coffee of the morning did little to abate the feelings of stress and fatigue that were now so familiar to me. You would think that so much coffee wouldn't help anyhow, and you would be right.

The truth however, was that although poured, the previous two cups had long since gone cold before I could get near them, hence the gulping down of this one. I had only just put the cup down when my secretary appeared in the door frame.

'I'm sorry Mr Shaw but she insisted that she must see you immediately' explained Nicola with a scowl, as one of my more fragile teachers pushed past her in floods of tears, saying something between sobs, about not being invited to a colleague's birthday party. Not exactly what I thought I was signing up for when as a relatively inexperienced twenty eight year old, I unexpectedly found myself as Principal of the now illustrious Causeway Academy.

Through a combination of ambition and fear of failure, I'd guided the school to considerable success and reputation so far, but it has come at a cost. My drive and energy have been replaced by a high blood pressure diagnosis and an increasingly expanding waistline. Not an ideal combination for a now, almost 40 year old parent of an exuberant three year old daughter. Still, at least it won't be long now until I leave for the day and Mr Shaw can become just plain Mark.

After putting the teacher at ease until her next crisis, probably within the hour, I managed to usher her out the door with the intention of putting a dent in some paperwork. Before long though, I found myself distracted from the monotony of administration by my own thoughts on my dinner plans.
I've been looking forward to this evening since I had the call from Uncle Sean last night. We haven't met up in quite a while and I was looking forward to catching up with the almost 70 year old eccentric reporter turned investigator. He did seem a little preoccupied when he asked me to dinner though. I wondered why, as he normally wasn't the worrying type. Maybe I'm being concerned for no reason. We've always been close so I'm sure he will speak to me about it later if there is anything wrong, preferably without spoiling my enjoyment of the peppered steak that I have been dreaming about since his call ended.

4.

The rain pounding heavily down upon him barely registered with Terror as he sat crouched in the dark, walled corner of what used to be the garden area of his former Primary School on the Falls Road. He had chosen the perfect vantage point to wait for the old man to leave. It was almost 19:00 so according to routine, Sean Brady would be exiting the building any time now.

The last of the rush hour evening traffic had tailed off and the area was eerily quiet. The old building had long since shed its use as a school, and after years of neglect and decay in the shadows of the imposing Divis Tower, had been bought by Brady, who had grand designs to return it to its former glory by converting it into a suite of offices. For now though, it remained virtually derelict, apart from the space currently used by Brady as a base for his private investigation agency.

It was a low rent operation, staffed by Brady himself. Being almost 70 years old, it was surprising to think that the old man hadn't retired. Surely at his age, business would not be brisk and judging by the figure that had just appeared in Terror's line of sight, neither was its sole proprietor.

Terror sprang forward toward the old man, pulling the knife from its sheath as he moved. The knife pierced his gut almost before Brady had realised he was under attack. Terror pushed him hard to the ground before stabbing him twice more.

Blood was pooling quickly as Terror removed the phone and

wallet. He could barely look his victim in the face and was struggling keep the hot tears pricking the backs of his own eyes, from rolling down his cheeks, as he heard the sickening, gurgling sounds as bloody bubbles erupted from a perforated lung. There was no pleasure to be had in this kill. No exhilaration, just sheer anguish.

As Terror ran from the scene, he fought the urge to spill the contents of his own stomach onto the pavement. Only his desire not to leave any DNA evidence in the area suppressed the urge. Instead he maintained a steady run until he reached the top of Tate's Avenue. Here he slowed to a walk until he reached his home at the bottom of Malone Avenue.

5.

The clock on the dashboard of my beloved 5 Series read 19:44 as I pulled off the Westlink at Divis Street. I had called home after work to change and check in with Beth and Alecia and ended up staying to tuck Alecia into bed, so was running a few minutes late. I'd thought about calling Sean to let him know but decided that he had probably already left and wouldn't be that far away from the restaurant now anyway, as it was quite close to his office.

I had wanted to try, "Happy Grillmore's" since Belfast-born celebrity chef, Jason Callum opened it recently in premises just facing the Royal Victoria Hospital. Sean had made a booking for us for tonight. It occurred to me that I should've offered to pick him up from work on the way past. I began to speed up a little to make up some time. Not only do I hate to keep anyone waiting, I was also quite hungry.

As I neared Divis Tower I had to brake sharply as I noticed that the road ahead had been cordoned off by the police. My heart almost reached my mouth as I realised that there seemed to be a lot of activity around the front entrance of the old St Comgall's building, my former school.

I pulled the car up tight near one of the police cars and got out. I walked quickly toward the nearest police officer and introduced myself. Having explained that I was en route to meet my elderly Uncle, who as it happened was the proprietor of the building they had sealed off, the young officer took me through the cordon and introduced me to a DI Black, who seemingly was in charge. Again I outlined who I was and my relationship as next-of-kin to Uncle Sean. Having listened to what I had to say, Black's expression tightened slightly.

'Mr Shaw, I'm afraid that we've just been alerted to the discovery of a body on the premises', he said.

I tried to speak but I couldn't find the words.

'We were called to the scene by a local tour operator who had been giving his final taxi tour of the day, and was speaking to his tour group, when he noticed someone in a dark hooded top run from the school. He's from the area and knows that the old building is often subject to vandalism from local youths. He was afraid that a fire may have been set, so left the tourists to take pictures of the murals while he checked out the school. That's when…'

'It can't be him. He would have already left by now', I said, wishing to myself that I was more sure.

Shaking at the prospect of what might be, I removed my phone from my pocket and quickly dialled Sean's number. This has to be a mistake, I thought. It couldn't be him. The phone went directly to voicemail. That's when I knew. Sean never turned his phone off. Everyone who knew him knew that.

I struggled to focus as I tried to process the information that Sean may be dead. I tried my best to listen as Black added that it looked like the victim, an elderly gentleman, had been violently attacked and robbed.

'I need to see him'. I pushed past only to be quickly restrained by Black and the assisting Officer who had introduced us.

Finding myself becoming increasingly enraged as I struggled to shake off my captors, I cursed them as Black tried to engage me rationally.
'Mr Shaw, the area is a crime scene. We cannot allow it to be corrupted'.
The fight in me quickly gave way and they loosened their grip as I collapsed into floods of tears. Black, his tone remaining calm, instructed me to go ahead of them to the morgue at the Royal Victoria Hospital. Once the crime scene had been processed, he himself would meet me at Reception and I would be called upon to identify the body.
The younger officer, whose name it occurred to me later, I hadn't even asked for, escorted me back to my car and asked if I needed directions. Unfortunately, this would not be my first visit to the city mortuary, so with the little voice I had left, I replied, 'No thanks, I know where I'm going'.

6.

My heart raced as fast as the car did as I drove the short distance to the mortuary area at the back of the hospital. Upon arriving at Reception I was informed that I was expected, and was shown into a private waiting area.

The passing of the next hour felt like an eternity as my emotions peaked and troughed between waves of anxiety and rationality. My impulse was telling me to call Beth but I didn't want anyone else to have to worry, perhaps unnecessarily. The arrival of Black sent my anxiety into overdrive. In the dark of the crime scene and in my state of shock, I had barely studied his features. Now, as he stood before me in the harsh lights of the waiting room, I studied his broad, solid six foot plus frame, his dark, serious features and the deep intonation of his voice as he explained the process for identification.

I could see how that despite looking like a relatively young man, he came to be in charge at the crime scene. The more I looked at him, the more I realised that his image, for good or bad, would be seared into my memory, and that I would forever associate him with the loss of my Uncle Sean.

Black led me through an adjacent door, down a short corridor. At the end of the corridor, to the right, was another door that opened into a small, windowless room. The covered gurney had been placed in the centre of the room under the harsh lighting. Black moved towards the sheet covering the body and after exchanging nods with me, pulled the sheet back a little. I was numbed as my gaze fell upon the face of what was once Sean Brady, the man I had loved and owed so much to. He was forever lost to me now and would never see his beloved Alecia grow up. Despite Black being at my side, the return walk along that short corridor was the loneliest journey I have ever taken.

7.

Terror sat still in the armchair he had taken refuge in upon returning home a few hours before. He shivered from the cold of his wet clothes, and the cold sweat that had enveloped him from the moment he felt the knife pierce the old man's flesh. His thoughts had been at war with one another since then also.

He tried to justify to himself that Brady posed a threat to his freedom with what he had seemingly unveiled. Terror's mission was too important to allow such a threat. Yet long before he had become Terror, Brady was such a good friend to his family and such a big part of his life. He had even saved him from himself after the death of his mother when he was just sixteen. That was before life took a darker turn, before his father had introduced him to his own alter-ego, The Ghost, and began his initiation into the murky world of the hired assassin.

Shortly after that time, Brady was to disappear out of his life, at least that was until a few days ago. He had resented Brady for all those years that they had been apart, blaming him for how he was treated by his Father, how he was forced to watch and later take part in orchestrated murders that would be conveniently looked upon as being unclaimed Loyalist or Republican attacks.

For a long time Terror could not have called which of the two men he hated more, his Father or Brady. Since tonight though, a sure opinion crystallised in his mind, The Ghost had made him what he was. He had created Terror, now he must deal with the consequences. Terror has arisen and the world would take notice.

8.

After four months, the day had finally come. As I stood on the stage in the school hall delivering what was to be my final assembly, I felt excited, but as I looked out at the audience of present and past pupils, parents and governors, I also felt fear and relief simultaneously at the prospect of my leaving. There was no going back now. My life had changed.

In losing Uncle Sean, I had gained his fortune, which was a vast and largely unexpected sum. I'd also gained a steely determination that I would see his killer pay for what they had taken from me, from us. If that meant the termination of my employment here, then so be it. I had been looking for a new challenge for a while and truth be told, although I liked my job, there were elements of the moral practices of the community that I served, that had bothered me more and more as the years had passed, though taking up the sole directorship at Farset Investigations had never before figured in my mind.

Having bid my final farewells, and now clutching the mandatory Bible presented to the lost alumni of the Academy's Headteachers, I gave a final wave to my successor and close friend, Caitlin Price, who had worked alongside me for many years and would, I was sure, have the skills to take the school on to even greater success, though I knew she shared many of my concerns.

I pulled out of the car park, deciding not to look back. Little did I realise the draw the place would have on me, and that before too long I would return in horrible circumstances. For now though, I had arranged to meet DI Black at the old St Comgall's building, my building, to be officially given the keys and have the placed signed off as a crime scene.

The police had found little in the way of leads in their investigation and to his credit, I detected a genuine note of disappointment in Black's tone, when he had informed me a few days ago, that the case was to be closed.

9.

'Mr Shaw, this is DCI Tom Ferguson from Merseyside Police, it seems that your Uncle Sean had tried to make contact with him in relation to a case he is working on,' said Black as I approached the entrance to the St. Comgall's building.
Ferguson, a pleasant looking younger man of medium build and fair complexion, extended his hand in greeting.
' Hello Mr Shaw. I'm very sorry to hear of your loss. Mr Brady left a message for me on my voicemail just a few days before his death. I had been trying to return his call a number of times and was trying to make contact with him ever since, until I found out through calling DI Black, what had happened. Your Uncle said he had some information for me regarding a case I'm currently working on, the murder of Owen Grant, are you familiar with it'?
'Of course. Practically everyone in Northern Ireland would be, though I don't know how Uncle Sean would be connected to the investigation. I'm about to have a look around the office myself, you're welcome to join me'.
'That'd be great, if you don't mind,' said Ferguson, his strong Scouse dialect reminding me of the former Liverpool defender, Jamie Carragher. With that, I thanked Black again for all he had done for our family. We shook hands and he departed with a solemn goodbye.
It had been a while since I'd been at Sean's office and was surprised at how warm and homely it was in comparison to the corridors and classrooms around it. The large oak desk,

presumably the Former Headmaster's looked impressive where it was stationed near the window. For a brief moment I felt a pang of regret at walking away from my own office but there was work to be done.

'OK, first thing's first', I said as I powered up the Mac on Sean's desk and began to unlock the drawers beneath it.

'I'll check his diary and recent documents, could you open the filing cabinets and see if you can make sense of the system? I want to start with any active cases he may have been working on, and we can see if there is any mention of Owen Grant or anything that might lead us to his or Sean's killer'.

'I thought I was the DIC around here', joked Ferguson, 'you're certainly starting how you mean to go on'.

I smiled at him, blooming with embarrassment as he took the keys and began matching the correct key to its corresponding lock, whilst I correctly guessed Sean's password on the first attempt. Alecia. Maybe I do have a flair for detective work after all.

Ferguson had quickly worked out that the files in the cabinets were either archived cold, or were solved cases from some years ago. Sean had always been keen to move with the times in some areas of his life I mused, though not quite so much in others.

'It looks like we are relying on what we can turn up from the computer', said Ferguson, as he quickly checked through the desk drawers on either side of me, 'nothing in here worth talking about either, that's strange!'

'Why?'

'There's no sign of any notebook or journal anywhere. All

detectives would carry some sort of book with them for when they are interviewing witnesses or suspects so there should be one somewhere'.
It suddenly dawned on me that he was right and that I knew exactly where it was. I hadn't been able to bring myself to open the personal effects bag when it was returned to me, nor have I since, but I do recall seeing a small, shabby-looking leather bound notebook through the clear polythene bag.
'I remember it. It's with his personal effects in my garage. I haven't been able to look at them yet.'
We agreed to continue to work at the computer for now, and that Ferguson would come back to the house with me for dinner, we could look at the notebook before he went to speak to Owen Grant's parents late in the evening, as he'd previously arranged.
I called Beth to bring her up to speed, then we began looking through the files on the computer. After about an hour, we had concluded that Brady had indeed been working on the Owen Grant case, and had also, according to his call log, been trying to call Ferguson. He only had one other case active, a young woman who was looking for her estranged brother. It looked like Brady had made some progress on this one and had been due to have a meeting with Patrick Rodgers, a medium at the local spiritualist centre, on the morning after his death. I decided to follow this up further and made up my mind to drop into the centre when it opened the next morning.

10.

Brian Wilson was sweating profusely, and had started to feel sick and disoriented, as he was about to take to the stage at Belfast's Waterfront Hall. As one of Northern Ireland's most successful former international footballers, he was about to move from his home in Cornwall, back to Northern Ireland, to take up his new role as President of the Irish Football Association.

He was here tonight at the premiere of a film chronicling his life, and as the guest of honour, he was to introduce it. He had come here directly from doing an interview with a local reporter at his hotel in the Titanic Quarter. He remembered how the young man had been so nice to him, insisting on buying him a pint of Guinness by way of a welcome home. He was regretting drinking it now though, as he wondered if it was perhaps interfering with his heart medication.

The MC introduced him, and as he took to the stage and began his speech in front of the packed house at the Waterfront Hall, he began to feel increasingly uneasy. He tried his best but knew he was stumbling over the words, slurring, and having trouble remembering what he had planned to say next. The last thing he saw was the MC, rushing toward him as he fell to the stage floor. After that everything went black, and the audience experienced an ending beyond the one burned onto the film biopic they were about to watch.

11.

As Terror sat in his seat in an upper tier of the auditorium, he watched as those around him frantically worked their phones to share the news. Some were even taking pictures and uploading them. He quickly followed suit and after retrieving his iPhone from his pocket , he logged on to his newly created Facebook account, using it to post links on both the Facebook and Twitter accounts of Brian Wilson successively, to a newspaper article linking Wilson to bribery and corruption.

Underneath the link, he typed:

#FamousForAllTheWrongReasons #TerrorAtTheWaterfront.

Terror knew full well that in providing a social media link directly to him, he had just created a following, and hoped that he would soon be able to bend some of them to his will. He had already been doing the groundwork on that in underground chatrooms for some months now. He also knew that without careful management, this link could be used as a means to catch him. He assured himself with the thought that he was intelligent and experienced enough to make certain that wouldn't happen.

As the Police were descending on the building, and the body of Brian Wilson was being removed, Terror logged out of his Facebook account, then into his work Facebook account as his alter ego, and like many other local journalists present on the night, quickly began to write a piece on the newsfeed on behalf of the Chronicle, not forgetting of course to highlight the fact that he had interviewed Wilson earlier in the day and that the interview would appear in tomorrow morning's edition.

12.

As we entered the house, Alecia came charging toward me, excitedly shouting, 'Daddy!', and ran into my usual hug. Beth smiled as she watched on. Straightening up, I introduced them both to Ferguson. The smell of Beth's speciality, slow cooked chicken stroganoff filled the air. It had been a long time since Ferguson or I had eaten, so we were quickly drawn to the dining room, where in between mouthfuls of our amazing meal, we recounted our day's events to each other. Beth and I got to know a little bit about Ferguson, and he us.

After spending a few hours with him today, I had already warmed to him and bizarrely, felt like we had been friends for a long time. He was now standing up well to the interrogations of both Beth and Alecia, as they wasted no time at all in establishing that he was single, an avid LFC supporter, and had a good working knowledge of the world of Peppa Pig, acquired via his young niece. It looked like he was a hit with the ladies of the house.

After dinner, Ferguson and I went out to the garage as Beth got Alecia ready for bed. I removed the package containing Uncle Sean's personal effects from a cupboard in a storage unit we keep there. Seeing his blood stained clothing brought me immediately back to that fateful night.

'Are you OK with this, would you like me to do it?' asked Ferguson, who must've sensed my discomfort.

'No, I have to do this,' I replied as I pulled open the glued seal

of the bag and fished out a small leather bound notebook.
I tried to finger through it but the pages were melded together with hard blood. Looking closer, I noticed that someone had already tried to separate the pages, but without any luck. I quickly reached the same conclusion that Black and the other investigating officers had no doubt reached previously. It had been saturated and had now dried, fusing the pages into a horrible paper mâché, that was never going to yield any clues.
'Great,' Ferguson growled, mirroring my frustration.
I dropped the book back into the bag and returned it and its contents to the cupboard, as Beth opened the door leading from the kitchen, to the garage.
'I think you two should come see this,' she hooked her thumb behind her toward the sitting room, where I could see the pattern of light reflected from the television screen.
We followed her into the sitting room, to the television that was locked on UTV's local news reporting on what was being suggested as the apparent murder of local footballing legend, Brian Wilson, and that it may be linked to the killer of Owen Grant.
'Looks like you may have a serial killer on your hands,' I exclaimed to Grant, who was already reaching for his phone to call Black.

13.

'Could be a late one', I said to Beth as I kissed her goodnight.
'Take care, both of you, she replied. 'Tom, I'll make up the spare bedroom, you're welcome to stay with us'.
I nodded my agreement and after expressing his thanks, Ferguson and I were soon cruising down the motorway, Belfast bound.
On the short journey, he called Owen Grant's parents and rescheduled his meeting with them. No doubt they would have by now heard the news and would've understood. He had arranged to meet Black at the Waterfront Hall and had amazingly convinced him that not only did he have some jurisdiction on the case, given the link to Owen Grant, but also, that there was an active link to a Farset Investigations case, so therefore I had the right to be an associate in the investigation team.
In the intervening months from Sean's death until now, I'd taken some online training courses and was now a licensed PI but had zero experience other than what I'd been doing today in working with Ferguson. I hoped that I was ready for what I was about to be thrust into.
When we arrived, a uniformed officer led us to one of the Hall's smaller conference suites, which was now doubling up as a temporary command centre. After greeting us, Black, who seemed more at ease with my presence than I was expecting,

ran us through the investigation to date.
The body of Brian Wilson had been removed for autopsy and the event organisers, MC, special guests, and media team were in the process of being interviewed, though nothing significant had turned up yet. They had decided against interviewing the audience, as they felt that it could hamper the investigation rather than further it. They had all witnessed the same thing but some would no doubt embellish what they saw or heard, leading to the waste of valuable time. For now it was a waiting game, to see if the remaining interviews or autopsy would throw anything up.
Ferguson asked if he could help out with the remaining interviews, quickly adding that I would be sitting in with him, after Black agreed. We were shown to a small room where local journalist Caleb Doyle was already waiting.
Ferguson introduced himself, and began to introduce me, when I interjected, 'It's OK, DCI Ferguson, Mr Doyle and I already know each other. We grew up together. Caleb's family and Uncle Sean were friends. Caleb's dad worked at The Chronicle with Sean before entering the world of politics. He's our Deputy First Minister now,' I said with a smile.
'Nice to see you Mark,' said Doyle as we shook hands, 'sorry I didn't get to speak to you at the funeral, I had to rush off after to file a story, I'm so sorry about Sean. He was such a big influence in my life. I really regret not seeing so much of him in recent years.'
'It's been such a loss for all of us,' I replied.
'So what has you working with the Police then? That's a bit of a departure from what you're used to'.

'Not so much as you might think,' I replied before explaining how I'd got this far.

Ferguson then began to ask about the events of the evening and upon discovering that Doyle had interviewed Wilson earlier in the day for The Chronicle, further probed for information likely to be of use to the investigation. I was looking forward to finding out what Ferguson's take on the conversation was, though I certainly didn't hear anything of great relevance myself.

'Well?', I asked as soon as Doyle had been ushered out the door.

'You tell me Mr PI, you're the one with the inside track on this. Could he have been involved'?

'I wouldn't have thought so,' I replied. 'He always seemed OK to me when we were growing up, and I know Uncle Sean had a high opinion of him. We haven't seen much of either him or his Dad in years though, not on a personal level anyway'.

'Any particular reason?' asked Ferguson.

'I don't think so, certainly not in my case. I wouldn't have much reason to see him now'.

'What about Sean?', asked Ferguson, his detective instincts kicking up a gear.

'I don't think he kept in contact with them. He had a major falling out with Michael Doyle, Caleb's dad years ago. Caleb would only have been a teenager at the time. It was shortly after his Mum had been found dead at home. Sean tried to help the family come to terms with what had happened but shortly afterward all contact ceased'.

'Did you ask Sean about it?'

'Yes, but he always just closed down the conversation immediately. I eventually stopped asking'.
'But that was before you were a detective,' joked Ferguson, lightening what had suddenly become a sombre atmosphere. He added, 'For what it's worth, I wouldn't rule him out completely, as he had personal contact with Wilson shortly before his death, but I don't think he's a major suspect'.

14.

Terror's mind was still reeling as he left the Waterfront Hall. He'd fully expected to be interviewed by the police but hadn't anticipated the Merseyside Police involvement. He'd quite enjoyed that realisation. It rubber stamped his becoming a fully fledged serial killer, like the ones he had read about and learned from. At the moment what was bothering him more was Mark Shaw's involvement. He definitely hadn't seen that coming. His presence stirred all manner of emotions within Terror, ranging from the happiness of their childhood friendship, sadness and guilt of the loss of Sean and what he had been forced to do to him. Overshadowing all of these other emotions however, were hatred and jealousy. He'd lost two of the most important people in his life to Shaw. Firstly, Sean Brady as a teenager, the Father he'd always wanted, instead of the piece of filth he had, then later, the love of his life, Beth Marshall, the beautiful and talented author who he had driven into the arms of Shaw. They were playing at happy families now. She'd married him and they had a child. Her writing career has gone from strength to strength and they've carved the perfect life for themselves, a life without him.

He'd thought about killing Mark Shaw many times over the last number of years. In the end he'd decided against it. He had work to do, a mission to complete, the incarnation into and rise of Terror.

What happens now though Terror thought? Mark Shaw had

forced himself back into Terror's life and not in a good way. He recounted the interview in his mind and concluded that he probably hadn't raised any major suspicions from either of the two men. For now though, he will need to keep a close eye on Shaw and Ferguson and he knew just how to do it.

15.

Beth Shaw put her iMac in sleep mode and pushed her chair away from her desk. Rising, she poured another cup of coffee and curled up on the corner sofa in her home office, or as she preferred to call it, her Creative Corner. This inner sanctum with it's grey brick effect wallpaper, framed memorabilia of her beloved Liverpool Football Club and an assortment of Rock memorabilia was the place where she had produced four best selling novels and had created a highly successful blog for new mums. This morning though, she had struggled to produce two sentences. She'd been troubled since Mark had told her of his meeting with Caleb Doyle when he got back. She'd said nothing to Mark at the time but was now feeling really conflicted about continuing to keep a secret from him. She loved Mark so much and their relationship was built upon honesty but she hadn't been entirely honest had she, at least not right at the start. She had hardly slept at all last night, consumed by the memories of her relationship with Caleb, memories which continued to invade her consciousness now. She'd been an undergraduate at Queen's University, fulfilling her wish to obtain a degree in English and become a writer. No-one else in the family had ever been able to get this far in education and everyone was so proud of her. Life was great. She was enjoying all that student life had to offer, had met Mark, who was a year above her in her English course at the time, though in their year long relationship, had since graduated and was now a trainee teacher at the Faculty of Education. His postgraduate course was very demanding of his time but she didn't mind that. They were both ambitious in their career aspirations which is why she had taken an evening class in creative writing. That's where she met Caleb Doyle, who was also studying for an English Degree, albeit at the University of Ulster. He had aspired to be a journalist, following in his father's footsteps, which was the reason he had signed up for this class.

She was drawn to him from the very beginning. Not only did they have so much in common through their studies, but he was so articulate and charismatic that she felt that she was learning almost as much from him as she was from the Lecturer. Of course the fact that he was so easy on the eye might have had some bearing also. Before long they had begun an affair. They had been together for around 3 months with her juggling her relationship with Mark at the same time. She'd felt conflicted then too, feeling that she was in love with both men and not being able to end her relationship with either. Not to mention that this was so unlike her. She definitely wasn't brought up to be that kind of girl. She'd even told Caleb about Mark. He had been so good about it, telling her that he understood and that she would make the right decision for her in time. What made it worse was that during this conversation, it became apparent that Caleb knew Mark and that they'd been friends until their mid-teens.

As it turns out, Caleb had been right. She did make the right choice for her in the end, though it was his increasingly aggressive, often violent and dominating behaviour that pushed her to it. She'd never told anyone about this, though she struggled to keep the signs from Mark. She thought that that part of her life was behind her and now feared that she was wrong.

The noise of the phone on her desk starting to ring startled her. She quickly composed herself and moved to answer it. 'Hello'.

'Hello Beth, long time no speak'. She instantly recognised the voice, its tone sending shivers down her spine. 'Who is this?' she replied, trying to disguise the tremble in her own voice which indicated that she knew exactly who was speaking.

'You mean, you don't remember,' Caleb Doyle replied, feigning hurt, 'I'm crushed'.

'What do you want Caleb? How'd you get this number?', she snapped?

'You can relax, it's not you that I want. Could you pass a message onto your beloved? I'd like to help in the Terror investigation and in the investigation into Sean Brady's murder'.

'Why don't you call him yourself, I'm his wife, not his PA,' she quipped, trying to keep her temper measured.

'I thought it might be more fun to have you pass the message on. How's domestic bliss working out for you anyhow Mrs Shaw or should I say Mum? Have you both shared all your secrets yet'? We wouldn't want little Alecia to end up in broken home would we?

With that Beth Shaw slammed down the phone and immediately burst into tears.

16. Part Two-Fear and Enlightenment

The smell of incense burning in the small reception area was overpowering as I sat waiting for Patrick Rodgers to become free from his current appointment. Still, it was helping keep me awake after what was a long and largely sleepless night. I was a bit concerned about Beth too. She seemed a bit off last night and seemed to be tossing and turning as much as I was. At last the door creaked open and in he walked. Dressed in a slate grey suit, an open necked white shirt which he had clearly chosen to make the most of his fake tan and compliment his neatly styled hair and designer stubble, he looked more like a contestant from The Apprentice than what I expected a Medium should look like.

'Mr Shaw, I'm surprised to see you here', he said as he grasped my hand in greeting. 'I wouldn't have thought that The Enlightenment Community would condone their Headteacher dabbling in the dark arts, and on a school day too, who would have thought it!'

I was stunned. 'I must admit, I was a sceptic, but you're good'.

He laughed. 'You don't remember me do you'?

'No, I can't say as I do, sorry' I said, studying his features in search of recognition.

He laughed again. 'That's OK, I was in my last year at the Academy when you first started and I certainly look a lot more worldly now. Of course, you would have known me as Jarl Mc

Manus'.

This prompted dozens of questions to flood into my mind, none of which had anything to do with why I was here. I opened my mouth to speak but he raised his hand in interruption. 'Let's go upstairs to my office, we can talk there'.

I followed him up the narrow stairs of what used to be a two up, two down terraced house. His office, likely the box room was cramped but cosy. There were two armchairs facing one another, with a small bamboo coffee table between them upon which was placed a jug of water and some glasses. Rodgers / Mc Manus gestured me to sit in the seat opposite the window, placing himself lightly in the seat nearest the door.

'So, our Receptionist said that it would be someone from Farset Investigations coming in this morning. Looks like a lot has changed for the both of us'.

I explained what had happened to Uncle Sean and why I was here.

'I'm sorry to hear about Mr Brady, but I'm afraid I can't help you. He did put Charlene and I back in touch when she first escaped but since she disappeared again I've been warned not to ask about her or to go looking for her'.

Again my mind was flooded with questions, though I had researched the Church of my former employers enough to suspect that I knew what he had been talking about. My face flushed, 'Escaped?', I asked, fearing the response.

'Please, Mr Shaw, I would've credited you with much more intelligence than that. You've worked for them for long enough, surely you're not that naive'.

'Sure I've googled the Church, read the pages that brand it a cult, which admittedly was most of them, and I've had my own views on their interpretation of Christianity and how they assert control on their members but…?'

'Sounds like you need a little history lesson Mr Shaw'.

'Please, call me Mark,' I replied.

'Thanks, and I'm Patrick. This all feels a bit strange. I feel like I know you through the school and the Community, though I don't really know you at all. I'm not quite sure where to start'.

'Why don't you tell me about you'?, I said, 'How come you ended up here, doing what you do?'

'Surviving and living a happy life is the short answer but I think that you need a bit more than that.

My family has been part of The Enlightenment Community for generations, so growing up we were used to all the control, and believe me there's a lot of control. We weren't allowed any contact beyond business with people outside our Community and were told who we could and couldn't associate with within the Community as well. We had to set up or work in Community businesses and give the majority of our income to the Prophet, who also forced us to set up Trusts and tax avoidance schemes. He even has his names on the deeds of our homes, schools and businesses. We were told what to think, how to act, who we could and couldn't marry. It was all supposed to be reflective of the teaching of the Bible but my Bible Study wasn't telling me that I should view myself and my fellowship as above all others in the eyes of God and it certainly didn't tell me that I should shun those that our Elders felt were sinners'.

As he talked, it became apparent that he was fighting back tears and his words were tinged with anger and frustration. My heart sank further with every word that he'd said. I abhorred everything that he was describing and yet in some ways, he was only confirming what I had always suspected. How could I have allowed myself to be involved with this Community? I'd always tried to fool myself by thinking that by being a positive influence in the lives of these children, I was making a difference. The truth was that in reality I wasn't making any difference at all. In fact, I was probably as controlled as they were. That was not the kind of person that I was and I quickly became aware that tears were pricking the backs of my eyes too.

'I'm so sorry'. I could hardly get the words out.

'You've nothing to be sorry for,' he responded, 'You've always acted fairly and did what you thought was best. You've always been liked and respected for that'. As we both tried to compose ourselves a little, he continued.

'My Father became an Elder in our area as we were growing up. This put more pressure on us to conform to all the demands of the Church. My Father enjoyed and was proud of his position, still is I expect. He was so consumed by his importance within the Church that he didn't seem to notice my Mother's descent into severe depression and alcoholism. Charlene and I were not far behind. Charlene was struggling at school, she still does I would think, and I was beginning to develop in both my gift and in my sexuality, both of which would see me withdrawn from and excommunicated'.

'Withdrawn from'?

'Yes, we would be locked in a house owned by the Church and not allowed any contact with anyone except the Elders, who would come to us every day to make us repent. It would be up to them when you were worthy to rejoin the Church or if you were to be excommunicated'.

'Is that what happened to you'? I asked.

'Yes, I've been withdrawn from in my life but I never gave them the opportunity to throw me out. I escaped after….after what happened to my Mum'.

From my recollection of dealing with the aftermath of this in the school, I feared I knew what he was about to say.

He lifted the glass of water from beside him and took a sip, his hands visibly shaking.

'We got up for Church one morning to find my mother gone. She had left us a note saying that she was sorry and that she could not continue any more. She'd also denounced The Enlightenment Community and all that they stood for. Her body was found hanging from a tree in the grounds of the Church. I think she wanted to make her message pretty clear.They had driven her to do what she had done. When I heard my Father pronouncing her as being evil and unworthy through her actions, I'd had enough.I hated him and his Church with every bone in my body. I waited until the early hours of the morning and left. I would've loved to have brought Charlene with me but I didn't know how I would cope myself at that stage and I thought that for the time being, she'd be safe. I'd always intended to go back for her, then a few months ago, your Uncle made contact with me through some other ex-members of the Community that he had found and told me that my sister had escaped and was trying to trace me. I spoke to her on the phone briefly but before we could set up a meeting, Charlene was captured by the Church and we were issued a message telling us to stay away from her if we valued her safety or our own. I know what these people are capable of, so I listened. I thought that when you had set up your meeting today, you had some news'.

'I'm sorry to have raised your hopes like that. I was hoping to get some kind of lead in my Uncle's murder, I didn't mean to…you've been through enough. If I can ever be of any help'. I stood to leave but was motioned to retake my seat by Rodgers.

'I know you didn't come here for mediumship but I do sense the presence of Mr Brady. It doesn't usually work quite like this but I get the impression that your Uncle was not the conventional type. He is giving us both a message. Do you want to hear what he has to say? I have to ask, it's what we are advised to do'.

I was elated and petrified all at the same time. 'Yes,' I replied, unable to get any other words out. A feeling of calm and security came over me and I knew that I was indeed in the presence of Uncle Sean.

'He is very proud of you and what you are doing. You will be an excellent detective and you will continually prove that throughout your new career. He knows who killed him but wants you to reach your own conclusions. You will bring Terror to justice. He says that you and I have more work to do together and that he approves of your other new colleague. You need to explore HQ more. There are some surprises in

store for you there that will help you realise what he always wanted to achieve and what you will achieve. And finally, that he very much loves you, Beth and Alecia'.
I was amazed and although I didn't leave my meeting with Patrick Rodgers with any answers, I felt that I had made a lot of progress. I was happy to have had contact with Uncle Sean and glad of the prospect of working with Rodgers again, not least because it might make me feel a bit less guilt about my association with The Enlightenment Community.
Now it was time to go exploring.

17.

Ferguson sat at the huge desk in what was Sean Brady's former office, remotely filing a progress report to Merseyside police. He had not long returned to the office from his rescheduled meeting with Owen Grant's parents and was trying to record the content and outcome of the meeting whilst it was fresh in his mind. Truth be told, there was nothing of great significance there, other than the fact that bizarrely, Grant's Parents had no inkling of his sexual orientation, putting his seemingly non-existent love life down to his being so career driven. Then there was Ferguson's own news. Earlier this morning, he had received an email telling him that as part of the necessary budget cuts that Merseyside Police had been forced by Government to make, he was being considered for redundancy. He was devastated. He knew that constabularies all across the country were having to make similar choices, so if he was selected for redundancy, it would effectively be the end of his career in the police force. This may well be the last case he works and he seemed to be getting nowhere with it. If this case gets put on ice, then his fate would likely be sealed. The only positive at the moment was that the local coroner had just reported back that blood and tissue samples taken from the body of Brian Wilson had unusually large concentrations of Hydrochloride. He had definitely been murdered and possibly by the same person who had murdered Owen Grant, but who, how and why?

Hopefully he will get a break in the case soon, the Lord knows, he needs one.
As he hit the send icon that would whisk his report off to Liverpool, the office door opened and Mark Shaw entered, followed by Caleb Doyle.
'Look who I bumped into in the car park,' he said as Doyle waved a hello. 'He'd like to work with us on the Terror case, what do you think'?
Ferguson was taken aback, he had worked with the Press before and could see the benefits but also the issues, and this seemed to have come from nowhere. It could certainly be beneficial to both parties, so maybe it could work he thought. His expression hardened as he addressed his response to Doyle rather than Shaw.
'What's your angle on this? Why Us and not DI Black?'
'Honestly… I do want to help but I won't deny that this could be big for my career. A potential serial killer with links to Northern Ireland. This could be huge.'
'You haven't completely answered the question,' Ferguson said with an edge.
'I thought that I could get the inside track from you rather than the police'.
'I am the police,' Ferguson's voice rose in anger at Doyle's implied dismissal of his role.
Doyle held his hands up in mock surrender. 'Look, we all want the same thing here. I want to help catch this guy. I'll consult with you all the way before anything goes to print'.
Ferguson looked dejected. 'Fine, so long as Mark is happy with the arrangement'. With the stare of both men firmly fixed

on me, I nodded.
'OK, but complete confidentiality at all times until we give you the ok to print. And before you go clearing the mantle piece for your Pulitzer Prize, remember, DI Black is the person in command in the Terror case'.
Doyle nodded and with that, he sat in with us as Ferguson recounted his morning's events to us. I decided to wait until Doyle had left, to fill Ferguson in on my meeting with Rodgers.

18.

Tears welled in Charlene Mc Manus' eyes as she put her head through the belt fashioned as a noose, that she had secured from the light fitting. She had been Shut Up for weeks now, spending all her time locked in the Shut Up House, her only visitors, the Elders providing her with daily food rations whilst they poured scorn upon her soul and tried to purge her of her sins. She had made a conscious decision that this would be her release and it would be on her terms. Even if she had been able to find a way to escape the house, they would always come for her. She realised that this was how her Mother must've felt in her last moments and was saddened at the pain of her loss. Now it was her time to be brave. She'd broken for freedom in the same way Jarl had and that hadn't worked. Now it was time to be free in the same way Mum was. She'll be rid from The Enlightenment finally and her Father will never be able to hurt her ever again. Closing her eyes, she kicked the chair out from under her feet. She immediately felt the belt tighten unbearably, squeezing her throat and impacting on her airway. She tried to block out the sensation of the life leaving her body by thinking of her brother. She hoped that he would understand why she had done this and could live with it. He had found happiness in his own small way and she didn't want to take that away from him. Suddenly almost every muscle in her body began to spasm as her oxygen deprived system entered the last throes of death. She

welcomed the pain. This would be her true purging and soon she would see real enlightenment. Momentarily the pain faded to numbness and then there was nothing.
15 miles away from her in the kitchen of his workplace, Patrick Rodgers was sweating profusely. The discomfort and pain that he felt around his throat could only be matched by the feeling of sheer anguish being placed upon his being. Overcome, he collapsed to the ground, momentarily blacking out. As he tried to open his eyes, he saw a hazy vision of a room. He'd been in the room before and was terrified by the reminder. At first it didn't make sense to him but then he suddenly made the connection. Snapping off his affliction, he rushed to reception. He needed Mark Shaw's help and he needed it now.

19.

I had spent so long trying to convince Ferguson that Doyle would be of value to us, that the remainder of my Subway Melt had lost both its warmth and appeal. He was willing to let him work alongside us but felt uncomfortable around him and wanted to make damned sure that I knew it. In truth, I shared many of the same concerns and had particular reason to do so, but Uncle Sean had such a soft spot for him that I felt that I owed him something.

'OK, let's just see how it goes and we'll both keep a close eye on him', I said, crumpling up the remnants of my unfinished lunch and it's packaging, and hurling them toward the bin in the corner. 'Let's see what secrets this place still has to give up'.

I had been on tenterhooks to find out what the message from Uncle Sean had meant regarding the old building and was about to look for the answer when my mobile rang.

'Hi Patrick, I wasn't expecting to hear from you again so soon'.

Rodgers spluttered, 'I need your help, it's an emergency, can you pick me up'?

Within five minutes Rodgers was clambering into the back of the 5 Series and giving us directions to a property on the Antrim Road. En route, he explained the visions that he'd had of the property and the fact that his Spirit Guide had instructed him to contact me. Ferguson who had tagged along to help if needed, was asking how and what he knew about the property. We quickly learned of its use as a Shut Up House and by deduction, had presumed that this was where Charlene was being detained.

I got us to the location as quickly as I could, bearing in mind the number of speed cameras on the Antrim Road. When we arrived, the driveway was blocked by a Silver Mercedes Vito people carrier, a popular choice amongst the Enlightened, I knew. The side door of the vehicle was open, as was the front door of the house. Rodgers who was beyond agitated at this stage, instructed me to block the Mercedes in. He was out of the car almost before it had stopped and was racing into the house. We quickly followed and when I entered, I was met with the sight of two young men, both former students of mine, carrying the limp, apparently lifeless body of Charlene down the staircase, whilst Rodgers had his hands around the throat of his father, another man, one of my former employers was trying to restrain him. The shock at seeing us and I would have imagined, me in particular provided enough distraction for Ferguson to look at Charlene. 'She's alive but her pulse is weak. We need to get her to a hospital now'.

With that Rodgers forcibly pushed his father into my former Boss, causing both men to crumple to the ground. Ferguson loudly announced his name, occupation and rank, as he produced his credentials. It was enough to convince the two young men to put Charlene down gently onto the ground. In one swift movement, Ferguson swept her up and we moved back toward the car. Moments later, we entered the Mater Hospital, where Charlene was admitted for what we hoped would be life-saving treatment. We stayed with Rodgers for several hours as he awaited news. Finally, late in the evening he was told that she would survive, though she had to be placed into a coma and put onto a life support machine as a means to stabilise her breathing until the swelling in her airways had gone down. She had also received an endotracheal intubation, whatever that was,to help her breathe. At this stage, it was too early to tell if there had been any brain damage, though her spine was intact. Although the outcome seemed hopeful, the news was still harrowing. How such a young girl could have found herself in this situation and to think that there may still be the risk of brain damage. On hearing the news, I just wanted to get home to my family and hold them as tightly as I could.

Ferguson and I left Rodgers shortly after he had finished speaking to the Doctors. Charlene was to be moved to the Royal Victoria Hospital to the Intensive Care Unit and he wanted to travel with her. We agreed that we would meet him there in a few hours, allowing him to get something to eat, rest and freshen up. I had managed to convince him that he would be of no use to Charlene without looking after himself and of course the unspoken message was that we all felt that someone should be there to keep her Father away, should he or any of his, 'Brothers,' turn up.

The journey home was a somber one, each of us lost in our thoughts. As we neared the house, Ferguson said, 'I was thinking… I'd like to stay on for a while and see if we can get

any traction on the Terror case. It seems a bit of a dead end at the moment but I could do more from here than I could from Liverpool.
Black doesn't have much space for me at the station, so I wondered if I could blag some desk space at Farset for the time being'.
'Sure, no problem. It's great to have you around and I could certainly do with the help. Since what you're working may be linked to what I'm working on so it makes sense.'
'Great, but I'll hire a car and sort out a hotel, I don't want to impose any longer'.
'Hey, you're welcome to stay with us as long as you need to, you know that'.
'Thanks, I appreciate it but I'd feel better getting a hotel. It'd probably be better for all of us'.
'Sure, no problem, as long as you know that you're welcome. Are you ok? I know we've been through alot today but you seem a bit off form'?
Ferguson recounted the content of his email. It looked like his career as a police officer was about to go into hiatus or possibly even come to an end.
'I'm so sorry to hear that'. I said. 'Though let's look at it positively. This gives us both even more reason to catch Terror and find Uncle Sean's killer. Surely the solving of a multiple homicide might take you out of the firing line'.
I smiled weakly and he returned the compliment, both of us knowing that neither we nor DI Black had anything much to go on.

20.

Alecia was having a sleepover with her Grandparents so the house was much quieter when we got inside.I had forgotten and after this evenings events, I was aching to hold her. Beth, hearing us enter, shouted down from her writing room, 'I'll be there in a minute. I just need to finish this paragraph'.

I went to the fridge, got Ferguson and I a beer each. 'I think we deserve this, don't you,' I said, handing it to him.

'Starting without me I see. Domino's for dinner sound OK'? Beth had appeared in the doorway looking amazing as always. I'm so lucky that sometimes I think I need to pinch myself.

'Sounds great,' we replied in unison, making all of us laugh. Ferguson excused himself, to freshen up and pack. After, he left us, I embraced Beth tightly then kissed her gently. 'I needed that, we've had a terrible day'. I was about to tell her what had happened when I noticed that she was fighting back sobs. The warm smile that had greeted us was now gone and her face crumpled into tears.

I embraced her again, asking what was wrong. As she tried to compose herself, we sat down on the sofa. I gave her a handkerchief from my pocket and as she dabbed her eyes, she began to tell me of the phone call she'd had from Doyle that morning and why it had been so upsetting. By the time she had finished what she had wanted to say, she was shaking and sobbing as she waited for my reaction. I leaned forward and kissed her forehead then smiled. Seeing puzzlement on her face, I explained that I had known about the affair at the time and although angry, I'd figured that I loved her regardless and if I were to break up with her, I would've lost her. I decided to take the gamble that she would eventually realise that I loved her more than anyone else ever could and come back to me. Her expression became a mixture of joy and relief. She kissed me hard and told me how much she loved me. I knew that and was counting on it because the next thing I had to tell her was that for Uncle Sean's sake, I'd agreed to work with Doyle. After the App had been tapped and the pizza ordered, Ferguson and I filled Beth in on what had been quite a day. She was amazed and intrigued by Patrick Rodgers, who she'd heard about through a friend, and was disgusted by ,The Enlightenment. She'd always had a dislike for them since she had researched them when I started to work for them. This had developed into a hatred as she heard more and more about their practices and witnessed their treatment of others. When the pizza arrived and as we ate, the conversation turned to Ferguson's predicament and the cryptic comment from Uncle Sean about what lay undiscovered at Farset. Beth was just as hyped to find out what it was, as I was, so Ferguson offered to take the next shift at the hospital so that Beth could come with me to see what we could find.

21.

'See you in a few hours, call me if you have any trouble,' I said to Ferguson as he got out of the car into the rain.

'No worries, see you later'.

As we pulled away from him Beth asked how we were getting along together.

'He seems a nice fella. We've been getting along great and he certainly knows his stuff. He got the measure of Caleb Doyle pretty quickly, not to mention how he handled the Enlightened earlier. I feel really sorry for him with the whole redundancy thing you know'.

'Yeah, I've been thinking about that too'.

'I wish there was something we could do to help'.

Beth laughed, 'For a PI you really don't have a clue sometimes'.

I looked sideways at her, 'What do you mean?'

'I mean, he likely needs a job, you've just taken over a detective agency and you're still new to the whole investigation thing… so you could take him on and see how it works out'.

The thought hadn't even occurred to me but as soon as she had said it I knew she was right. I decided to put the proposal to him later.

I parked at the back entrance of Farset, as the thought of entering through the main entrance on a dark and rainy night still pained me deeply. This meant having to unlock a set of

heavy double gates, which led onto a vast concreted area that used to serve as a playground. I don't think that health and safety these days would have approved. Getting half drenched by doing this, I was about to return to the car, when it started to move through the gate. Beth had slid across into the driver seat and was parking up as close to the rear entrance as she could, probably to avoid getting her hair wet I laughed to myself. I secured the gates again, then joined her.
'Nice park job, Goldilocks but you'll still need your umbrella,' I said as I pointed to the two small outbuildings that bookended the top and bottom of the play area which used to be referred to as, 'The Yard'. 'First things first though, we need to turn off the alarm in the main building.
The back door opened into the basement of the building. I quickly swiped my electronic key fob across the alarm panel, disabling the alarm. We entered the building and I locked the door behind us. I grew up in this area and knew that we had to be security conscious, which was another reason why we came in this way, the car would be more secure. Beth turned on the light. She hadn't been down this part of the building before. 'How cosy… not'! She pulled the collar of her coat tighter around her neck as we proceeded up the dank basement corridor. After a short while we came to a staircase which led to the classrooms which were on the boys side of the school. Another staircase leading to the girls side, lay further on down the corridor.
We alighted the stairs and headed for Sean's office. I'd already been through it with a fine tooth comb, looking for a lead in Sean's murder case but we searched again nonetheless. There

was nothing to be found there, so we progressed through the school, room by room on both the boy's and girl's side. All we could see were derelict and abandoned classrooms, staff rooms and the office of the former headmistress. 'I wish we had some idea what we were looking for,' I said.

'At the moment, what I'm looking for is a warm fire and a glass of wine. Let's give it up and come back tomorrow when its light. This place is giving me the creeps'.

Conceding defeat, I nodded and moved towards the staircase outside the Headmistress' office. 'This is the opposite of the one we came up earlier. It'll take us down to the basement again and we can go through the corridor and outside. I'll have a quick look at the outbuildings and then we'll call it a night'.

'Sounds like a plan,' replied Beth, 'we could be in our PJ's and curled up on the sofa in front of the TV by ten. Maybe another episode from the West Wing box set'.

'Not with me you won't' I smiled, as we went downstairs. 'My turn at the hospital remember'!

'What's that noise'? Beth asked as we reached the bottom of the stairs. I suddenly became aware of a humming noise, almost a drone. There was an old metal door to our left. I pulled down the handle and pushed the door but it didn't budge.

'This used to be the old boiler room, maybe it's the boiler making the noise,' I thought out loud, 'but wait, the heat in Uncle Sean's office runs from the electricity, surely the boiler hasn't been on in years'.

'Look,' said Beth, pointing to something on the wall to the left hand side of the door frame. I could just about see a very faint green light emanating from the shadows. I looked closer to see that it was an alarm panel, similar to the one I'd used earlier. Hoping for the best, I removed the keys of the building from my pocket and held up the electronic fob in front of the panel. There was an almost inaudible beep followed by a loud clang as the lock on the door released. I opened the door and we walked in. The door behind us clanged shut and the lock on it rearmed, startling us. The space in front of us then began to light up as what looked like energy saving lights kicked in, steadily getting brighter. I couldn't believe what I was seeing. In front of us was a huge opened planned space which stretched almost as far as the eye could see. The huge expanse was partitioned using plexiglass into distinct working areas, offices and a Boardroom. Each area was kitted out in the latest technology and computer equipment, most of which I didn't even know what its use was.

'What on earth…'?

I had always heard an urban legend growing up about a bunker under the school from wartime but I certainly hadn't imagined that it actually existed, never mind what Sean had apparently transformed it into. At the far end of the space there was a solid bare bricked wall with a set of double doors at the end of it.

'This is amazing. He's gone and he's still managing to surprise us,' said Beth in shock and disbelief.

Looking to my left I saw on the wall, a very corporate looking sign depicting the Farset Investigations logo. So this was the real dream eh, I thought, welling with pride for my Uncle. We walked through the space, almost afraid to touch anything as we did so. I tried the double doors at the end and they opened. They led to a hallway area with four further sets of doors, two facing us and one each to our left and right. The doors facing us each had conventional keyholes. I matched each to the keys on my keyring and opened them. To our further shock, they each turned out to be modern, self contained one bedroom apartments. The door to the right was a large staff leisure area, again open planned and equipped with a huge kitchen and gym.

Finally we came to the last door. It too had an alarm panel and again my key fob worked. The door opened and as before energy saving lights slowly went from dark, through dim, to stark white light. I didn't think I could have been any further surprised tonight but I was wrong. What we were looking at was a huge garage with a large, corrugated warehouse style rolling shutter at the back of it. That wasn't the remarkable part. That took the form of ten brand new vehicles, mostly BMW models from across the range, with the exception of two VW Passats and a Mercedes Vito Van, that adorned the garage floor.

'You look like you've died and gone to heaven,' said Beth.

I laughed. 'Though I'm sick of the sight of those Vito's,' I tutted mockingly. 'What on earth was he thinking'?

'Oh, those are the type favoured by police'. I looked at her with a mixture of surprise and disbelief.

'What… I'm a writer. We do research you know'!

Seriously though, what was he thinking? I couldn't get my

head around any of this and I knew that Beth was thinking in much the same way as I was.

I suddenly remembered Ferguson. Our exploring probably took longer than I'd intended. I took out my phone and called him.

'Sorry, we got a little held up,' I apologised when he answered.

'I'm on my way now… cancel your hotel and car hire. You won't be needing them. You're about to get a better offer'.

22.

Beth decided to stay behind and poke around a little further while I returned to the hospital. When I arrived Ferguson was sitting slumped asleep in a chair beside Charlene Mc Manus' bed. Standing over the bed, I couldn't help but think how frail and fragile she looked lying there with all those machines hooked up to her. She was a shadow of the gregarious young girl who was never afraid to add a bit of humour to my English lessons with her class. I couldn't even begin to comprehend the turmoil she must've been in, yet she covered it so well.

Thinking back, I enjoyed the majority of my time at Causeway Academy. I momentarily toyed with the idea that maybe the interaction that my staff and I had with the students did make a positive difference to the students lives. Our students did well and we certainly had some laughs. At the back of my mind though, I couldn't shake the expression of Drew my former boss' face when he saw me in the Shut Up House earlier that evening. His eyes burned through me and he had neither said nor done anything to help Charlene. Clearly it was he and the other Enlightenment Elders who had driven her to do what she had done. I couldn't help but wonder where they were taking her when we arrived. Why hadn't they rang for an ambulance? My train of thought then brought me back to the day that Drew and some of his colleagues had broken the news of the death of Charlene's mother to me in my office. It had felt a bit odd at the time and I remembered getting the distinct impression that they were covering something up or hiding something. At the time I put it down to my perhaps being paranoid, or my reacting to the fact that Enlightenment people do not mourn their dead, believing them to have been called by God. It wasn't unusual therefore that after burial, I would rarely if ever hear the name of a deceased member again but in the days and weeks that followed Charlene's mother's death, my colleagues and I couldn't help but notice that the students were behaving differently. Nothing was ever said about the bereavement and it looked like Charlene was becoming increasingly isolated from her peers, something which they were actively, though silently advocating. Could my colleagues and I have done more for her? The answer was probably yes, though given the confines of what we were dealing with, I'm not sure what. Hot streams of tears began to streak down my face as my gaze remained fixed on her. I was so glad to have been part of her rescue and I will now do all that I can to help both her and her brother I silently promised myself. I hurriedly wiped the tears away as Ferguson's low snores subsided and he stirred awake.

'Well, if it isn't sleeping beauty'. I smiled as he was startled by the sight of me. 'Sleeping on the job, tut tut'. A slight blush spread across his face. 'A quiet shift I presume'. Before he could answer, the figure of Patrick Rodgers filled the doorway. He thanked us again and despite my protests, sent us on our way. I returned to Farset with Ferguson, filling him in on what we had found on the way.

23.

When we returned we saw that Beth had stationed herself in what looked like the Master Office at the corner of the open planned work area. She barely registered our arrival except for a quick wave of acknowledgement. The light of the computer monitor reflecting on her face showed that she was deep in concentration on something, so I left her to it for the moment and began to take Ferguson on the guided tour. He was blown away by what he saw, as I continued to be as he explained what some of the technology on display was used for.
'I've only ever heard of half of this stuff from watching CSI, no Station I've ever trained in or worked at could dream of being able to afford this kind of kit'. This really is cutting edge standard'.
'I'm glad you feel that way,' I replied. 'Because there's something I want to ask you. How would you feel about working here, or at least for Farset anyhow'?
I know it would mean moving over here but it would give you a bit of job security for a while and to be honest I could be doing with the help and your expertise. Did I mention the company car and living accommodation'?
'Wow! That's a bolt from the blue. I really like the idea but I'd need to think about it'?
'I know, it's a bit much to be asking you to move over here away from your family and turn your back on your career but…'

'No, it's not that, the only family I have are my brother and sister in law and my niece. Both my brother and sister in law are in the army, so they move around a lot with my niece and I don't see much of them anyhow apart from via Skype.
Moving away from Anfield would be more of a worry,' he laughed, trying to lighten what had quickly become an awkward situation. 'But seriously though, it would be a big step for both of us. I mean, it's a great facility you have here but beyond what we're already working on we don't really have a client base and you haven't really got much experience yet. I buy into the dream, I really do, but there is no real vision in place for Farset yet so I don't know what I would be coming into'.
I was a bit taken aback at his response but in truth, he was right. I'd taken on Farset as a means to get justice for Uncle Sean. Now I was getting lost in the aspirations Uncle Sean had for the business, and for me. I hadn't really thought beyond what would happen if or when we found our killer.
'You're right, I'm sorry. I just...'
'I know, it's fine and I really appreciate the offer. I will think about it and we'll talk more about it before I make my decision. I hope I haven't let you down. You've been a good friend to me in the short time I've known you and I want us to still be friends. After all, we've got a killer to catch'.
He held out his hand and I shook it. 'That'll do for now,' I said and smiled at him, 'though at least in the meantime, use one of the apartments here to stay in and one of the cars. Now that I know this place exists, you'd be doing me a favour to stay here to keep an eye on it'.

'The place is like Fort Knox,' he laughed, 'but I know what you mean, and sure I'd be glad to'.
'It's agreed then, let's go catch up with Beth. She looked entranced when we came in'.
Beth's eyes were still locked on the screen of the computer when we approached. It sounded like she had been watching a video clip, which she paused as we sat down in the seats at the opposite side of the desk from her. Finally looking away from the screen and making eye contact with us, she began to speak.
'OK, so when I started up the computer I noticed that it had a link to an iCloud account. After a bit of guesswork, I was able to work out the login details and open it up'.
'And'?
'And it looks like Sean was definitely investigating ,The Enlightenment Community. From what I have been able to put together so far, it looks like his contact with Charlene and your link to them through the school had sparked an interest with Sean and he was working on an expose´'.
'Once a journalist, always a journalist I suppose. Was he getting anywhere with it'?
'I would say that he was more than getting somewhere, look at this'! After a few clicks of the mouse a nearby printer hummed into life and shortly after, spat out two pieces of A4 paper, which she retrieved and handed one to each of us. It was an article, the headline reading, 'PROPHET AND LOSS,' and the sub-heading following with, 'Enlightenment Church Exposed As Corrupt and Wicked Cult'.
I began to feel sick as I read on. After a short bio of the

Church, its leader and it's practices, Uncle Sean then went on to level, then support with evidence, accusations ranging from tax evasion to money laundering and outline various reports of physical, sexual and emotional abuse, before ending the article by describing how families are broken up and the use of practices such as being shut up or withdrawn from. I looked up at Beth, knowing that she would be aware of exactly how I was feeling, then across to Ferguson, who looked like he was still trying to process what he had just read. 'It all checks out,' Beth broke the silence, 'or at least it looks like it does. He has surveillance footage, taxation records, accounts from past members, copies of property deeds, police reports, medical records, everything, and it looks like he had only just scratched the surface'. Beth's tone suddenly got a little more serious than it already had been. 'Mark, there's a few other things that you should know. Some of this research predates Sean's coming into contact with Charlene Mc Manus and… and it looks like Sean had you under surveillance for a while as well'. Her revelation sent me reeling. 'What,' I exclaimed! She turned the screen around so that we could all see it, then brought up various pictures and video clips of me in various school situations, all of which had me interacting in conversation with adult members of The Enlightenment. Some had been captured outside their businesses on what I recognised as Work Experience visits, where I would go to check on students on placement. Others had been captured outside the school or at the local sports centre at school events. 'Why'? I thought aloud, and, 'How could he have done this especially without my realising?' Ferguson

interrupted, 'It makes sense, he was clearly a professional and needed to eliminate you from any wrongdoing, especially since his expose´ would have serious implications for you'.
I could see his point, though I couldn't help but still feel a little betrayed by Uncle Sean even if I did see the logic. 'At least now I know why he was so uneasy when we last spoke,' I said. 'And it explains why there is a Vito minivan in the garage,' Beth added with a mood lightening smirk. 'So what do we do now'?
'Head home for some sleep I suppose, I think we all have a lot to think about. We'll start fresh in the morning'.
I took out my keys, uncoiled a key for one of the apartments off the keyring and tossed it to Ferguson. Beth furrowed her brows in question. 'Come on Goldilocks, I'll explain on the way'.

24.

After pouring another Filter Coffee from the jug stationed at the corner of his office, Caleb Doyle returned to his cubicle at, The Belfast Chronicle, or as the locals had dubbed it, The Chron'. He was feeling pretty groggy this morning, having not had much sleep. Still, it had been a very productive night. He had spent many of the hours of darkness in virtual conversation with some of his followers, exchanging information on possible future targets. The question was, how far were these people prepared to go or were they just fantasists? Only time would tell. When he did eventually make it to bed in the very early hours, he couldn't settle. He was glad that he had been able to secure a situation where he had an inside track at Farset but there was something about Tom Ferguson that really bothered him. Obviously, he'd been interviewed by Ferguson as part of the Brian Wilson murder and obviously the Terror killings were being investigated by Ferguson so he had a natural reason to dislike him.

It wasn't that that bothered him though, it was the fact that Ferguson clearly did not like him either. He had always been able to charm people into liking him, at least at the start That hadn't been the case this time. For the first time in his adult life, Terror felt exposed. Maybe he was being paranoid but he needed to be wary of Tom Ferguson. This thought still preoccupied him as he sipped at his coffee and scrolled through the inbox of his work email account. The most recent email was marked with a red flag. It was from the Stormont Communications Office. An Assembly debate on Welfare Reform which was due to take place this afternoon, had been brought forward and was about to start. He would need to hurry if he was to make it to the media gallery on time. This was a pretty high profile debate with high levels of interest UK wide. His reporting of it and any associated press conferences held by any of the parties later could potentially be good for his journalistic career. Just like his alter ego, Terror, Doyle was ambitious. It was just a pity that his ambition and career prospects were still in a way linked to his Father and his actions. Soon he will be watching his Father hold court in the assembly, trying to upstage himself at the expense of the First Minister. No doubt, his speeches will be filled with rhetoric alluding to the Terrorist past of other MLA's whilst painting himself and his party colleagues as being beyond reproach. In truth they were up to their necks in corruption and that was before their Leader, and Deputy First Minister's alter ego was considered. The Province's best kept secret will be exposed someday though. When the time was right, either Caleb Doyle or Terror, depending on the circumstances, will make sure of it.

Before long Doyle's Seat Leon was pulling into a slot in the media car park behind The House on the Hill. Time to get to work he thought.

25.

The smell of bacon filled the air as I came down the stairs. Beth had been up and dressed a while before I was and was busily packing a bag of supplies.

'I thought we'd have breakfast to go this morning. I've spoken to Dad and he and Mum are going to take Alecia to nursery. They're picking her up and giving her dinner as well, so that frees me up all day'.

'For what'? I asked, smirking to myself, already knowing what the answer was.

'Don't give me that Mark Shaw, I'm coming with you. There could be a new book in this for me. Besides, how else could I trust you to keep a bacon sandwich for Tom'?

Not before long, we had convened in the subterranean board room at Farset and between mouthfuls of bacon sandwich, were talking about what Beth had found on the cloud drive the night before as well as still trying to get our heads around our new base, or "The Batcave" as Beth was now dubbing it.

'How could Sean have been able to do all this? I mean, I was shocked by the amount of money I'd inherited from him, but this is a whole new level'.

'I'll see if I can look into his finances if you like,' said Ferguson. 'And you and I can look at the cloud drive,' added Beth. I nodded agreement, 'but first we need to think about what we do about The Enlightenment Article. The more I think about it, the more I think we should publish it. He may

have been murdered to suppress it'.
'That's what I'd been thinking too,' agreed Beth, 'but I must admit, I'm worried about the possible consequences'.
'I can see where you're both coming from but I think I would be against that idea, at least for the moment'. Ferguson continued, 'The way I see it, is that we want to see if The Enlightenment were involved in your Uncle's murder, right?' Beth and I nodded. 'So why would we play our trump card so soon? If they were involved then they probably think that Sean's threat died with him. Why don't we let them know what we have and use it to stop them coming after Charlene again? Depending on their reaction, we might be able to start building a case, but either way, we'll have given Patrick and Charlene some breathing space'.
Yet again, Ferguson was right and was outlining the most sensible and logical option. He made me realise all too quickly that I did have a lot to learn and I could see why he had reservations about coming to work with me.
'I think you're right… and I think that this particular nettle is one that I'll enjoy grasping. I'll go call my old friend Drew'!
'Wait, do it here' said Beth as she pointed to the teleconferencing unit sitting in the middle of the table. 'I'd love to hear how the smarmy slime ball reacts. I've never liked that creep'.
'OK, let's call it therapy then'!
'Or we could call it evidence gathering' quipped Ferguson, as he moved toward the recording equipment at the side of the room. I dialled the number from memory, having done it hundreds if not thousands of times before. I was a little

anxious as I heard the ringing tone but found myself smiling as the call was answered and the recorder whirred into life simultaneously. 'Hello Drew… it's Mark Shaw. I would say it's been a long time but…'

26.

Although neither Drew nor myself ever really liked each other, we had developed a good working relationship and the truth be told, it was through his growing trust in me over the years, that I really got an insight into the wrongdoings of The Enlightenment. The more we had talked, the more familiar to him I became and he began to drop his guard somewhat. I had developed an understanding of him and bizarrely, a grudging respect. That of course had disappeared the instant I saw him in the Shut Up House. By the time I had finished the call with him, I was seething and from the look of the faces of Beth and Tom as they listened in, I wasn't the only one.

Learning of the existence of the expose did not phase him in the slightest. He instead boasted of the strength of the legal team that represented the Church and also of the PR Consultancy firm they had links with. The power and experience of both I had already witnessed first hand. He even went so far as to suggest that the release of the article would damage the reputation of Farset more than it would The Enlightenment. He had brought the call to an end before I had even managed to draw him on Charlene by reminding me that I had worked for The Enlightenment long enough to know it's power. He also reminded me that many members of The Enlightenment held me in very high regard and that it would be a shame to lose that respect, especially since I lived within such close proximity to The Enlightenment

Community. It had come across with an advisory tone, almost sincere, but the veiled threat within it was clear. The question was, what was the true level of the threat. Being shunned when I met them in Tesco I could live with but I now knew that these were truly dangerous people I was dealing with.
He had really angered me but I responded with calm and measure, threatening that he would only have 3 days to prepare before the story went to print and that Farset were happy to live with the consequences. As I pressed the Clear Call button on the conference phone Beth could not contain herself any longer. 'How could you speak to him so calmly? You've always been the same with him. He's a snake' she snapped'.
'Yes, and as I've said to you before, when you have to handle a snake, the last thing you want to do is anger it'?
Clearly still annoyed, she questioned, 'Then what was the purpose of the call then'?
'To make him feel threatened. To force a reaction' I replied calmly. Remember, I'm the one that has worked with him for years. I'm the one who spoke to him every day and got to know what makes him tick, or at least I thought I did'.
'So what's your gut reaction now, having spoken to him' interjected Ferguson.
'He's rattled', I replied. 'In my experience The Enlightenment will automatically deploy a legal team and a spin doctor when there is something to hide. That would suggest that the contents of the expose´ are all true. What I still don't know, is whether they would have killed Sean to cover it up. Deep down, I think not, especially if we consider the way in which

he was murdered'.
'I agree' said Ferguson, 'still, we've rattled the cage, so lets wait for a reaction'.
Beth looked a little deflated.
'Don't worry, they'll get what's coming to them. In the meantime, let's get looking at the cloud drive'.
'And I'll follow up on your Uncle Sean's bank records', said Ferguson.
After a few hours of searching we found that although the cloud drive held other folders, they were mostly for cases that had been solved. The only active folder seemed to be that of The Enlightenment and with the exception of a few screen grabs from blogs relating to them in cult forums, there wasn't much that we didn't already know. The more I thought about the call with Drew, the less decided I was that ,The Enlightenment could have been responsible for Uncle Sean's death, but then I kept thinking back to what Patrick Rodgers had told me and to what we saw in the Shut Up House, not to mention the image of Charlene lying in that hospital bed fighting for survival. I couldn't possibly be sure of what they were capable of.
'I've been thinking', I said to Beth. 'If we are going to run this article in a few days time, I'm going to need to speak to Patrick and see if he is happy about it. I'm sure he would be but we have to consider the possible consequences for Charlene'.
Ferguson, who had been working at a nearby station within earshot, added, 'I can't believe I'm going to say this, but we'll probably need to fill Doyle in on all of this. After all, we'll

need to rely on him to get it to print'.
'I'll email him and ask him to come around to the office upstairs later. I'm not sure I want him to know about this place just yet'.
'Or ever', replied Ferguson, gruffly.
I whispered to Beth, 'You ok with that?' She nodded and I leaned over and pulled her into a hug, kissing her lightly on the cheek. When I released her from the hug, she looked up at me and smiled. A few phone calls and a bit of time later Ferguson got up from his work station and walked towards us. He pulled up a nearby chair and sat facing us. 'So, I've been looking into your Uncle Sean's accounts and financial dealings. About 10 years ago a vast sum of money was deposited into his personal account, which you already know. At the same time and every year since, 5 million $US has been deposited into the Farset account. I've traced the money that went to both accounts to a US Bank but it seems to be a Government account and the details of the department or holder are sealed. I also managed to get hold of the details of Sean's accountant to see if he had any clue to the benefactor's identity. He wasn't able to tell me much other than the existence an agreement between Sean and a Mr Michael Dean, that in the event of Sean's death, the transactions to the Farset account would continue under your directorship. He had presumed that Sean had told you that. I've tried to find out who Michael Dean is but I'm coming up against a brick wall'.
I was stunned. 'I've never heard him mention the name before. Things around here seem to get more bizarre by the minute'.

'I know, and there seems to be a new mystery at every turn' said Beth.

'Well, what else would you expect in a Private Investigations Office' joked Ferguson, though the humour was lost on me. I was still deep in thought, trying to make sense of yet another newly uncovered secret from Sean. I loved him dearly but at this stage I was wondering if I had ever actually known him at all.

'I'd better e mail Doyle' I said, trying to shake off the doubts I was feeling about Uncle Sean. 'Then I suppose I'll go see Rodgers and Charlene'.

'I'd better go and pick up Alecia from Mum and Dad. Tom, you're welcome to join us for dinner later'. Beth rose and lifted my keys off the desk. 'I'll take our car home if that's ok. I'm sure you're dying to try out one of your new company cars anyhow'.

'You know me Goldilocks, see you back at the house'.

'I'm going to make tracks too' said Ferguson. 'I want to try to speak to the tour guide who reported your Uncle's attack to the police. I'm going to walk up to the murals and see if I can get hold of him. I'll check in with you both later'.

27.

I decided to walk the relatively short distance from the St. Comgall's building up the Falls Road to the Royal Victoria Hospital. That way I could accompany Ferguson on the short walk up to the traffic lights at the top of Albert Street where the murals faced. There were a few black taxi tours stopped there at the time, with tourists eagerly taking photographs and the taxi drivers either chatting to each other or telling the tourists about the murals. It was already beginning to get dark and approaching the time of the evening that Uncle Sean had been attacked. The murals were beautifully up-lit so it was not unusual for them to be the last attraction of a Belfast Tour, particularly in the Autumn and Winter months. I left Ferguson to it and continued to walk up the Falls Road, past the library, crossing the top of Leeson Street, the street that led to the cul de sac that contained my family home growing up. I had already been feeling a bit brooding since Ferguson told us of Sean's mystery benefactor but somehow, walking up here made it worse. I haven't walked through this area in a long time. I felt like a ghost from my own past. In some ways it was a nice thing to do. It made me appreciate how the area looked so different with the passing of time, yet in so many other ways, it hadn't changed a bit, neither things had I noticed before when frequently driving through. I got to wondering that maybe it was me who had changed but was soon interrupted from my thoughts by the fact that I had arrived at the Royal Victoria Hospital, known locally as the RVH. Having bought two coffees in Reception I made my way to Charlene's ward and was about to enter the small room at the start of the ward, when I noticed Patrick Rodgers gesture to me from just inside the main ward. I arrived to see that Charlene had been moved into the main ward, though she was still unconscious.

'She's improving quickly' said Rodgers excitedly. The swelling has gone down quite a bit so they have been able to reduce her medication and she's breathing on her own'.

'Fantastic' I replied. 'Have they said anything about any possible brain damage'?

'We won't know until she regains consciousness and they are not sure when that might be'.

'Based on her progress so far, lets hope for the best'.

I handed him a coffee and gestured for him to take a seat beside the bed. I lifted another chair from a pile stacked nearby and sat facing him. As we drank the coffee, I filled him in on what had been discovered on the cloud drive, my subsequent conversation with Drew and the concerns that it had raised. His response was one of anxiousness.

'Frankly, none of what you said about the contents of the expose is surprising to me, and if you are asking are they capable of murder, then I would say the answer would be yes, though not really in the way that you are thinking. Charlene is almost testament to how they commit murder and my mother certainly was, but I would doubt that they would have been responsible for your Uncle's death. At least they wouldn't have set out with such a bloody and violent attack in mind. The situation may have escalated, who knows, but I would doubt it. If you are minded to run the expose in the media, I would be glad to see it and I know Charlene would too. I would agree however, with your worries about Charlene and I. I think any connection to us should be kept out of it'.

'You have my word on that', I replied. Finding Uncle Sean's killer is still my first priority in running the article, but I have to say that I feel that I owe it to you and Charlene and those like you who were and are trapped by evil'.

Rodgers leaned forward and put one hand on top of mine. 'You owe it to yourself and your family too. Your involvement with The Enlightenment hasn't been easy on any of you I would've thought, but don't take any decisions lightly. If you do this you will have a fight on your hands'.

'I am worried about that', I conceded, 'but it's a fight I think I'll have to accept and win'.

'Then rest assured you will have us in your corner. You've been a good friend and you have an excellent aura. Do what you need to do but don't expect it to be their downfall. Others have done similar things and failed, but if it raises local awareness, at least it will damage the local Church'.

Little did I realise, that the plans of others in the not too distant future, would make my concerns pail into insignificance.

Rodgers drained the last of his coffee and rose, taking my already empty cup out of my hand. He walked behind me to a nearby bin and I heard it open then close after he had deposited the cups. My gaze however, had not left Charlene since he got up. I hadn't been sure at first but now I was. She was waking up. I turned to tell him but he had already noticed and had raced to her side. Rodgers collapsed quickly into the seat beside Charlene's bed. He took her hand in his and raised it to his mouth, kissing it softly as his eyes filled with tears. He tried to call her name but it came out in a choked whisper. Charlene's eyes opened and after blinking a few times to adjust to the light, she looked at him and said his name in a similar choked whisper to that which he had just uttered. They both smiled and as I rose, lifted my coat and left the ward, without either of them noticing, I was smiling too.

28.

Tom Ferguson had watched as Shaw continued to walk up the Falls Road. They had developed a strong bond in the short time they had known each other and Ferguson wondered how Shaw could possibly be dealing with the chain of events that had occurred in his life since learning of his Uncle's passing. He wanted to do all he could to bring Brady's killer to justice for his new friend, regardless of whether there was a link to the Owen Grant murder or not. Turning to the business in hand,he had eventually been able to get hold of the taxi driver who had initially raised the alarm. Once Ferguson had explained his position, the man, who had identified himself as Frankie Woods was eager to help, recounting what he had initially told the police, even down to the vague description of the man fleeing the scene and in what direction. After quickly scanning his whereabouts, Ferguson concluded that it would be unlikely that there would be any sources of CCTV footage, though asked Woods about it just in case. Woods backed up what he had already thought, though added the interesting fact that up until a few years ago there had been a British Army outpost stationed on the roof of Divis Tower which ran 24hr CCTV monitoring of the entire area. The post had long since been abandoned since the troubles had ended but the surveillance equipment had only been removed within the last year, when in response to the booming tourist industry in Belfast, a developer took advantage of the views afforded at the top of the Divis Tower and leased the roof space, turning it into a huge American style smokehouse. Impressed, Ferguson made a mental note to check it out. It would be cool to send his Army family a picture from the former outpost.

Ferguson then went on to ask about who Woods had been giving the tour to at the time and whether or not they would have seen anything. He had remembered that it was a couple in their forties. The man had originally been from the Falls Road area, though he now lived in Dublin where he had met and married his wife. Ferguson had asked what contact details if any he would have had for the couple and Woods had agreed to pass on the contact e mail address of the person who made the booking, when he returned to the office the next morning. Ferguson gave him his card with his contact details on it before making his way back down toward Farset.

As he neared the building he saw that the light was on in what they had originally taken to be Brady's office. Through the window he saw Mark seated at his Uncle's desk, in conversation with Caleb Doyle. He thought to himself that he should probably join them but thought better of it, not really wanting to spend any more time in Doyle's company than was necessary. He couldn't really put his finger on why, but as much as he had gotten to like Mark Shaw since they had met, he had also grown to harbour a strong dislike for Doyle since their first encounter. He continued past the office and made his way down to through the basement corridor into Farset. He sat down at the work station he had been working from earlier and booted up the computer. As the Mac whirred into life, he realised that he wasn't actually sure if there were any

other angles he could be working on. Remembering their visitor upstairs, Ferguson decided to log on to the Chronicle website and see if the acclaimed journalist, Caleb Doyle was worth his salt. When the website had loaded, Ferguson firstly looked at Doyle's coverage of the Owen Grant murder. The article was pretty much as he had expected it would be, so he then moved on to the coverage of Brian Wilson's death. Doyle had written a few pieces around this story, including his interview with Wilson before he died, but it was when he was reading the coverage of the actual death, that he saw it. There in black and white was a small detail that had been overlooked and yet it provided a connection between Grant's murder and Wilson's murder that could blow the whole case wide open.
Ferguson took out his phone and called Shaw. The call had only just connected when it was answered.
'Hey Mark, Are you still with your visitor'?
'Yes, I'm still with Caleb. Where are you? I thought you'd have been back by now'.
'I am back, I'm downstairs. I've been looking through Doyle's coverage of the murders and I've just noticed a possible lead'.
'Great, what is it'?
'Well, Grant's body was found in, The Majestic Hotel, part of the Titanic group of hotels, right'?
'Right'.
'Doyle makes reference to where Brian Wilson was supposed to be staying on the night that he died. The Hotel was in the Titanic Quarter'.
'The Titanic reference linking the two…'
'I know that the killings were linked by the

#FamousForAllTheWrongReasons, but the Titanic thing could be worth looking into. Maybe one motive is a smokescreen for the other'.

'The plot thickens further still. Obviously both victims are from Northern Ireland, maybe the Titanic connection just underlines that… or it could mean that any further victims will be Northern Ireland Celebrities with something to hide'.

'Or that Terror is a local'.

'I think you should fill Doyle in on this. It would be good for him to run a piece that asks the questions about the possible connection. Tell him to hold off on going to print though until we've cleared it with DI Black and Merseyside Police. I'll make contact with them now'.

'Will do. That'll be the second story he has gotten out of us today. Lucky him!

Any luck with the taxi driver'?

'Not really but I'll fill you in on that when you get down'.

Ending the call with Shaw, Ferguson made the necessary calls to allow any story to go to print. Thankfully both forces were agreeable and upon Shaw's return to the office, he was able to contact Doyle, giving him the green light.

29.

Drew Pinkerton was really beginning to feel the effects of prolonged sleep deprivation as he took his seat in front of his office computer at 04:00am. Like most other members of the Community, he had been concerned at the latest directive from, The Prophet, but had followed it unquestioningly. Like all the other adult males in The Enlightenment, he was now surviving on less than four hours sleep per night and had been for some time. Eighteen of the remaining twenty hours left in the day were to be spent at work, leaving two hours a day for Church Meetings. Some had innocently sought clarification from, The Prophet and his apostles on this, as the new regime left virtually no family time, family being a cornerstone of their faith. They had been told that they must make sacrifices to strengthen the Church position and that they largely work with family anyhow, so they need not be concerned. It didn't stop them from falling out of favour with, The Prophet though, nor had faith in the new directive stopped the large number of car accidents and instances of illness caused by prolonged lack of sleep amongst the Community males. Still, Drew was compliant. He had enough worries with the Mc Manus situation and Mark Shaw's threat without adding this one. He booted up his computer and logged into the webinar, joining some prominent local and UK Enlightenment Priests. They were about to take these matters in hand before reporting to, The Prophet. He doubted that this meeting would end well for his friend, David Mc Manus, particularly since he as another prominent Priest in the Community, had not been told of this meeting or its agenda. He also wondered how he himself would fare given his relationship with Mark Shaw. He had little doubt that many would blame him for the situation with Shaw and that he may well be held accountable for it. His chest tightened as the screen was divided into the twelve live camera feeds of his colleagues. The meeting had commenced.

30.

Having had his latest instalment in the Terror saga approved by his Editor at, The Chron, Caleb Doyle was smiling to himself, as he now held a hard copy of today's edition with his story gracing the front page. He was elated. His work on the Terror stories had certainly increased his favour with the Editor, and definitely raised his career profile. What was more important though was that Terror was being granted credibility in his notoriety. Now it was time to take things up a level. His would be captors were playing up the Northern Ireland connection and suggesting that he himself may be from the Province. Perhaps it was time to put his powers of manipulation to work again. He lifted his iPhone off his desk and began to compose an e mail. Within minutes a similar smartphone located in New York, pinged to indicate that an important e mail had been received. It was time.

31.

Closing the front door of her lavish apartment on the Upper West Side of Manhattan, Helen Walsh donned her expensive headphones and began her usual morning jog. She had always loved to pound the pavement but was finding it particularly enjoyable lately, as it helped her deal with the stresses of her recent move to New York with her fiancé. He had wanted to continue his professional football career, here but she still hadn't settled to the place. She should be happy. She was planning their upcoming wedding, not to mention being in rehearsals for her imminent Broadway debut. She was living her dream, so why was she finding it so difficult to settle here?

It was still quite early as she entered Straus Park, a favoured part of her route. In US terms, the park was quite intimate and usually quite quiet. She enjoyed the small expanse of greenery nestled near the heart of the bustle of Broadway and the temporary sanctuary that it provided. She had stopped at her usual bench to take on some water when she noticed the young man on the hoverboard coming towards her. She'd read a bit about this latest must have tech but she'd never seen one in real life before. It could move a lot quicker than she realised. She was so mesmerised by the gadget, that she didn't pay much attention to the pilot, nor the small pistol with silencer he now held. At least not until it was too late anyhow.

32.

I reached for my phone immediately when I heard the notification alert. I dreaded to think what awaited as I tapped on the Facebook app. Any new post from Terror was not likely to be good. I wasn't wrong. The picture showed the body of a young woman jogger, posed to mimic the position of the statue behind her. She had apparently been shot. Beneath the picture read:

#TerrorInTheStates #StrausPark #HelenWalsh
Was she #FamousForAllTheWrongReasons? You decide.

I was horrified. I put the phone down and turned my attention back to the Mac. I was about to start typing when, 'Mark' Ferguson said with urgency as he rushed into the room. 'I know' I replied. 'You take Straus Park and I'll take Helen Walsh'.
'I'm on it' he said and was out the door as quickly as he had come in.
After a quick Google search I learned that Helen Walsh was an aspiring actress who came originally from Coleraine, though until her recent move to New York, had spent most of her adult life living in London. She was due to be married in the next few weeks to her long term partner, former Premiership turned MLS footballer, Robbie Cahoon. She was also about to make her Broadway debut as the female lead in,

"Starman" a new musical based around the life of the recently deceased Glam-Rock star, David Bowie.

I was struck by the tragedy of her murder. This young woman had everything to live for and it was all taken away from her on the whim of a monster. On learning of her connection to Northern Ireland, I also felt guilty at the thought that the article that we had asked Doyle to write may have led to her death.

Remembering the #FamousForAllTheWrongReasons, I began to dig a little further. As it turned out, Miss Walsh had been engaged to be married before, to a dancer she had attended drama school with. She had quickly ended the relationship upon meeting Cahoon though, prompting accusations of her being a gold digger. Beyond that, I couldn't see anything untoward. After a quick conversation with Beth who had just seen the Terror post and called, I poured two coffees and headed off in the direction of Ferguson's work station to compare notes. From his end, he had found out that Straus Park was in New York. It had been named after Isidor Straus, a prominent American Politician and former owner of Macey's department store. The statue, a woman gazing over a body of water, was erected in memoriam to Straus and his wife, who had both lost their lives in the sinking of the Titanic.

'He's playing us isn't he'? I asked Ferguson. He nodded. 'But how?' he added, leaning forward across his desk. 'It's obviously not a coincidence that after we have a story published suggesting possible links between Terror, the Titanic and Northern Ireland, that a woman from Northern

Ireland is murdered in America and her body left at a Titanic Memorial'.

'So either he's a fast traveller or…'

'Or there's more than one Terror' said Ferguson, finishing my thought.

'We'd better share this with DI Black, though I'm sure he may have had the same thought already' I said, still feeling some weight of responsibility for the loss of Helen Walsh's life'.

'I'll report in with my CO as well, then we can…' Ferguson stopped mid-sentence as my phone pinged another notification alert from Terror. 'Please, not another one' I said as I lifted the phone. With that, Ferguson's phone pinged an alert also.

Thankfully, there had not been another victim, though what we saw was just as frightening. Terror had posted a statement. It read:

So why did the beautiful Miss Walsh have to die today? Was she #FamousForAllTheWrongReasons? In a way, yes she was, but had I planned to kill her, the answer is no. At least it would have been, until my would be captors decided to try to use the media to smoke me out. Not a clever move really, I'm sure Mr Cahoon would agree. Still, as my dear departed Mother used to say, 'You've made your bed, now you must lie in it'. So, DI Alan Black, DCI Tom Ferguson and not forgetting Farset Investigations own Mark Shaw and the illustrious Belfast Chronicle hack, Caleb Doyle, the way I see it, you all have blood on your hands. You were complicit in the murder of the lovely Helen and now thanks to the power

of social media, you are famed for it.
Some would refer to you as being #FamousForAllTheWrongReasons #LegitimateTargets.
As for the rest of you fake little stars and starlets with something to hide, I know your secrets and I know where you live. I'm sure even you have by now worked out that I have a worldwide following, eager to carry out my wishes. "Terrorists" they call themselves. Cute isn't it! #LookBehindYou.

The fear I had initially felt on reading that our lives had been threatened quickly gave way to a level of anger that I had never experienced before. How dare he attach blame to us, for his sick and twisted deeds. How dare he bring us down to his disgusting level.
Part of me knew that I was reacting in this way because I had already felt some degree of guilt for Helen Walsh's death as it was. It wasn't only that though. On reading his post, I had concluded that not only was Terror the type of person that he himself was purported to despise, but also, with the news of the, "Terrorists" existence, we now had two dangerous cults on our hands.
'What do we do now?' I asked Ferguson. He looked tense.
'Be more careful in future' he replied.

33.

As he stirred the simmering pot of chicken soup, Patrick Rodgers was smiling to himself. Not only had his sister Charlene, survived her recent ordeal, she had done so without any lasting physical damage. And to beat that, here she was convalescing in his apartment. She was free from The Enlightenment at last… they both were. He was looking forward to getting to know her again as he nursed her back to health, and to helping her find her way in a new life beyond the control of, The Prophet. He filled a bowl with the soup, then placed it on a tray, carrying it to his guest room, where she lay in bed. She was asleep, so he set down the tray at the side of the bed, trying to decide if he should wake her. He quickly decided against it and was about to lift the tray away again when he felt a heightening of his psychic senses. He became aware of Charlene's aura.It surrounded her as vibrant and colourful as it had always been. As he watched though, the colours began to blur into one another, losing their distinction and darkening until they reached total blackness. His senses spiked with fear. He had never seen anything like this before personally but he had heard enough to know that it wasn't good and that he should be worried for the safety of his sister and perhaps himself. She stirred awake and his senses began to dampen down as what he saw gave way to her smile.

'So, how's the patient? I'm sure some rest will do you good.

Here, I've made you some soup. It'll help you get your strength up'.

Charlene sat up, and he placed the tray on her lap.

'Thanks… Patrick. You know I'm still not sure what to call you'.

'It's Patrick, definitely Patrick but we'll talk about that later. For now though, your soup is getting cold.

'So you cook now'?

'Oh yeah! Just wait until your throat has recovered enough for you to have solid food. You're in for a treat, now eat up. I spent ages on that soup. I even opened the tin myself'.

Closing the bedroom door, Rodgers thoughts immediately returned to the blackness he had seen in his sister. If it was what he suspected, he hoped that they would both have the strength to deal with it, if and when the time came.

34.

The mood had been tense between Ferguson and myself all day. The deadline I had given Drew and ,The Enlightenment was due to expire in less than an hour and we still had heard nothing from him or them. The topic had remained unspoken of as we tried to track Terror's activity online, without much success. Still it permeated our consciousness nonetheless. With just a few minutes until the deadline expired, I had a call from Caleb Doyle.

'Hey Mark, I'm at the office but there's no-one around. I have some news'.

'Hang on Caleb, we're almost there, just give us a few minutes'. I still wasn't sure how much to trust Doyle, so continued to keep him in the dark about our true location. Ferguson and I quickly donned our coats and left via the garage area, taking the short walk from the corner of Ardmoulin Street onto Divis Street toward the Falls Road to the front entrance. Within a few minutes, we were seated in Uncle Sean's Office.

Both Ferguson and I were on tenterhooks to hear what Doyle had to say but wanted to wait until we were safely in the privacy of the office before I asked,

'So, what is it? Did The Enlightenment contact you?' Doyle was flushed and visibly angry.

'No, they didn't contact me but my Editor did. He's pulling the story'.

'What, why?' Ferguson and I said in Unison. 'I thought he was on board with all this' I continued.
'He was. I think he still is, but he pulled me into his office earlier and told me that he'd been ordered by the owner of the newspaper group, to pull the story and bury all evidence that it ever existed'.
'He can't do that' snapped Ferguson.
'He can and he has' replied Doyle, dejectedly. 'Obviously the owner has bowed to political pressure though I'm not sure why'.
'I agree, that's most likely what has happened. At least it most likely rules out any involvement on their part in Sean's death'. I too was dejected at the thought that they could quash the article so easily.
' I don't understand' said Ferguson. 'What has…'
'…the story got to do with Politics?' I finished his sentence for him. 'It's an easy answer when you think about it. I just wish I had before I put us in this situation'. Now both men were staring at me, perplexed.
'Go on, you're the expert in all things Enlightenment' said Ferguson.
'Ok, so The Chron is owned by Dawson Media Group. Its majority shareholder and CEO, Jeffrey Dawson is a prominent member of the UPNI party, an offshoot of the UK Conservative Party. For a few years now there has been speculation that The Enlightenment have been making donations to the Conservative Party to the tune of millions of pounds'.
'How'? Doyle was intrigued.

'And why, sure they don't even vote do they'? Ferguson added.
'No they don't, but you never know when you're going to need a politician to help you secure charitable status or tax breaks or even grant you planning permission for your latest business premises or Church building for that matter. It's all confirmed in Uncle Sean's investigations The Enlightenment have put their weight behind political campaigns worldwide. It's one of the ways they have become such a wealthy organisation'.
'And deceptively powerful' added Ferguson.
'It looks like we've been burned on all fronts. Both Terror and The Enlightenment have placed us firmly back in our box and we're still no closer to finding Terror or Sean's killer' said Doyle.
'I spoke to DI Black earlier' replied Ferguson. 'He's had his tech team doing much the same thing we were, in trying to track Terror's online presence and who he has been in contact with'.
'And'? I asked.
'Much the same as we came up with. There were a few people claiming to be Terror in some chatrooms. It's hard to work out what's real and what's not. Some will likely be getting a knock at the door regarding their web activity, though most likely they'll be teenagers with too much time on their hands'.
'Like the one in New York' said Doyle sarcastically. 'Look how that turned out'.
'Black and I had a conference call with the detective investigating Helen Walsh's murder. There was no mention of

any teen suspect' Ferguson fired back.

'Maybe not but the US media are reporting that a witness has described a man dressed in dark clothes and riding a hoverboard as being the killer. You wouldn't need to be a DCI to make the presumption that he's a teen'.

'Maybe it's just as well that you're not a DCI then because we deal with facts and evidence, not presumption' snapped Ferguson, clearly riled. 'If all you can bring to our investigation is presumption then perhaps you no longer need to be here'.

'Tom, hang on, that's…' I began.

'It's fine Mark, I'll go.' Doyle got up, lifted his briefcase and overcoat and made for the door. 'I'll be in touch'.

'Ok Caleb and thanks for coming today' I replied as he left.

'I'm sorry' said Ferguson as soon as Doyle was gone'.

'It's fine. I suppose he did provoke you a little'.

'Yeah but still… I'm sorry'.

'Forget it. Look, maybe you're right. Maybe we shouldn't involve him anymore. He provoked you deliberately and we can't afford that kind of distraction'.

'Or any distraction for that matter'.

'Let's leave it at that then' I said extending my hand to him.

'Done' replied Ferguson, shaking my hand.

35.

Terror was furious with himself as he left Mark Shaw's office. What a stupid mistake to have made reference to the fact that Helen Walsh's killer was a teen. His quick thinking had made up for his error but it had done nothing to improve his relationship with Tom Ferguson. Not that it was ever likely to improve anyhow. Still, though, little errors like that could be dangerous. Little errors like that could get him caught. A little error like that had cost Sean Brady his life.

The reminder of his having to kill Brady pained him deeply. He had tried to suppress all thought of it since that horrible night but had struggled to do so. He had been haunted by what he had done ever since and even now as he got into his car, the image of Brady's lifeless body sprawled in front of him pervaded his consciousness and had streams of tears flowing down his cheeks. Trying to compose himself, he wiped the tears away but it didn't help that he had chosen to park his car directly opposite the old St. Comgall's building where Brady had met his end.

Staring ahead at the heavy metal door Terror replayed the events of that fateful few weeks in his mind. Was there any way he could have avoided the course of action that he had taken? He remembered the email he had received from Brady at, The Chron, just after he had finished his story reporting on the death of Owen Grant. Brady had asked to speak with him urgently and had included his mobile number within the email.

Terror had treated the e mail with scorn and in his reply had told the old man that he had nothing to say to him and was not interested in hearing anything he had to say. Within seconds another email from Brady had landed in his inbox. This one read, 'We need to talk'. It had an attachment, which when opened revealed some pictures of Terror and Owen Grant in Grant's hotel room moments before Grant's death. He had allowed the pictures to be taken. They had helped lead Grant toward a false sense of security, though Terror had ensured that he had deleted the pictures after killing Grant, before removing all evidence that he had been there from the room and destroying Grant's phone after having used it to announce his demise .

On seeing the pictures Terror had then immediately called Brady. It had transpired in their conversation that Brady and Grant had been friends and that Brady had recently been teasing Grant about an apparent drought in his love life. On the night of Grant's murder Brady had received the pictures and a text message from Grant, with the message, 'Drought's Over'. Presumably this had been done while Terror was pouring drinks from the mini bar and had been momentarily distracted.

What had also transpired was that Brady had no doubt that Terror was capable of the murder of Owen Grant and suspected his involvement. Brady had wanted to report what he knew to the police but felt that it would be better for Doyle, or as he suspected a.k.a. Terror, to contact the police himself. After all this time, Brady had still wanted to help Doyle, so the two men agreed to meet up later that evening so that they could talk the situation through. Brady had even offered to accompany Doyle to the Police Station. It was at that point where the fight or flight instinct had kicked in with Terror. He had agreed to meet Brady but had resolved to himself at that point that Brady had now posed too great a threat to allow him to live. Having replayed the chain of events in his mind, Terror concluded that although he regretted what he had done, the only way it could have been avoided was if he had been more careful with Grant. 'No more slip ups' he said aloud thumping the steering wheel in frustration before edging out into the heavy Friday evening traffic.

36.

Having lit the barbecue I took a seat at the patio and reached into the large ice bucket, retrieving myself what was now a perfectly chilled bottle of Bud. I cracked it open and took a swig before leaning back in the chair. As I waited for the flames and smoke from the barbecue to die down, I watched Alecia play on the grass in our back garden. She has been excited all day at the prospect of what she was calling our, "Barbecue Party". In truth, I was a little excited about it myself. Beth and I had decided that it would be good to invite Rodgers, Charlene and Ferguson along with a few of our closest friends and family out to the house for the evening. Beth had decided that it would be good for Charlene to meet some new people now that she was feeling a lot stronger and that it would do Ferguson no harm to widen his social circle a little. I was just looking forward to spending a relaxing Saturday evening with family and friends and forgetting all things Farset related for the weekend.

'Alecia,time to come and get dressed for the party' shouted Beth from the window. 'Mark will you put a tablecloth on the buffet table and bring the salads and dressings out of the fridge. They'll be here soon'.

After a quick check on the barbecue and laying out the food I quickly changed and had returned to my seat and my beer when my girls appeared at the patio doors.

'Look Daddy, we're so pretty' said Alecia gesturing towards

herself and her mum in their summer dresses. I got up and crossed over to her, scooping her up in my arms. 'You certainly are pretty' I said kissing her on her forehead before leaning over to kiss Beth, 'both of you'.
'Daddy looks handsome too doesn't he Alecia'? Beth said.
'Yes, Daddy you do' she replied before pulling both of us into one of our family hugs, reaching round both mine and Beth's necks as I held her in my arms. 'I'm so excited about our party'. We laughed and I set her back down on the grass just in time to hear someone call, 'Knock, knock' at the gate. Looks like it was time to get the party started.

37.

David McManus placed the book he was reading down on his lap before reaching for the Whisky bottle on the table beside his armchair. He refilled the heavy glass tumbler beside the bottle, set the bottle down again and took a large gulp from the glass. He returned his attention to the book, a bound printing of the latest volume of sermons given by The Prophet. He had always found comfort and solace in the words of The Prophet but was starting to struggle to do so lately, especially since it was clear by the actions of the rest of the Church Community, particularly The Elders, that he was being punished for not keeping his family in hand.

Since Charlene had joined her brother Jarl in the world of sin, beyond The Enlightenment, he, David Mc Manus, one of the highest ranking and most respected members of the Northern Ireland faction of The Church, had been asked to give up his seat at the front of The Church and to take a place nearer the back. This very public humiliation had been followed by some members of The Church cutting business ties with him. Although he hadn't been shut up or technically withdrawn from, he may as well have been. Even now, this Saturday evening, Church members would be gathered together in groups in the homes of some, in a social gathering, for dinner and drinks. He had not been invited to attend any such gathering since Charlene had tried to end her life. Still, he would keep his faith strong and pray that The Prophet will return him to favour in due course. Draining the contents of the glass with another large gulp, he again tried to focus on the teachings of The Prophet. Before long though, he was overtaken by the effects of the alcohol and had fallen asleep in the chair. Dreaming, he relived some of the high points in his life. His being invited to meet The Prophet in person, his reaching the positions of Priest and Elder in the Community, his reputation and standing as a successful businessman within the Community. Before long though, the high points were replaced by memories of the low points. The suicide of his wife, the defecting of his son to the world of sin, the petulance and disrespect shown by his daughter toward the Church, to the point where he had to routinely beat her, to stop the Devil getting in. That's when it happened. David McManus sat bolt upright in the armchair awake and fully conscious as the pain exploded in his chest. His movement had knocked the glass from the table and the book from his lap. As the glass shattered on the hard wooden floor, surrounding the book with tiny sharp splinters, his heart beat it's last.

In the front room of a house a few doors down, a group of The Enlightenment were gathered around a piano, drinks in hand, united in song and merriment. Tomorrow morning they will give thanks that the soul of their Brother David has been taken home to the Lord. Very few however, would feel the weight of guilt that they had collectively contributed to his demise.

38.

From a cursory glance around the assembled company, I think that it's safe to say that our Barbecue Party is a success. Charlene certainly seems to be getting on well with Beth and her friend Susan. I even heard talk of a possible shopping trip tomorrow as I checked that everyone was ok for food and drinks earlier. Alecia and Susan's daughter Jo were having a great time flitting from table to table in between dancing and torturing Ferguson to play Little Mix on the sounddock again. He seemed to be having a good time too. Being with the girls probably reminded him of his niece I thought. Both Alecia's parents and mine had already given him the seal of approval, having eaten with him earlier and were even more enamoured now as he took the time to keep the children laughing and happy. That was something that hadn't gone unnoticed by Susan either by the look of things. I smiled across the garden at Beth then nodded in the direction of Susan, who had now become assistant DJ. Beth returned the smile then gave me a cheeky wink. I smiled again, shaking my head in mock disbelief. Beth had been playing matchmaker for Susan since her divorce was finalised a few months ago. It looks like Ferguson had made it onto her hit list.

After lighting the patio heaters and lighting the candles in the lanterns that Beth had strategically placed around the garden earlier, I took a seat beside Rodgers, who had just returned from having a cigarette in another little garden area that we

had at the side of the house.
'Those things will kill you, you know' I said jokingly. He shrugged his shoulders then laughed.
'Well, it's not like you can expel me now is it… Sir'?
Since our recent meeting in his office it had become a source of amusement that in a former life for both of us, I had been his Headteacher and he, a student of mine, despite not that much of an age gap. Whilst we could see the funny side of it, it was clear from dinner earlier, that Charlene was still embarrassed to be around me socially.
'So, how are you both holding up'? I asked, taking advantage of the chance to speak relatively privately.
'Yeah, we're ok I think. I mean it hasn't been easy but we're getting there. At least, physically, she's healed'.
'And emotionally'? I ask. 'It must be difficult enough to adjust to life outside,The Enlightenment, let alone the other things she's been through lately'.
'And not just lately either. I've really tried to talk to her… tried to get her to open up to me but she just keeps closing the conversation down. We're getting along so well and we're both really happy that she is free. We're so close to each other again but at times I can see a real distance between us. She's hurting so much from the past and she's isolating herself. I can't reach her'.
'Maybe she just needs time' I suggested. 'It can't have been easy for you when you first left either'.
'No, that's true but…'
'But what'? I asked.
'It's nothing…I'm not sure you would understand'.

'Hey, do you remember where I used to work'? I joked, trying to lighten the mood. 'Try me'.

'Her aura. I've never seen anything like it before'. Rodgers then went on to describe a blackness that had been surrounding his sister. He felt that her life force had become suppressed by something dark, something evil. He feared that since returning from her near death experience, a dark side to her personality had developed and he was worried it could consume her. He was right, I wasn't sure I understood either but after seeing him use his psychic gift first hand, I believed him.

'Maybe a distraction would help. She seems to be enjoying herself tonight OK'.

'Yeah, probably because she's escaped me for a few hours'.

'Well maybe that's it. You've been cooped up together for while now getting her back to strength. Maybe it's time for you to get back to work and giver her some space'.

'I'd love to but I don't like the idea of leaving her alone at home for so long. Not until we figure out what to do next anyway'.

'I wouldn't worry about that so much. Maybe you won't have to figure out what to do next'.

'Why'?

'From what I can remember, she is an intelligent and hardworking young girl. If you're happy with it and she is agreeable to it, then I don't see any reason why she can't be Farset's first receptionist and administrator'.

'You'd do that, really'?

'Of course, what are friends for? Besides, she'll be a real asset

to the place'.
'Thanks Mark replied Rodgers. 'I'd say she would love the idea. Looks like I'll be shelling out for some work clothes as well now.'
'All the more reason for you to get back to work my friend' I replied before topping up both our wine glasses.

39.

The barbecue had continued on into the small hours of Sunday morning, so Beth and I had gone straight to bed after waving everyone off and clearing up. It was only now as we ate a late breakfast of porridge and coffee, did we get time to compare notes on the success of the evening. A good time seemed to have been had by all and perhaps some new friendships formed. We joked at Susan's less than subtle flirtation with Ferguson and his attempts to keep her at arm's length. He had certainly been a hit with everyone, as had Rodgers.

'Everyone was really taken with Charlene as well from what I saw and heard' said Beth. 'You know, she really has a wit, intelligence and charm beyond her 17 years'.

'That was the influence of her English Teacher for all those years' I quipped. 'It sounds like she has certainly won you over'.

I told Beth of my intention to make a job offer to her, which she was delighted about.

'That's just what she needs. It could be a good fit for both of you'.

I agreed, filling her in on the conversation I'd had with Rodgers and his concerns.

'That kind of fits with something she said to me last night' said Beth appearing to grow concerned herself. 'I just put it down to her needing to deal with some of the things that have

happened to her but…' Beth appeared lost in her thoughts.
'But what? What did she say'?
'That she sometimes has dark thoughts'.
'Of what'? I asked, hoping that Charlene was not still considering suicide.
'Of vengeance' Beth replied. 'She said that since she woke up from the coma, she has wanted to make them pay. She has wanted her father and The Enlightenment to suffer for what they had done to her and her family and what they drove her to try to do to herself'.
'What did you say'? I asked.
'I said that it was only natural to feel angry after all that she has been through and that the best way to get vengeance was to do what Patrick has done and create a new, happy life for herself beyond their control. I suggested that she could become a new person, just like he has, even create a new identity as he has'.
'How did she take that'?
'That's what worries me, now that you have told me what Patrick has said'.
'What'? I asked, becoming increasingly anxious myself.
'She said that if she was going to take on a new identity it would be as an alter-ego in the same way that Terror has done. She said that perhaps The Enlightenment might come to know her as Fear. I thought she was just venting but…'
'It may well be, but I think we need to keep a close eye on her all the same. She obviously has some issues to deal with and we need to make sure she doesn't do anything dangerous. Are you still going shopping with her today'?

'Yes, Alecia and I are going to meet her this afternoon then Susan has invited us over to eat with her and Jo after'.

'Could you ask her about the job offer for me? If she's interested she can come down to the office tomorrow morning and I'll meet with her to discuss it'.

'Sure'.

'I think I'll give Rodgers a call when you're all out and bring him up to speed'.

'Fine, but tell him not to mention anything to Charlene. The last thing that either she or we need, is for her to feel that I've broken her confidence'.

40.

Charlene's revelations to Beth were still churning in my mind as I ran through Antrim Castle Gardens. I had taken up running shortly after Uncle Sean's death and usually found that it helped me destress and clear my head. Not today though. Today would be better described in the words of Macbeth. "Oh full of Scorpions is my mind". My first preoccupation was with Helen Walsh. I have thought of her plight and my role in it every time I've pulled on a pair of running shoes, since her death. Where was this Terror thing going to end? Then there was my earlier conversation with Beth about Charlene. When I had phoned Rodgers to tell him about it, his increased fear for her was palpable. Was there any real substance to what she said about revenge on ,The Enlightenment? I spent the remaining distance between Antrim Gardens and home, pounding the pavement hard in the hope that it might provide me with the answer to that question. It didn't!

When I got home, I quickly showered, changed into a pair of sweatpants and t shirt that I wear to lounge around the house in. I'd put in a good run so decided to treat myself. After all, Beth and Alecia were eating out this evening and wouldn't be home for a while yet. Before long I was sitting in my favourite chair in the lounge with a cold beer beside me, a plate of my favourite M&S duck spring rolls and crispy chilli beef on my lap, and the latest episode of Elementary which I had recorded, filling the TV screen. Not for the first time, I wished that Holmes and Watson were consultants of Farset rather than the NYPD. I must have had the volume up a little too high, as I mistook a text alert received by Detective Bell in the show, for a text alert from my own phone. When I lifted my phone to check, I noticed that I'd missed a call from Ferguson. He'd left a voice message explaining that his family had been given some unexpected leave and would be returning to Liverpool tomorrow. He had managed to get a seat on a flight back home this evening and was packing for the journey now. Not sure exactly what time his flight was, I sent him a text message, wishing him a safe journey and my hopes that he will enjoy spending time with them. I also added that I would let him know if we had any developments but would try not to disturb him.

It was after I had sent the message to Ferguson that I'd noticed that a new email had come into my personal account. I hadn't received an email from this source in a relatively long time, so it was with a mixture of surprise and shock that I opened it to read what Drew Pinkerton had to say.

In his usual curt tone, Drew informed me that David McManus, father of Jarl and Charlene had been, "taken". His remains were found in his house this morning. His funeral was to take place tomorrow morning at 06:00 am and I was to tell my new friends, his children, that under no circumstances would they be allowed to attend. My head was swimming. How was I going to tell Ferguson and Charlene? Then, in a second of clarity, it hit me. "My new friends". How could he have known my connection to Mc Manus' children unless he

or other Enlightenment had been watching me, or them?
I quickly changed again into a pair of jeans and a hooded top. I'd thought this kind of news would be best given in person, so was going to drive down to Rodgers' apartment. I was just about to call Beth when I heard the car pull into the driveway. By the time I had got out the front door, Beth had lifted Alecia, who was asleep, out of the car, and was carrying her towards the house.
'I think all of the excitement was a bit too much for her. She's been asleep the whole way home'. I moved to the boot of the car and took out the shopping. Judging by the number of bags, I could see why Alecia was worn out.
'It must've been quite a shopping trip' I said, setting the bags down in the hall. Alecia was now sprawled across the sofa, still asleep and Beth was unbuttoning her coat.
'We had a great day. It's funny to see how Alecia is starting to have her own sense of what she likes. Charlene had a great day too. She was buzzing when I told her about the job. I'd say she'll be there in the morning before you get there, she was so excited'.
'Good, I'm glad. Actually, I'm on my way to see her and Patrick now'. I showed Beth the email. She was horrified at the news, not to mention, riled at Drew Pinkerton's tone.
'How can these people be so cold? Christians! How Christian is it to deny someone access to their Father's funeral? Evil scum'!
'I'd better go break the news' I said solemnly. I knew Beth wanted to come with me to be there for Charlene but it wouldn't be fair to drag Alecia out again.

‘Pass on my condolences and tell them I’ll speak to them tomorrow’ Beth said as she pulled me into a hug. ‘Take care’.
‘I will. I’ll be back as soon as I can’. Within minutes I was on the motorway, trying to figure out how best to break the news.

41.

Patrick Rodgers didn't seem that surprised to see me despite the fact that I'd turned up unannounced on what was now Sunday night. I wondered if he had already new that something was wrong via his psychic gift, though his actions didn't betray anything of it if he did. He greeted me warmly and invited me in, motioning me to take a seat in the sitting room area of the open planned apartment.

'Was it Charlene you were looking for? She's so excited about the job. I thought she was supposed to meet you tomorrow morning. She's in her room. I'll go get her'.

'No, wait Patrick. I need to tell you something first'.

He barely reacted as I told him the news and extended mine and Beth's condolences, though his gaze remained locked on me throughout. He asked to see the e mail and I showed it to him. He read it silently then handed the phone back to me without speaking.

'I'm sorry' I said again feebly.

'Thanks Mark. I appreciate you coming to tell us'.

'It was the least I could do' I replied. 'I did wonder if you'd sensed anything about it'.

'No, not a thing. I mean, I knew how The Enlightenment would likely be treating him but frankly I'd closed myself off from feeling anything for my father on any level a long time ago'. I heard a door open then close in the distance and figured that it must be Charlene.

'I'd better…' Rodgers moved for the door and managed to intercept Charlene in the hallway. I heard him explain what had happened in a low voice, then immediately after, heard Charlene begin to cry. I felt like I was intruding on their grief and wanted to leave, but at the same time, I didn't want to go out into the hallway for fear of disturbing them so I remained seated. After a short time the crying stopped and Rodgers and Charlene were speaking to one another softly. I didn't wish to eavesdrop so took out my phone and busied myself by looking at my Facebook account as a distraction. Momentarily Rodgers returned.

'Sorry Patrick, I didn't want to intrude or interrupt' I said.

'That's fine. Don't worry. She's gone to bed. It'll probably take a while to register with her'.

'It'll take a while to register with you both I would imagine. I'd better go and leave you to it. I'll give you a call tomorrow but if there's anything I can do in the meantime, please let me know. Tell Charlene not to worry about coming in tomorrow. I'll catch up with her another time'.

'Thanks Mark. I really appreciate all you've done for us'.

'No problem, I'll speak to you tomorrow'.

Rodgers let me out the front door, closing it behind me. As I made my way back to the car I noticed a dark coloured Skoda Octavia parked across the street. I could just be being paranoid, but I thought I recognised it as belonging to a more elderly member of The Enlightenment. The fact that on realising I was looking toward the car, the driver turned the headlights on full beam to obscure my vision of him or the number plate of the car made me feel justified in my feelings of paranoia. Disgusted, I waved mockingly in the direction of the car before getting into my own car and driving home.

42.

Even before I went to bed I knew that I wouldn't get much sleep. Since the beginning of my journey home, my anger at Drew Pinkerton's email and the fact that I was being spied upon at Rodgers' house, had me near boiling point. I was also angry at myself. After all these years and despite my no longer being in their employment, they had still been able to manipulate me into doing their dirty work. I tossed and turned into the early hours of Monday morning, consumed by anger at The Enlightenment and how they were able to permeate evil under the guise of Christianity and not be held accountable. I thought about Sean's expose and how easily they were able to quash it's being revealed. I thought about Charlene and Rodgers and how they were not only being denied the right to attend their Father's funeral, but also, in all likelihood, any inheritance they might have had from his assets, would be swallowed up by the Church. Finally, I thought I was tired of being pushed around by them, which was why, by 05:30 in the morning, I was parked up in a space just facing their Church with a camera in my hand. I had decided to continue with Uncle Sean's investigation and was determined that I would find a way to get his findings and my findings out into the public domain.

By 05:50, the cavalcades of Enlightenment vehicles were making their way into the Church car park. I made no effort to conceal my car, my camera or myself as they passed me and although subtly, my presence had been duly noted.

43.

By 07:00 I was already seated at my desk in the glass booth in the corner, that had now become my subterranean office at Farset. I was feeling a lot calmer now, having completed my stakeout of David McManus' funeral. I logged into Uncle Sean's iCloud account with the intention of going through some of his evidence sources from his investigations into The Enlightenment and the Owen Grant murder myself. I was hoping that I might find something, a name, anything that might give me a lead on who might have killed him. By 08:30, I had come no closer to a suspect and was beginning to wonder had I set myself an impossible task in trying to find his killer. After all, the PSNI had closed the case, believing the perpetrator to be an opportunist thief or a desperate junkie. They were obviously more experienced than me in conducting investigations. They had explored all related avenues and still they were unable to find the identity of Sean's killer, so why did I think I could do better? I wondered about speaking to DI Black about the true Farset HQ in the bowels of the school boundaries. It may give him a fresh perspective on the case and perhaps give cause to have it reopened. I called the Grosvenor Road Police Station and asked if DI Black could call me when he was able to. In the meantime I decided that my time would be best spent continuing to work the case, though I'd had my fill of looking at Enlightenment related documents for a while. I put a fresh pot of coffee on to brew and returned to the computer with the intention of going through the other folders and files in Sean's cloud. In the last number of days Ferguson and I had already started this task but still had quite a few files to see, so I decided to crack on. I opened my desk journal at a new page and was about to open a new file when my mobile rang. It was Rodgers.

'Hi Mark. We've been ringing the Farset number for a while now and there is no answer. Charlene and I are outside the office. Are you nearly here'?

'Yes... sure. Have you been waiting long?'

'Just a while but...'

'Don't worry, I'll be right there'. I ran upstairs from the school basement, along the corridor and opened the main door from the inside, not a moment too soon, as it was now raining heavily. I led them both into Sean's former office and turned on the electric fan heater in the corner.

'Sorry it's so cold, it doesn't usually take long to heat up though' I said, hoping to distract their attention from the fact that I was already inside the building but had not answered the phone.

'Take a seat. I was going to call you later to see how you both were. I hadn't expected to see you today'.

'I know, but Charlene and I had a talk last night and she would like to start today if that's ok'?

'Of course. Welcome to the team Charlene' I smiled, 'Well, a team of two for the moment'.

'Thanks', Charlene smiled 'Even a small team needs a PA, I'm looking forward to it'.

Rodgers shifted uneasily in his seat and in doing so, caused

Charlene's smile to fade. He leaned forward.
'The thing is Mark' he began,'We had a really good and really long talk last night after you left. Hearing about the things Charlene has had to endure since I left, what happened to her recently and talking about what The Enlightenment have done to us and our family, we've decided…' Suddenly consumed with emotion, his voice broke and his eyes brimmed with tears. Charlene continued on his behalf.
'Mr Shaw, Patrick has told me about the work your Uncle had done to expose The Enlightenment, and about the article. We want to help. We want to do everything we possibly can to help bring them to justice, everything we possibly can to weaken them and expose them'.
She was very calm and measured in her tone but there was no mistaking how serious she was. She meant business. I'd never seen her like this before. She bore little resemblance in her character to my vivacious and bubbly former student and she was certainly nothing like the frail, weak young woman I saw in the hospital bed just weeks ago. By contrast, Rodgers, who had began to compose himself, was a shadow of the tanned and self assured character, he liked to present to the public. I quickly brought them up to speed on the fact that the article had been blocked and my suspicions how. They both defeatedly agreed with my conclusions, confirming that bribery of political officials was not unheard of within their community. I went on to tell them of my being followed home from their house and by my subsequent decision to continue Uncle Sean's investigation, including my, "attending" their father's funeral. Both were visibly elated at the

continuation of the Farset Investigation, particularly when I added that we would work together to explore other means of lifting the lid on the activities of The Enlightenment.

44.

I was surprised when Charlene used the internal intercom built into our phone system (which until she showed it to me, I didn't know existed), to inform me that I had a visitor. It turned out that rather than return my call, DI Black had arrived in person. I asked Charlene to show him down to the main office. Having overcome my earlier reluctance I had already given Rodgers and her the guided tour and had furnished her with a necessary security fob to allow her to fulfil her duties. Upon his being ushered into my office by my already invaluable assistant, I rose to greet him.

'DI Black, I'm glad you came. I wanted to talk to you about… this' I gestured around the bunker area, not sure how best to describe it. 'We've only fairly recently discovered it ourselves and I was thinking today, that it might perhaps have some bearing on Uncle Sean's case'.

'It really is an excellent facility' he replied awkwardly, perhaps unsure how best to describe it himself, or possibly embarrassed that it had not been uncovered in the investigation. After conducting my second guided tour of the facilities in one morning and bringing Black up to date on everything that he wasn't already aware of all that had come to light since we discovered our new HQ, which admittedly was not much, we returned to my office where I poured two coffee's and took a seat at my desk, gesturing Black to sit down.

'So, what do you think? Is there anything that you've seen or heard that you feel would merit further investigation'?
'I'm sorry Mark, but I would really have to say that the answer is no' he replied curtly. 'Even if there was anything, I would have a hard time in convincing my superiors to do anything with it, especially now'.
My heart sank even though, truth be told, deep down, I wasn't expecting to hear anything to the contrary. The last part of his statement however, had confused me a little.
'What do you mean especially now'? I asked, perhaps a little naively.
'Take a look around you Mr Shaw', Black's tone had quickly gained formality. 'If I talk to my superiors I'm going to have to tell them about this place. A state of the art crime lab located virtually under their noses, containing thousands if not millions of pounds worth of equipment, whilst we are struggling for resources and having to make decent police officers redundant because our operations budget is being squeezed beyond belief'. His face was flushed and although he was trying to contain himself, it was clear that he was angry. I empathised, but still, none of this was my doing. Regardless, I decided not to respond. He leaned forward and opened the briefcase he had left on the floor beside his chair earlier. He opened it, removed a thick file from it and placed it on my desk.
'One of the reasons I came today was to give you this' he said tapping the file with his index finger. 'This is a copy of the file on the investigation on your Uncle's murder. As far as I'm concerned, we've done all we can. As next of kin, you have a

right to see the file and out of courtesy I made this copy for you. Its up to you if you want to continue the investigation' he said, trying less hard to hide what I could only now judge to be contempt for my new found situation. I was left with the distinct impression that he would not be so willing to work with me in the future, than he had been of late.
'Thanks' I said. 'I appreciate all that you've done'. He nodded and moved toward the door.
'Wait, you said one of the reasons you came today. What was the other'?
He stopped just short of the door and turned toward me. He sighed heavily then spoke grudgingly. ' I had a call from the New York State Park Police today. They arrested Helen Walsh's killer last night. Waylon Matthews. Kid about 17. His sister got suspicious and called him in. He has already been charged but isn't giving anything up on Terror'. He made toward the door again.
'I'll show you out' I said before walking silently alongside him down a corridor, not for the first time, though I suspected the last. On returning to the office, the phone on my desk was ringing. The dial tone was one specifically used to alert me that it was Charlene on the intercom. I picked up the receiver but before I got the chance to speak I heard her say, 'A Mr Doyle here to see you. He said you would know what it's about'.
'Thanks, I'll be right up' I said before returning the receiver to its cradle. 'Great' I said aloud to myself. 'Today just keeps getting better and better'!

45.

Charlene smiled and waved at her brother as she saw his car approach the rear parking area at Farset. She was glad to have finally unburdened herself to him last night after hearing of the death of their father. He had been so supportive and understanding but also blamed himself for leaving her behind. She'd never blamed him though and was glad to have resolved those feelings for him. They had always been close and both were glad to be finally moving on from The Enlightenment together, though both had agreed that they needed some kind of closure. Mark Shaw had agreed to help them out with that this morning, though she did wonder what closure had actually meant to Patrick. Her only feeling on learning of her father's death, was one of relief and on telling Patrick why, he had understood. So why had he insisted that they visit the grave after they had finished work? Why were they on their way there now? It must be something that he felt they needed to do so she didn't question it, she just got into the car.

'So, how was the first day'? Patrick asked excitedly.

'It was great. Mark is really nice to work for once you get past the fact that he used to be your teacher'.

'And you don't have to call him Mr Shaw' Patrick laughed.

She felt her face flush a little. 'I'm certainly going to be busy. He made the unfortunate mistake of asking for my input on improvements to the office, to make it a more user friendly space for me and any visiting client'.

'I bet that was a costly mistake. What did you suggest'?

'Well, lets just say that the office and the two nearest rooms to it, are being completely remodelled, with me as Project Manager'.

'Into what'? Patrick asked, surprised.

'A reception area and office for me, a meeting room and an office where Mark can meet clients. That way, the bunker can remain secret'.

'Great idea. Sounds like he was right, you will be an asset to the place'.

She felt her face flush again.

'Anything else exciting'?

'No, I just met a few clients, that's all. Nothing else to report'.

Her face flushed for a third time. It was just as well Patrick was concentrating too much on his driving to notice, because that wasn't all, was it?

She hadn't told him about her new friend Caleb Doyle had she?

She smiled to herself, though before long her thoughts had begun to turn sombre again, as they made their way toward Carnmoney Cemetery. They both remained silent throughout the rest of the journey and had barely made eye contact with one another as they walked the short distance from the car to the graveside. Dusk had begun to descend and the rain had started again. Patrick crouched down on his knees and touched the headstone that had been erected for their mother. He was forcing back tears unsuccessfully as she looked on. For her part, all she could do was watch him. She still missed her mother, yes, but she was under no illusion that the reason

Patrick had brought her here was so that they could both say goodbye to their father. Misplaced respect on Patrick's part she thought as she watched the now heavier rain bounce off the small puddles that had formed in the newly turned soil. Truly, they had lost their father a long time before today. The only feelings she had for the remains of the person lying six feet beneath them were of hatred and anger. She put her hand on her brother's shoulder.

'I'll wait in the car' she said before turning her back on her father, just like he had done to them.

46.

Terror removed what had once been Sean Brady's iPhone from the toolbox in his garage where he had stashed it. He had gone through it shortly after the murder and had learned all the information it had contained,which was nothing of any real interest apart from the incriminating photograph of him. After deleting everything, he had checked to see if the phone was connected to a cloud drive. It wasn't, though that didn't surprise him given Brady's age. The SIM card had long since been burned, as had the leather effect cover. Taking a seat at the kitchen table, he removed the new SIM card,charger and case that he had bought earlier, from the bag. He carefully used the tool that came with his own phone, to insert the new SIM before snapping the pink plastic protector case onto the back of the phone, connecting the charger and plugging it in. He watched as the familiar Apple icon appeared on the screen of what now looked like the phone of a teenage girl. The perfect gift, he thought to himself, before removing his other purchases of the day from their bag, a pink metallic gift box and some silver tissue paper.

Tomorrow he would return to Farset and give the phone to Charlene, the new Receptionist and the latest to succumb to his charm. It had been easy to engage her in conversation, especially when he had noticed how she had initially looked at him, then became awkward and bashful in her words and movements. It was at that moment he sensed an opportunity that could be exploited. Who would have thought that another visit to Mark Shaw, in an attempt to get back on the inside track at Farset, could yield such a result? Terror knew that Charlene would not only prove useful as an insider, she also had the potential to influence things in his favour, should he ever need it. All he had to do now was win her over and based on their initial conversation, that shouldn't be too difficult. She had obviously been lonely for a very long time and after learning from him that he had been involved in trying to bring Sean Brady's investigation of The Enlightenment to the attention of the public, she had been quick to trust him with some of her experiences of life inside the cult. The journalist in him had been keen to find out more, though he was all too aware that he would get nowhere with his Editor. Still, he had managed to ingratiate himself with Mark Shaw again and further still, had offered to help in the continued investigation into The Enlightenment. Now he had an excuse to spend more time at Farset and an opportunity to further his plans. The phone would give him a personal link to Charlene which would make things easier still. He'd been surprised that she didn't already own one, until her learned that within The Enlightenment, all mobile phones, computers and tablets must be bought from a supply company owned by, The Prophet, and were implanted with technology allowing him to track the movements and behaviours of his flock. Despite having no qualms about manipulating her, he did feel sorry for her. Having spent her life under the control of a cult, she thinks she has found freedom. It wouldn't be long though before she would be under his control.

47.

I had to credit her, the change to the former Headmaster's office and the rooms adjacent to it made them barely recognisable by the time Charlene and the team she employed had finished. To top it off, it had all been completed in just four days. To any unsuspecting potential client there was no indication that the vast majority of the rest of the building was virtually derelict. She had even upgraded the external doors, gates and security system around the entire perimeter of the building and had CCTV cameras fitted internally and externally in all areas occupied by Farset, including the bunker. Now anyone I chose to give access to, could log in remotely to the CCTV from anywhere via their mobile internet or broadband. She truly was a marvel. She had even stayed within the budget that I had set for what she had dubbed the, "Farset Upgrade". Even now, as I was leaving through the front exit, she had sign writers fitting a very corporate looking sign above it, much like the one in the bunker, except this one included contact details.

I wish that I could say that I had made as much progress in my investigations but I hadn't. It was not for the want of trying though. I had gone through the copy of the murder file that had been compiled by the PSNI meticulously and could find nothing that would give me any new leads, at least that was until this morning. Having read the CSI's report for what must've been the 20th time and having continually poured over it's accompanying pictures, it suddenly dawned on me. The scene had been left too clean. There had been no DNA or fibre transfer between Sean and his killer, which indicated that Sean did not realise he was under attack until it was too late. They had obviously lain in wait for him but there were no footprints in the mud found anywhere around the building despite the fact that it had been raining heavily that night. That suggested that the killer came in directly through the front gate and made their way to the old garden area.It had become overgrown over the years, so would have provided cover and accounted for the lack of footprints.There were no photographs or mention of this area in the report though. The CSI had found no discernible fingerprints, DNA transfer or anything else for that matter that could be classed as evidence on the murder site whatsoever. This led me to reach the conclusion that this was no random mugging, the killer was a professional who knew exactly what he was doing. Sean had been deliberately targeted, of that much I was now completely sure. What I still couldn't fathom though was why and by who. Another couple of things that I was now sure of was that none of The Enlightenment that I knew of, had the skills of an experienced assassin and that DI Black and his team should have been able to reach the same conclusions I had. That in particular, bothered me. For now though, I had agreed to pick up Ferguson from the airport. I'd been keeping him up to date with all the other happenings since he left, by e mail. All except my recent deductions of course. I was looking forward to having him look over the file, to see if he agreed. From his end, return communication had been fairly brief. I got the impression that perhaps not all was well but I'm sure he would talk to me about when the time is right.

48.

After what seemed like hours, Ferguson finally looked up from the file.

'Well?' I asked anxiously before giving him the chance to speak.

'I think you're right. It certainly looks like your Uncle was targeted deliberately and by someone who knew what they were doing. Discounting The Enlightenment, the only other thing that we know that he was involved in was, the Terror murder of Owen Grant'.

'Which implies that Terror is the most likely to have been responsible. It doesn't fit with his MO though'. I'd been mulling over the same thought but couldn't reconcile it to the other murders attributed to Terror or Waylon Matthews, his disciple.

'True' replied Ferguson 'but Owen Grant's death is the first to be attributed to Terror. What if Sean knew or at least suspected he knew who Terror was? He could well have been targeted by him if Terror was aware that this was the case'?

'Which might possibly explain our account of the crime scene and the lack of defence wounds on Sean's body' I questioned aloud ?

'Exactly'.

'So what now'?

'The thing that makes most sense to me now in light of all this is to work with a criminal psychologist or profiler. I'd already been thinking along those lines while I was away. I mean, this guy has only just come out of the woodwork and is labelling himself as Terror. He wages war on celebrities with something to hide, yet in reality, three arguably minor celebrities have met their demise. Horrible I know, but it's hardly striking fear in the hearts of the glitterati. It's hardly even made national news, yet alone global'.

'True, I suppose, though I doubt we would have access to the services of a psychologist or profiler, especially now that the PSNI have cut their ties with us'.

Ferguson looked pensive. 'I did have a little bit of training in profiling a few years back, nothing much though, but maybe I could work something up'.

'I have a little bit of training on criminal psychology from my online course as well. Then of course I know a fair bit about psychology and behaviours in the Education field. I'm sure that between us we could put something together'.

As I was finishing the sentence my mind was racing away ahead of me. I remembered what Patrick had said about Uncle Sean indicating that Patrick and I would work together again in the future. Maybe this was what he meant. Ferguson was nodding his agreement to what I had just said when I added, 'Hey, I'm just thinking out loud here, but what would you think about working with a Psychic Detective?'

'You mean ask Patrick, I think that would be a great idea. I mean, we've nothing to lose and the more information we get for the profile the better. Besides, we've both seen him in action, he's great right'.

I immediately texted Patrick. I didn't want to call him for fear that he may be with a client. Within seconds he had replied that he would love to help. We agreed to meet at Farset at around 7pm. He hadn't seen Charlene's handiwork yet as they were both busy, so this would be a good chance. Besides which, I thought that being at the scene of Sean's murder, near the time of the evening that he had lost his life may well enhance Patrick's ability to make a connection, like I was an expert in these things!
'Well, that's that sorted. He's going to meet us here around 7 o'clock this evening'. I glanced down at my watch'. 'So, I'm due to meet Beth and Alecia at Beth's parents house for dinner at 17:30, it's 16:00 now, that should give us enough time'.
'You want to start work on the profile now'?
'No, I think it would be best kept until tomorrow, after we see what happens with Patrick tonight. No, what I meant, Tom my friend, was that it will give us enough time for you to tell me what's going on with you'.
'What do you mean?' asked Ferguson as he leaned back in his seat, trying to appear comfortable and relaxed, though the fact that he had folded his arms across his chest, suggested a defence mechanism to me. Hey maybe I might be good at this psychology stuff all right.
'I mean that any contact I had with you when you were away was met with minimal response. You hardly spoke a word in the car when I picked you up and you barely reacted when you saw all the work that Charlene had done to the place. There's also the fact that you have hardly mentioned your trip back to

Liverpool and that every time I tried to ask you about it, you've just clammed up. So, what gives?'

Ferguson leaned forward again and placed his elbows on the desk. 'I got called into the station when I was there. My Superintendent broke the news I've been dreading. I'm definitely amongst those being made redundant. They're putting together packages for us and it should all be finalised within a few weeks'. He lowered his eyes from mine and fixed his gaze on the surface of the desk. I was gutted for him.

'Tom, I'm so sorry. If there's anything I can do to help, you know I'm here and you know there'll always be a job for you here if you decide to take me up on my offer'.

'Thanks Mark, but I'm afraid there's a bit more to it than that. My Brother and Sister in law have just taken a fixed posting at the British Embassy in Sydney. They'll be moving out there permanently so I'll hardly see much of them or my niece Emma unless… I apply to emigrate there myself. I could get a job in the police force there easily enough and my Super says that the forces between here and there could work with emigration to speed the process up, but'. He shrugged his shoulders.

'You're not sure about it though.' He shook his head.

'No, I can completely see that it would be great for them and it would give Emma such a great childhood and lots of opportunities when she grows up and that's fantastic. It would give Michael and Maria a better life too, the chance to finally put down some roots, maybe have more children'.

'It could be great for you too you know' I said. 'I mean, you would still have the opportunity to advance your career there and you could maybe meet someone and start putting down a few roots yourself, who knows'. He smiled.

'I know. I'm probably not being rational. It makes perfect sense to take the opportunity but there's just something holding me back and I wish I knew what it was'.

'What did you tell them?' I asked.

'That I would think about it and I will give it serious thought, which I will. They are flying on out in the next few weeks. If I decide to follow, and if everything goes according to plan with the emigration process, then I could be there within a few months. Like I said, I'll think about it. In the meantime we have a killer to catch'.

49.

The smell of takeaway fish and chips filled the kitchen as I took my seat at the rather crowded dining table. It had become a mini tradition since I had started at Farset, that Beth, Alecia and I would meet up and have a meal with either my parents or Beth's parents at their house one night each week. Sometimes, as it was with tonight, both sets of parents would get together with us at the same time.

The food from our preferred "chippie", Cafe Fish on the Lisburn Road was amazing as always and as we ate our meal the conversation flowed from talk of a mini-break that my Mum and Dad had booked with Beth's Mum and Dad, to the visit of a guide dog and handler to Alecia's class in Nursery, which had happened to coincide with Beth's voluntary day as Parent/Helper. I had already said when I had first arrived that I needed to go back to Farset for a 7 o'clock meeting, but had been thankfully interrupted before having to explain why. My Dad has been struggling to cope with the loss of Uncle Sean, let alone the circumstances, to the extent that it has had a negative effect on his health. He has also been worried about me giving up my career to take on Farset and what dangerous implications that might have for us in the future. I think that deep down he is proud that I have been investigating his brother in law and best friend's murder but I know that he is uncomfortable talking about it, which is why I normally try to avoid it. Not tonight though as it turns out, as invariably Beth's inquisitive nature was bound to get the better of her.

'So, who are you meeting? Have you had a break in the investigation'?

'I'm meeting Patrick. He's going to do some psychic investigation for us'. Unsurprisingly this little nugget of information set off a flurry of questions from almost everyone around the table, except Alecia. Oddly, the number of my interrogators included Dad.

After explaining a bit about what I'd deduced from Sean's case file and the subsequent conversation between Ferguson and I, I went on to explain that we had hoped that Patrick might be able to give us something else to add to our existing information which was why I was meeting him. Patrick had texted me again a little while ago and asked if possible, could I bring something personal of Sean's with me if I could, as he had hoped to try some psychometry also.

'Do you have anything'? Beth asked.

'Yes, I have a Parker pen we got him from Alecia at Christmas. It was in his desk drawer so I presume he must've used it a fair bit'.

At that moment Dad unbuttoned the top few buttons of his shirt. He took a chain from around his neck, removed something from it and pushed the object into my hand . I opened my hand to find a small gold ring, identical to the one presented to Alecia by my parents on her Naming Day. The ring that Alecia had been given had belonged to my Mum as a child. It was bought for her by her parents for her Christening and as it was now clear to me, they had done the same thing

for Sean at his.
'This might have a bit more personal meaning' he said as he wiped away a tear and turned his attention to Alecia, asking her about her latest story book.

50.

Patrick Rodgers pulled up the collar of his overcoat. The weather had been unusually cold for the time of year and he was definitely beginning to feel the chill in the air. He now stood alone outside the Farset Building having explained to Mark, Tom, and Beth, who seemed a little disappointed, that for him to maximise the potential of what he was about to do, it would be best if he were to be alone. He had already began to sense the presence of the spirit of Sean Brady, though as he had already suspected would be the case, there had been no dialogue between them. It had already been made clear by Brady in an earlier connection, that he was fully aware of the identity of his killer, but that he wanted the Farset Team to reach their own conclusions.

As Rodgers paced around the former garden area, the spirit placed upon him a sense of foreboding. There was something else though. Something he had only experienced a few times before. He could sense the emotions of someone else, someone who was still alive. He remembered the ring that he was holding in his hand inside his pocket and wondered if he was picking up on Mark's father's grief as the now wearer of the ring. He opened his hand and let the ring fall inside his pocket. Physically losing connection with it, had not changed the feelings that he was experiencing, so it must be something else. It was only when he reached the corner of what was the garden in previous years, did he fully realise that he was experiencing a psychic imprint. It all made sense to him now. After all, something truly heinous had happened here, so it shouldn't be surprising that an imprint had been left of it on the surrounding walls and terrain. Realising that the second set of emotions that he felt were those of Sean Brady's killer, Rodgers tried to focus on these in particular. The feelings that were being put upon him were ones of anguish but determination, anger and hatred, yet love and affection. Momentarily he saw a flash of Sean Brady's figure appear in the doorway of Farset and sensed a speed of movement toward him. As he physically made his way toward the door himself, the feelings intensified vastly with each step. By the time he had reached the spot where Brady had lost his life, not only was he completely overwhelmed by the emotions of the killer, his physical being was also being subjected to the violence of the murder, feeling every stroke of the knife. Finally, in a state of physical and emotional despair, Rodgers was overcome. He lost consciousness and fell hard to the ground. His next sentient awareness was of voices around him. Mark, Tom and Beth he thought. This was confirmed as he opened his eyes to see all three crouched around him. Shaken but otherwise feeling compos mentis , he sat up, assuring them that he was OK. They helped him to his feet and assisted him into the office. After a short rest and a strong coffee, he had regained his composure enough to relay what he had experienced, whilst Beth took notes at furious pace. Mark and Tom hung on his every word, ironically looking like it was they who had seen a ghost.

51.

As I listened to Rodgers recount what he had seen and felt to us, I couldn't help but be in awe of him. Not just because of his gift, but of the resilience with which he bore it. He had put himself in physical danger for us tonight and this was something that I would not forget in a hurry. We had all been shaken as we watched him through the newly installed CCTV and saw his violent collapse. It almost looked like he had been pushed by an invisible force, which I suppose, to all intents and purposes, he had been. I was relieved he was ok, we all were. I was grateful too, that he was able to give us the insight into Sean's killer, Terror, presuming our linking the two was correct.

There was a short silence after Rodgers had finished speaking, filled only by the noise of Beth's pen strokes as finished off her notes.

'So, he was conflicted then. Terror felt conflicted'. I said, trying to process what I'd heard in my own mind.

'It certainly seems that way' replied Beth.

'And to emotional extremes it felt' added Rodgers.

Ferguson nodded sombrely, clearly he had been affected but what had happened to Rodgers, as much as Beth and I were.

'Like he didn't want to do it but felt that he had to' again I wondered aloud.

'It would confirm that Sean knew his killer and implies that he

cared about them, or at least the killer cared about him' Ferguson finally spoke.
'Not enough though' I said as I stared through the window into the darkness. 'Not enough'.
'I'd better go' Rodgers broke what had probably become an awkward pause in the conversation.
'Are you ok to drive Patrick'? Beth asked. 'I mean, we could take you if you like'.
'No, I'll be fine, though I better bring Charlene's phone' he said as he stood up. 'She left it behind here by accident earlier. Honestly, I'm surprised, cos it never seems to be out of her hand since she got it'.
'I'm glad to hear it' laughed Beth. 'Sounds like she's becoming a regular teenage girl'.
'I suppose so' Rodgers smiled.
'I hope you're still saying that when Alecia's that age' Ferguson joked.
'No way. She's not allowed to grow up. She's going to be Daddy's little princess forever. Isn't that right Beth'? I moved toward Charlene's desk and lifted the phone handing it to Rodgers. I wasn't quite prepared for the response I was to get though. As soon as he took the phone from me, he collapsed violently again, momentarily losing consciousness in doing so. What was actually just a few short moments, felt like forever, as he regained consciousness and began to compose himself for the second time that night.
'It was exactly the same feeling that I'd got when I was outside the door' he finally said as we watched him expectantly. 'It must just be some residual energy. That can happen

sometimes. I'll be fine'. He said it like it was the most normal thing in the world.
'Maybe' said Beth, ' but you need to rest. Let's get you home. We can get your car to you tomorrow'.
Patrick opened his mouth to speak but was preempted by Beth.
'No arguments Mister! I'll take this for you'. She bent down and lifted the phone from where it had landed on the floor. 'Let's go'.

52. Part Three- Terror and Fear.

The last four weeks had been amazing for Charlene McManus. She couldn't remember ever feeling happier. Having been so impressed with how she had project managed the Farset upgrade, Mark had asked her to oversee an extension of the project and now the renovation of the entire Farset building into commercial premises was almost complete. He had even trusted her to work with a local letting agent in securing tenants and to date they had already agreed terms with a GP's Practice, a Solicitor's Practice and a Recruitment Company, to set up residence. That was in addition to her brother Patrick's new Spiritualism Practice. As he was now spending more time as an associate investigator for Farset, it seemed the next logical step. At least that's how Mark had persuaded him anyhow. It wasn't just her job role or the rekindling of the relationship with her brother that was making her happy, although both were important. It wasn't her developing friendships with Ferguson and the Shaw family either, those all these people had accepted her readily and were beginning to mean a lot to her. It wasn't even the company car, a sporty red BMW 1 Series that she was now sitting in. What was making her so happy was that for the first time in her young life, Charlene McManus was in love!

Although older than her, Caleb had quickly become her soul mate. He had understood her from the moment their

relationship had begun and had helped her come to terms with her past and use what she now understood about it, to help shape her future. He had even encouraged her to embrace the darker feelings of revenge which she harboured and the identity of Fear. It was natural he had said, realising how she felt conflicted about having evil thoughts, though had supposedly been brought up with strong Christian beliefs. He had encouraged her to see that The Enlightenment were even more evil than even she had realised. He had shown her that through what she had thought at first to be a macabre interest in serial killers. She was becoming interested now herself though since learning that one of the most prolific serial killers in European history was from Enlightenment stock. Bhrams Howden had killed 14 members of the Church in Sweden in 1967. He had called it an act of Redemption when he was apprehended. He later died in prison in suspicious circumstances. The Enlightenment Community in Sweden had since disbanded, joining up with neighbouring European branches of the Church. As with what had become the norm, Howden and his deeds were covered up by the Church and was swept under what by now must be a huge Enlightenment rug.
Pulling in to Caleb Doyle's driveway Charlene buzzed in anticipation of seeing him. Soon, his medium, muscular frame filled the doorway and he was smiling at her. He was cooking dinner for her this evening and she was later going to experience a trip to the cinema for the first time. Everything was perfect. Well, almost. She wished that she could tell the world about her relationship with Caleb but he had asked her

to keep it a secret for now. It concerned her, but she was willing to go along with it, at least for now.

53.

Terror smiled as he watched Charlene McManus' face light up at seeing him. He too had been enthralled with her and at the relationship that he had cultivated with her, now beginning to blossom. It wasn't about love for him though. It was more infatuation. What had started as a means of infiltrating Farset Investigations, had quickly taken a darker and more interesting turn, when he learned of her feelings of hatred for and desire for revenge upon The Enlightenment. This made her much more interesting to him and this coupled with the fact that she had been so easily manipulated so far, meant that he had begun to invest a lot of time in their relationship. He found himself fantasising about the acts that Fear would commit in vengeance on her former oppressors and had already started to put plans in place to allow the first of these acts to happen. For now though, he must concentrate on continuing to lead Charlene down the path that would lead her to the incarnation of Fear. This in itself has been a delight and it hasn't hurt that she is so pretty to boot. The fact that the relationship is going on under the nose of Mark Shaw sweetens things further.

Despite all of that, Terror was troubled. He was concerned that in spending so much time with Charlene, that his own cause was being neglected. He was also concerned at a comment that Tom Ferguson had recounted to her, from an earlier conversation with Mark Shaw. Ferguson was clearly of the opinion that Terror was a minor player who despite the murder of some minor celebrities, had not exactly lived up to his name. He had been furious at this remark at the time and had silently vowed to make Ferguson pay for it, a pledge which he still planned to fulfil. The more the remark played in his mind though, the more he thought that it might have some substance to it. That was why he had to decided to raise the stakes, starting tonight. Whilst he spent an enjoyable evening with the delectable Charlene, his followers would be executing his plans to the last detail. Later, he too would join them in their revelry and he too would take a photograph of someone who had been #FamousForAllTheWrongReasons.

54.

Although it seemed that we weren't much closer to catching Terror or learning his true identity, the last few weeks had proven fruitful. Charlene had all but finished in the refurbishment of the Farset building and we had acquired enough tenants to ensure that the building was not only more secure, but at last becoming economically viable and worthy of the money I had invested in it. The place had a buzz around it and the day to day operations of the businesses within, made our movements less conspicuous to the people of the surrounding area. Not only that, I was beginning to feel like a proper investigator. Rodgers had joined the team as an associate Psychic and he, Ferguson and I had started to put together a profile of Terror, which now donned the newly installed plexiglass board that police dramas on TV had led me to believe that no criminal investigations suite should be without. We had begun the profile based on the information we already had gathered, coupled with Patrick's observations relating to Sean's murder. We had also obtained, with some considerable difficulty from local quarters, copies of the investigation files of Brian Wilson and Helen Walsh, to add to that of Owen Grant, which Ferguson already had access to and had shared with us. As we each combed through the files, applying our own skills and experience to each, Ferguson often joked that what we were doing, despite our surroundings, was just good old fashioned police work. What

was old fashioned about a soon to be redundant DCI collaborating with a former Headteacher and a Medium, I couldn't quite work out, but still, it was working. I finally felt like we weren't just spinning our wheels. Each of us had been operating independently on composing an overview of our findings and had been working to a deadline of 10:00am tomorrow morning, where we would each present our conclusions and see what connections we could make, if any. I still hadn't quite finished, which was one of the reasons why I was here so late. The other was that Beth is hosting her book club at the house this evening. The opportunity to take Ferguson out for dinner and a few drinks sounded like a much more enjoyable prospect to me. After all, he needed cheering up, right? My decision had absolutely nothing to do with the prospect of playing Butler to a group of late thirty something women, some of whom usually seemed to spend less time discussing the merits of the latest James Patterson or Mary Larkin offering, than they did talking about the most recent episode of, The X Factor or suchlike.
After typing the last sentence of my part of the presentation, I brought up the website of Howard Street Restaurant to make sure that it had not been booked out. The place was a favourite of mine, though its close proximity to the Grand Opera House meant that it could often be busy, even on a weeknight. I could hear a shower running in the distance, so figured that Ferguson must've finished in the gym and we could soon be on our way. Before long we were walking down into the city centre for our night on the town. Given the hours we'd been putting in lately though, it was likely to be a short

night out. Still, it could be the last opportunity we might have, if Ferguson decides to join his family in Sydney. He had been quiet on the subject since we had first spoke on it and it was only through mine or Beth's occasionally asking him how his family were getting along in their new lives Down Under, was the topic ever mentioned.

Howard Street was bustling when we arrived, with its usual mixture of families, couples and friends all availing of the friendly service, great atmosphere and amazing food. Our table however, was situated in a relatively quiet spot near the back of the restaurant, which suited our mood entirely. To my surprise, upon being seated I noticed that the table neighbouring ours was occupied by James Dowell, a well known film and TV actor who originally hailed from Bangor. He was accompanied by equally well renowned local director, Martin Phillips. Neither man had called Belfast home for some time, so it was good to see them both on home turf, if not a bit of a shock. It was difficult not to be starstruck or stare, but I figured that they were both out for a quiet meal so I directed my attention to the menu instead as Ferguson had already done, without paying the slightest attention to the people at the table beside us.

Before long we were sharing a bottle of wine as we waited for our rib eye steaks and sides. We had previously agreed that shop talk was banned this evening so we were in deep conversation about Ferguson's current favourite topic, Liverpool's chances of beating Seville in the upcoming Europa Cup Final. As a lifelong Manchester United Supporter, I was giving him a hard time about the subject and of course pointing out the irony that he himself bore the surname of the former United and arguably club football's most successful manager. It didn't take long before Dowell and Philips, both avid United supporters and in Dowell's case, a season ticket holder, joined the conversation and two tables for two became a table for four. All plans for a relatively short and quiet night out were soon abandoned as our countless selfies, check in's and Facebook posts bore testament to the following day. It had been a great night though and bizarrely, I realised later, that despite being in the company of two celebrities I had not once thought of Terror.

55.

After dropping Alecia off at Nursery, Beth joined us in the Meeting Room in the Farset Bunker. I had asked her to come along this morning as I knew she would be able to give us an objective outlook on our findings and perhaps help crystallise our final profile of Terror. After Ferguson and I sat through a bit of ribbing about our night out by both Beth and Rodgers,it was time to get our game faces on. Taking a seat at the head of the table, Ferguson clicked open the PowerPoint presentation he had prepared on the desktop beside him, wherein it was immediately displayed on the large screen behind him, each slide showing a summary of the points he was making as he went.

'So, if we look at the crime scene reports of each of the victims, we can see that in each case, it would appear that they were deliberately targeted. In the case of Brian Wilson, the killer was clearly aware of his movements and had close proximity access to him before his death. With Owen Grant, Sean Brady and Helen Walsh, their killers were aware of their movements and habits and thus were able to lye in wait. We can also see that in each case, the crime scene was completely free from any CSI evidence of any form'.

'So, each murder was meticulously planned, reconnaissance undertaken and carried out by an experienced professional' stated Beth.

'Well, it's highly unlikely that it was Terror himself who killed

Helen Walsh, especially with the confession from the kid, Waylon, whatever his name is, which would rule out all being committed by someone experienced. However, I would say that Terror coached him in every last detail of the execution of the plan, including posing the body'.

'What about the methods used, can we learn anything from these'? I asked.

'The methods used differ for each victim. Again this would suggest experience. One thing that did stand out though was that the methods used with Owen Grant and Brian Wilson suggested that Terror liked to have power and control over his victims. He wanted to enjoy watching their suffering, savour the moment. Sean Brady and Helen Walsh on the other hand were about getting the job done quickly and effectively.

'If Sean was someone he knew or cared about, I suppose it would make sense that he took no pleasure in killing him, which was certainly what I felt' said Rodgers.

'And if he couldn't do the job in New York himself, I suppose his main concern was making Helen Walsh's killing, foolproof for Waylon to do the deed' I added.

'Exactly' exclaimed Ferguson. 'You're up next Patrick' he said as he threw the remote clicker for the PowerPoint at Rodgers, who caught it awkwardly as Ferguson vacated the seat at the head of the table. Rodgers moved to the front of the room, set the control down and put the Mac in sleep mode.

'My presentation will be a little more low tech I'm afraid' he said and we chuckled in response.

'You're all already aware of what I experienced here and what we learned from the psychic imprint on the building here.

What I did after that was to use photographs from each of the crime scenes, as well as Waylon Matthews' signed statement. The energy that I picked up from his fingerprints and signature would lead me to believe that he was guilty of Helen Walsh's murder. There were feelings of fear and anxiety but also excitement that he had been brave enough to carry out the killing, and happiness that he would have pleased Terror. The feeling of pleasing Terror was particularly strong from the picture of how and where the body was posed.
With the killings at The Majestic and The Waterfront, I would agree with what Tom has said about Terror getting a kick out of controlling his victims and making them suffer. Those were certainly the impressions that I picked up'.
'Anything else strange'? Beth asked.
'Yes, there was one thing. Although Terror's experience as a killer can be felt, I kept picking up a feeling of insecurity, like he was new to all this or he was looking for …?'
'Validation' I said. 'It sounds like he's looking for validation of his reputation as a serial killer, or looking for someone's approval'.
'That's it! That's exactly it! That's what kept coming across' replied Rodgers.
With that, I launched into my report, using the transparent board that I had set up at the side of the room earlier. I took the team through the psychological impressions that I had formed of Terror from the reports, adding to it the conclusions we had reached from Rodgers and Ferguson's presentations. Within a few hours the thought cloud I had drawn (which was the latest Teacher speak for what most

people would remember as a good old fashioned Spider Diagram), had enough information for us to summarise into a criminal / psychological profile of our killer. It didn't make for pleasant reading either. My own overview painted a picture of a sadistic narcissist who had problems with celebrity and an inferiority complex, the latter likely stemming from his childhood treatment by a parent or caregiver at my best guess. What I found harder to cope with however, was that I agreed completely that Terror in some way was connected to Uncle Sean. Finding out what this connection was, in my opinion, still key to breaking open the investigation regardless of the other information we had gathered for the profile. The others agreed, so as Beth returned home and Rodgers returned to his office upstairs, Ferguson and I began the painstaking work of again delving into Uncle Sean's life and movements for the weeks and months before his death and as Caleb Doyle had dubbed it in his first report on the matter, "The Rise of Terror".

We were not at work long however, before the sickening news of what social media had revealed to the world whilst we were all in our meeting was relayed to us via the prompt return of Rodgers to the bunker. We had all put our phones on silent in order to be able to concentrate on the meeting. Neither Ferguson nor I had thought to look at ours since. Rodgers had though, and what he revealed to us stunned us beyond disbelief.

56.

The photographs had already gone viral on virtually all social media platforms and as we were discovering, occupied virtually every live media outlet. Terror had certainly elevated his status, of that there was no longer any doubt.
Four high profile celebrities had lost their lives between late last night and early this morning, and their remains had been posed for photographs all bearing the #FamousForAllTheWrongReasons, #TheRiseOfTerror and #Terrorists twitter tags. Again there were links to documents outlining hidden crimes and misdemeanours which had led to their execution. The first victim, Tyrell Jones, US billionaire businessman and TV Executive, and in the views of many, President elect, had been accused of corporate espionage. The second and third victims, Neil McCarron and Dave Tohill, both members of The Rolling Stones nearest rivalling band, The Tupelos, had been accused of deliberately infecting groupies with the HIV virus. It was the final victim that I struggled with most though. Well known Northern Irish Actor, James Dowell, had been found strangled to death in the Glenvine Hotel this morning by his friend and colleague Martin Phillips. He had stood accused of funding paramilitary organisations. One of the men that Ferguson and I had been out with the night before had died at Terror's hand. I couldn't help but think that inadvertently, for the second time, I had

been implicated in a murder in Terror's name. I only realised how much when Charlene arrived in the bunker with DI Black and one of his colleagues, who promptly brought Ferguson and I to Grosvenor Road Police Station for questioning.

It was five hours later that we were eventually discharged from the station having being alibied by the vast CCTV coverage in the city centre. I could understand that having been amongst the last to see Dowell alive, why we would have been questioned about our movements and conversations etc from the previous night, but for Black to take the aggressive manner of questioning that he had done and to keep us in custody for the length of time he had, seemed excessive. Ferguson agreed, though pointed out that in fairness, it was a murder enquiry and that he did not do anything that was beyond his power to do. It certainly marked an even deeper rift in the relations between Farset and the PSNI and I was concerned that we would have trouble in getting access to files from any of the new murder scenes now. Thankfully, one short email to his superior officer (for now) from Ferguson, made that problem disappear and it was agreed that all law enforcement agencies involved in the investigations would be bound to share information with Farset, on agreement that we did likewise.

By the time we got back to Farset, I was too tired to think. It had been a late night last night and a long and difficult day today. I decided to call time on it and urged Ferguson to do the same, though not before agreeing that we needed to process any information we could get from the crime scenes as quickly as possible. Ferguson suggested that tomorrow morning we divide our efforts. He suggested that he would work on processing the newest murders and add evidence gathered to our profile, whilst I continued to try to find a fresh perspective on Uncle Sean's final weeks.

57.

It was 07:30 am when I first stirred. I heard Beth calling Alecia downstairs for breakfast and realised that I hadn't even heard her get up. Getting out of bed, I walked out onto the landing and saw Alecia through the open door of her bedroom, tentatively pulling the duvet down a bit, looking vaguely in the direction of the doorway, then pulling the duvet back up over her head. I moved quietly toward, then into her room and before she knew it had thrown the duvet off her and was tickling the backs of her legs, where I knew she was most ticklish.

'Come on Wee Madam, time to get up'! I was laughing almost as much as she was as she tried to push me away and make a grab for the duvet again. 'You heard Mum'.

'Leave me alone Daddy! Just five more minutes! ' she said in a mixture of annoyance and mirth that when added to her bed head hair, made the situation all the funnier and her all the cuter.

Within a few minutes we had both joined Beth at the breakfast table and were wolfing down our cereal whilst doing our best to ignore the small glasses of dark green liquid that Beth had filled from the Nutri-Bullet and placed in front of us. We both knew deep down though, that neither of us would escape our daily dose of vitality if Mum had anything to do with it.

It was nice to have a family breakfast together. When I was a

Headteacher, I was usually out of the house too early to enjoy times like this and was grateful that my Farset role allowed me the flexibility that it did. Despite yesterday's events, I was feeling positive today. A lot of that was to do with having a good night's sleep and a bit of family time. The rest was down to the conversation I had with Beth when I arrived home last night. As is her gift, she made me realise that Terror was going to commit these atrocities regardless of my actions or connections. He had set out his intentions when he killed Owen Grant, before he even came onto my radar, or me his.

Not long after breakfast, I was on the motorway joining so many others on the morning commute into Belfast. The U105 breakfast team had just announced an increase in the station's listening figures and I was pleased for them. I have been a fan of the station since it's first day of broadcasting and it seemed to be going from strength to strength. Within a short time though, my attention had begun to wander back to Uncle Sean. We had cleared and sold his house in the months after his death, after the PSNI had conducted a number of searches on the property in relation to the investigation of his murder. Needless to say, they had yielded nothing. I wondered if anything had been missed and toyed with the idea of breaking off my journey to Farset and trying to gain access to the property from it's new owners. I decided against it for the moment, thinking that they might either have already left for work, or were about to leave and the last thing they would have needed at this point of the morning, was me turning up. Instead, I continued to Farset. The early morning traffic on the Lower Falls was hectic, so rather than spending an extra

20 minutes sitting in it in order to park at the front of the building, I turned onto Ardmoulin Street and used the electronic control that Charlene had ensured that all Farset related vehicles was now fitted with, to open the heavy shutter that led into the underground garage. Ferguson was already seated at his desk when I entered.

'You should see this' he said with some urgency on noticing my arrival. 'I think we may have caught a break'.

I took a seat beside him and saw that he had a piece of video footage on pause on his monitor.

'Couldn't sleep huh?' I asked.

'Nope! I got up around 4am and found this in my inbox, from the PSNI'.

'What is it'?

'It's the CCTV footage from the Glenvine Hotel'. I looked at the screen curiously as Ferguson continued. 'The layout is similar to most hotels. There is no coverage on any of the hallways but there is a camera in each of the guest elevators, stairways, in the reception area, bars and service entrances. This is Dowell and Philips entering from outside into the Reception. They go straight to the elevator and presumably to their rooms. The camera doesn't show anyone in the elevator with them, which got me thinking that the killer either followed them later or was already on the premises'.

'Maybe another guest'? I thought aloud.

'Perhaps, though based on the likely timeframe of the murder, which until we get the Coroner's report, we have to assume is a little before the photograph was uploaded onto the internet, no-one enters or leaves the elevators or is seen on any of the stairwells'.

'What about Philips'?

'According to the police reports, he was devastated. He held up well at interview and even offered to take a polygraph. They don't have him in the frame'.

'So…'?

'So that brings us back to the only 2 real possibilities. Either the killer was waiting in the room before he got there, or was able to get access to his room afterward somehow, without being seen, either of which would imply a staff member or someone who would have staff level access without question'.

'I suppose that would be police, emergency services, maintenance people and that kind of thing'? I surmised.

'Exactly'!

'Anything from any of the other cameras'? I asked.

'No nothing that I can see so far. I've started to look at the CCTV footage from the Majestic again. Nothing so far there either, other than the fact that Owen Grant was alone in the elevator when he went to his room. I'll keep on it and let you know. In the meantime though, I'm going to go over to the Glenvine to try to hook up with the PSNI Team, see if I can work the crime scene. I'll be in touch if I find anything'.

'Sounds good. Take some pictures if you can. We can hopefully go through them with Patrick later'.

'No worries, will do'.

When he left, I made my way to my office, unlocked the new filing cabinet that I had begun to use and removed Uncle Sean's file from it. I must have been through it 1000 times already since it came to my possession but this time I was hoping that I could unlock some new information from it. Bizarrely, as soon as I took the seat at my desk and opened the file, I noticed a new lead staring me in the face.

58.

Caleb Doyle looked coldly at his Father, Deputy First Minister Michael Doyle, as he and his colleague and First Minister, Peter Lafferty took their places at the podium in the Great Hall at Stormont. The two men had called for a press conference earlier this morning and now stood in front of the assembled media as they jostled for position to be able to answer follow up questions. The cold look from his son had not gone unnoticed by Doyle senior. The two men had been estranged from one another for a considerable time now, a situation that appeared to suit them both. As expected the press conference centred around a new strategy for Education that was being rolled out following an Executive reshuffle and the appointment of a new Minister for Education. The two men were merely endorsing the appointment and strategy document as well as informing those gathered, that the new Minister would hold a further press conference later today. Doyle immediately left the assembled throng as they attempted to pepper questions at those who held our First Office. He knew that to remain would be a waste of time, as in truth, the, "new" strategy had existed in draft form for a long time and through his contacts within the political arena, he had already had sight of it. His time would be much better served getting ahead of the game with this, "Breaking News". He could return for the other press conference later. Besides which, he couldn't bear to spend any more time in his Father's company than was absolutely necessary. Just seeing him in the flesh made Doyle feel consumed with an anger and hatred that he could barely control. He soothed himself by allowing his alter-ego, Terror to come to the fore. With that, all negative feeling was washed away and replaced with feelings of elation and excitement. The multiple executions could not have gone more smoothly nor created more impact. Terror now occupied more media air time and copy space than he could have hoped for, some of which he had even contributed to himself as Caleb Doyle. The world of Celebrity was living in fear of his next move it would seem, though some of it's inhabitants had been either vain enough or stupid enough to make comment on the situation, unknowingly or perhaps uncaringly putting themselves in the kind of spotlight that could be fatal. They would be safe for now though, as his latest goal had been achieved. Now he could concentrate on Charlene and the soon to be incarnate, Fear. Terror against his better judgement was starting to develop feelings for her, feelings that were felt all the more strongly after she had chosen to spend the night with him. What a special night that had turned out to be, especially as unbeknownst to her, before they had returned to his home, Terror had left her alone for a short time in the Glenvine Hotel bar to go and take the life of James Dowell. It had been a relatively easy kill. The seat in the Bar room that he had deliberately chosen for he and Charlene offered a good view of the Reception area as well as being a CCTV blackspot. All he had to do was wait for Dowell to arrive back to the Hotel that a Chron contact had mentioned he had been staying at for the last few days. True to form,

Dowell would have availed of the nightlife afforded by Belfast any time he was in the city. When he finally returned, Terror watched as he and the other man, whom he vaguely knew but couldn't place, drunkenly crossed the Reception and pressed the button to call the elevator. When the doors closed, Terror watched from his seat to see what floor the elevator would stop at.

When he saw this, he quickly made his excuses to Charlene and made his way to the Service elevator, gambling that in their drunken state, it would take Dowell and his friend a while to reach their rooms. He was right, though when the Service Elevator opened on the eighth floor, it was only Dowell who remained in the hallway, drunkenly trying to slide the plastic key card into its slot. Terror moved slowly at first, unnoticed by Dowell. Then as the door clicked open and the light on the lock had turned green, Terror sprang forward and violently pushed Dowell forwards into the room as he had pulled down the handle. In the actor's drunken state, the rest had been easy and within a few short minutes Terror was again seated beside Charlene, engaged in conversation with her whilst silently wondering if his chosen Terrorists had completed their tasks so easily. Snapping back to the present, Terror smiled broadly before saying out loud to himself, 'What a night indeed!' before crossing the front of the physically imposing building and making his way to the car park.

59.

Well, this was certainly another new experience for me, I thought to myself as I announced my name to the security guard at the Ormeau Avenue entrance to UBC Northern Ireland. I was told to make my way to the fourth floor where Miss Boyd would be expecting me. On the short route I had met and awkwardly greeted a considerable number of local media personalities before finally coming face to face with Miss Dana Boyd. Though casually dressed, she looked every bit as striking as she does on her weekly current affairs programme, Unreported Ulster.

'Mr Shaw' she extended her hand in greeting. 'Sorry that we are meeting in such difficult circumstances. Your Uncle was a good friend and an excellent colleague. I miss him a lot'.

Shaking her extended hand, I found myself gazing perhaps a millisecond too long into her piercing blue eyes. Beth had often made jokes to me about my having a crush on Dana Boyd. I quickly composed myself.

'Thank you Miss Boyd. It has been tough without him. I suppose that's kind of why I'm here. I've been investigating his death and was wondering if I could ask you a few questions'.

'Yes, I'd heard you had taken over at Farset, certainly, anything I can do to help, though I have already spoken to the Police… a DI Black, I think'.

'That's right. He was the investigating officer. From his notes on the file I was aware that he had spoken to you and that you had been eliminated from his enquiries, but what I couldn't find any information on, was why there were so many telephone calls exchanged between you and my Uncle in the weeks leading up to his death'.

'We had been working on a story together. We often collaborated if budgets and mutual interests permitted'.

'Could I ask what the story was'? I noticed that she flushed slightly and broke off eye contact following my question.

'I… I'm not sure that I can, Mr Shaw'. An experienced journalist and presenter should not be so easily thrown I thought to myself. She obviously had something to hide.

'Please, call me Mark' I said with what I hoped would be a disarming smile. 'Look, whatever it is, my Uncle may have lost his life as a result. You say he was your friend, if that really was the case, the least you could do is help me bring his killer to justice'.

Tears began to brim in her eyes. I offered her a handkerchief which she dabbed at the corners of her eyes in an attempt to stop her mascara from running.

'No, it's not that, not that at all. I'd be happy to see whoever was responsible pay for what they've done. It's just…'

That's when it dawned on me exactly what the story must have been about. It was the expose´of The Enlightenment. I decided to cut to the chase.

'Miss Boyd, if it's about The Enlightenment movement, I'm already aware of what my Uncle had been working on, including his surveillance of me. Believe me, you can trust me, I wasn't involved with them other than foolishly being in their

employment for a time'.
The look of relief on her face was palpable. She took me to her office where I filled her in on the article penned by Sean and the supporting evidence we had found, as well as how and perhaps why The Enlightenment had been able to suppress it. As it turned out, she was already aware of the article and other files , which begged my next question.
'If you were aware of all this stuff, then why haven't you done anything with it?
Did they block you?' I felt my temper begin to flare a little.
'Block me? No, Sean had most of the material evidence. The plan was that Sean's article would be published on the UBC Newsline website on the same night as a related episode of Unreported Ulster. We were in the process of making the programme but then Sean was killed and I could no longer access the material to finish the programme. I couldn't ask you as I knew you had been under surveillance as part of the expose´so I had to just let the story die'.
'Not any more you don't. I came here hoping you could help me. Now it looks like we can help each other'.
It was obvious by the look on her face that the cogs of her mind had already started turning. Within the next few hours, not only had I given her permission to access Sean's article and the related evidence, I had also told Boyd about the plight of Charlene and Rodgers, got agreement from both of them to be interviewed for the programme and had given a recorded interview about my time with The Enlightenment myself. All of this coupled with excerpts from related YouTube videos, which included testimony of ex-members

worldwide and global media investigations, made for the components of an excellent programme which would leave audiences in Northern Ireland and their UK and Republic of Ireland neighbours in no doubt, that an evil and dangerous cult lived amongst them. I was buoyed by the time I was ready to leave. I still may not be much further in finding Sean's killer but I'm a lot closer to fulfilling at least part of his legacy and maybe my own too. In Dana Boyd I think I'd found a useful ally and potential friend, to boot, but before I left one final question sprang to mind.

'Miss Boyd, do you know if Uncle Sean had ever approached any of The Enlightenment directly? Could he have met or gotten to know anyone in particular?'

'Not to my knowledge? Why do you ask'?

'My colleagues and I are pretty sure that his killer was familiar to him. We've reached the conclusion that The Enlightenment weren't involved but I just wanted to have it confirmed for sure'. She shook her head.

'No, I don't think he would have made contact without telling me. We were working pretty closely on this. The one thing I can be sure of though, is that these people are dangerous'. Little did either of us realise that we would shortly experience just how dangerous. I nodded and motioned to leave.

'By the way' she said. 'Enough with Miss Boyd. My name is Dana'. I flushed a little as I realised that I had again made eye contact for a little bit too long.

'Goodbye Dana. Speak to you soon' I said awkwardly before closing her office door and making my way back down to the security point.

60.

'Sounds like you had an interesting afternoon' said Ferguson in greeting to me as I arrived back to the office. I looked at him perplexed.

'Charlene filled me in, plus, Patrick called in earlier and we ate lunch together. He'd brought some food for you too, thinking you'd be here. I put it in the fridge in the staffroom for you'.

I had been so filled with adrenaline at the prospect of exposing The Enlightenment that I had forgotten about lunch, but I was glad of the Doorsteps sandwich waiting for me in the staffroom. I poured some coffee and took it and the sandwich back to where Ferguson was working at his desk. I sat down across from him.

'That was nice of Patrick, I wasn't expecting him today and he didn't mention anything when I called him earlier'.

'No, I think it was just spur of the moment. I think he was looking for some advice more than anything'.

'Advice, on what? I asked.

'Parenting I suppose. Charlene didn't come home last night. He thinks she spent the night with her new boyfriend. She didn't call him to say she wasn't coming home and when she got back this morning to shower and change before work, she didn't say anything about where she'd been'.

'Did he ask'?

'No, he wasn't sure how to handle it, I mean she is a young

adult'.

'True, I suppose' I said. 'Still, after the type of upbringing she's had and all that she's been through, she needs looking out for'.

'That's pretty much what he thought too but just wasn't sure how to go about saying it without upsetting her'.

'What did you say to him'?

'Just that he needs to sit down with her and set some ground rules if they were going to continue to share the apartment. She can't expect him to be lying awake worrying about her just because she didn't afford him the respect of a text message or call. He's going to speak to her tonight.'

'Good call. I suppose this new man explains some of the reason why she's been so upbeat lately ,especially today. It's a worry that she's being so secretive though. I mean, does anyone know who he is or anything about him for that matter'.

'I certainly don't. Patrick has asked her about that though. She says that it's early days yet and if things continue to go well between them, then we'll meet him soon'.

'Well, if last night is any indication, things are continuing to go well, so who knows, we might meet the mystery man in the near future. And speaking of mystery men, Dear Abbie, did you spent your entire afternoon playing agony aunt or are we any nearer to finding Terror'?

Ferguson laughed. 'Well, as it happens, I did manage to get something you might be interested in'.

Today just seemed to be getting better and better. I was all ears.

'What is it'? I asked intently.
'The crime scene at The Glenvine wasn't quite so clean as the others. There was a long blond hair found on Dowell's body'.
My initial excitement at the prospect of a lead dampened a little as I processed what Ferguson had just said in my mind.
'But he died in a hotel room that he had been staying in for a fews days before he was killed. The hair could be anyone's, a maid, a previous guest and that's before we even factor in his reputation as being a bit of a Lothario'.
'True, but you didn't let me finish. He was found face down on the ground just clear of the door and there had been no sign of any struggle, despite the fact that he had been strangled. The hair was found on his back'. Suddenly it all became clear to me where Ferguson was coming from. I thought aloud.
'So, he comes back to his hotel room and if Terror is true to his MO, then he was waiting for him. He likely pushed him into the room from behind to retain the element of surprise, then strangled him where he fell'. Ferguson nodded and I continued with my train of thought.
'He would have had to get close to, if not nearly on top of Dowell to be able to strangle him, which means the hair transferred from Terror to Dowell in the process'.
'Exactly' replied Ferguson. 'So the hair is either Terror's or someone he came into close contact with before killing Dowell. Given the length and colour of the hair, it's unlikely to be that of a man, though we can't yet rule it out. Either way, it has been sent for DNA testing, then to be ran through the National Database. It's a slow process but we should have

the results back within a few weeks'.
Again what Ferguson said started my mind churning. Up until now, everything pointed to Terror being male, something that Rodgers had also confirmed. The new evidence and something else about what Ferguson had described from the crime scene bothered me though. I leaned forward toward Ferguson.
'I don't think Terror did this personally. It must have been one of the Terrorists. We've just presumed because of the timeline of the murders so far and the fact that there are similarities between Dowell's and Grant's killings, that Terror himself was responsible but lets face it, a woman could easily overcome and strangle a drunken man, but would she necessarily have the strength to lift a dead weight single handedly. Some women would I'm sure, but I'm thinking in general terms. Why wasn't the body posed in this case? I think that may be the answer. Perhaps Dowell tried to smuggle her into his room unnoticed, not realising what he really had in mind'.
By the time I had finished theorising, Ferguson was beaming from ear to ear.
'You're absolutely right in reaching the conclusions you have and I had been thinking along the same lines originally myself'.
'I sense a but coming'.
'You may still be right but I showed the crime scene photographs to Patrick earlier and he confirmed that it was definitely a male energy responsible. From our profile of Terror, I don't get the sense of a killer who wants to be

caught, as some do'.

'So the hair and the fact that the body wasn't posed would suggest that he is either getting sloppy, which I doubt, or more likely, was in a hurry'. Ferguson smiled and applauded softly at my musings.

'Congratulations Detective, you're really developing a knack for investigation, which is good because there is something else I'd like to talk to you about'.

61.

The next few weeks were a whirlwind of activity. Dana Boyd had almost become part of the furniture at Farset and the recording and editing of the programme on The Enlightenment was coming together really quickly, especially with Patrick and Charlene on hand as interviewees and resident experts. I had become more at ease in the company of Boyd, though received much ribbing about my supposed feelings for her whenever she wasn't around, led mostly I might add, by Beth.

I think it would be fair to say that we were all buzzing at the prospect of unmasking The Enlightenment, though there remained an undercurrent of fear as to the possible repercussions.

There had been more rapid changes at Farset also. Ferguson's decision not to join his family in Australia thrilled us all and I decided to reward it by making some changes to the management structure. There were now 3 company directors, Ferguson (who would not accept the role unless he was allowed to invest his redundancy settlement into Farset), Beth and I. Rodgers' associate partnership had been formalised and Charlene's role, pay and benefits were amended, as in addition to being Personal Assistant to the Directors, she now had responsibility as a Business Development Advisor. One thing I learned about The Enlightenment from when I worked for them, was that business acumen had been virtually bred into each of it's members, so despite Charlene's relatively young age, she was more than a match for the role.

We had put together a three year development plan, though had agreed that it would not come into effect until Terror had been caught and brought to justice.

We'd also had some developments in relation to the investigation too. The now high profile Terror case had come under the remit of the FBI and we were expecting a visit from Agents Ross and Curtis by the end of this week.

Unreported Ulster was due to air tomorrow and Uncle Sean's article, which was now referenced several times in the programme, was set to go live at the same time. All that remained to be done now, was for Dana Boyd and a small TV crew to go along to an Enlightenment Meeting, inform some of the assembled members about the programme, confront them on its contents and try to get some comment from them. I decided to go along with them and was quite looking forward to my role as agent provocateur.

62.

Although it was allegedly a place for public worship, the heavy iron gates blocking the entrance and the tall, barbed metal fencing around it, did not suggest that the public would be very welcome in The Enlightenment Church Building, or Meeting Hall as they preferred to call it. As usual, the gate was manned by a number of "heavies" comprised from the late teen to early thirties male contingent of the Church. They each wore walkie talkie devices and high vis jackets, which by anyones standards, was probably a bit odd for a midweek, run of the mill Church Service. The Enlightened entered almost in convey as per usual, each vehicle being waved through the gates upon recognition of its occupants and for a short time the area was gridlocked with traffic. As each vehicle passed I could feel several sets of eyes burning into me and my assembled company. From the look on Dana Boyd's face, she was shocked at the spectacle playing out before her eyes but whenever the last people carrier had the gates closed behind it, she moved forward, undaunted.

'Hi there, my name is Dana Boyd and I'm here representing UBC Northern Ireland. I was hoping to speak to Mr Drew Pinkerton'. In a swift movement, the heavy gate opened slightly and two men came out to us. I recognised them from school events, though did not know them by name. The older of the two came to engage Dana in conversation. I stood by her side, whilst out of the corner of my eye, I could see the younger and more physically imposing of the two, trying to stop the conversation being filmed.

'Do you have an appointment to see Mr Pinkerton, Miss Boyle'?

'Actually, it's Boyd, my name is Boyd and no, I'm afraid I don't have an appointment' Dana replied evenly, not rising to his mocking jibe.

'Well, Boyd, I'm afraid that it's not going to be possible for Mr Pinkerton to see you this evening' he replied derisively.

I looked at the younger of the two men again. Despite his best efforts to strong-arm the crew, they were clearly more experienced than he was, and I would hazard a guess, considerably more intelligent, as the camera was still rolling.

I seized my opportunity.

'Is he here'? I asked, trying my best to sound deliberately naive.

'Mr Shaw' the younger of the two men had decided to give up trying to stop the filming and instead try his intimidation tactics on me, which at the moment included standing in an aggressive stance, way too closely to my personal space.

'I would've thought you would have had more self respect than to be involved with these people'.

'You would be surprised just how much my levels of self respect have increased since severing ties with you people' I quipped with a smile. He was riled and came closer still to me before his colleague interjected in a tone much more officious than that he had adopted for Dana .

'Mr Shaw, I'm afraid Mr Pinkerton is not here this evening'.

'I'm sorry, all those years involved with the school and I don't believe we've been officially introduced, Mark Shaw' I said outstretching my hand to shake his. He looked warily at the camera before deciding not to introduce himself ,nor did he accept the handshake.

'It doesn't matter to you at this stage what my name is Mr Shaw, I think it unlikely that our paths will cross again in the future'.

'Fine, just being friendly' I said, 'but that's OK. Seems a bit strange that Drew isn't here now, when I saw he and his family drive in, and his car is still parked up over there'. I pointed toward a black VW Caravelle. 'Still, I have an idea! We'll come in and join you for the service and who knows, by the end of it, Drew may have turned up. Besides, it'll be nice to see some old faces again'. I strode forward confidently toward the gate, which had remained slightly ajar, knowing full well, what would happen next, and I was right. I was immediately grabbed and pulled back from the gate by the two men, who were clearly determined that I would not set foot onto Enlightenment property.

'I guess that sign on the gate must be outdated Mr Shaw. It says that the public are welcome when it seems that's not actually the case' Dana addressed the comment to me, but was looking squarely at the camera, which after her remark, panned onto the sign. The two men looked fit to be tied but were trying to remain in control due to the camera. She continued, 'Really we were just hoping to get a comment from Mr Pinkerton regarding a programme due to air on our channel. Still, perhaps either of you would care to comment'. She then went on to outline the content of the programme.

'There will be an article penned by the late Sean Brady which relates closely to the content of the programme. He had been looking into, your organisation for quite some time, though you already knew that didn't you' she smiled before adding, 'Any comment?'

After a pause, I added, 'No? Didn't think so. Perhaps if you want to come back to us after the programme has aired. Oh no wait, you won't see it will you? After all, it is only those tarnished by evil and unworthy of The Enlightenment who would watch television isn't that right? Still, I'm sure you'll all huddle around the screens you keep hidden in your attics and basements, for fear of being caught by, The Prophet. Give me a break'. I turned to walk away, again knowing the likely reaction I had provoked. Within an instant the younger of the two men was upon me. He grabbed me by the shoulder and spun me round toward him, before landing a punch squarely on my jaw. I fell to the pavement and watched from there as the elder of the two men grabbed his colleague and dragged him to the relative safety of behind the gate, where the locks were immediately clicked into place. I stood up and dusted myself off, before taking a handkerchief from my pocket and wiping some blood away from the corner of my mouth.

'Thank you for your time Gentlemen. That's what we in the business call, the money shot and it'll be available again for you to see tomorrow night, in glorious technicolour'. With a glowing smile and a wink, Dana Boyd calmly walked away toward the UBC van, with her crew and myself following closely behind.

63.

After styling her now blonde hair and applying the finishing touches to her make up, Charlene McManus stood up from the dressing table and walked over to the full length mirror that stood in the corner of the room nearest the wardrobe. She adjusted the black cocktail dress that she was wearing a little before fully taking in her appearance as it was reflected back to her. She liked what she saw. Gone were the long skirts and frumpy clothes of her Enlightenment days. Gone was the mousy brown hair and pasty complexion. Gone were the feelings of suppression. She smiled to her reflection. Soon enough, Charlene McManus would be gone too. She was going to tell them tonight at the party, after the show had aired. From this evening onwards she wished to be known as Gillian Rodgers. She had always liked the name Gillian. It reminded her of a girl who was always really nice to her at Primary School. She'd decided on Rodgers, so that she would continue to share a surname with Patrick. She even intended to make it legal, just like Patrick had.

When she had discussed it with Caleb, he had as usual, been very supportive of her, though as far as her name change was concerned, he had already given her the pet name, Fear. Another sign of how he really got her, she had thought to herself. He had understood the need for her to leave Charlene behind. That wasn't who she was any more. Now she was an independent, attractive and successful young woman in her own right, who was enjoying her new life. She still desired vengeance though and supposed that in some ways, she would get that tonight. Would it be enough for her though? Fear was a part of her personality and Caleb got that too, encouraged it even. She wished she could have brought him to the party tonight but he was insistent. Her friends and family would meet him soon enough, just not yet.

64.

The underground bunker area at Farset looked magnificent. Beth and Charlene had done a wonderful job in transforming it into a party venue for this evening. You could have been forgiven for mistaking the room for a function room in a top class hotel, especially with the large round banqueting tables that had been so elaborately dressed and the eloquent mood lighting, not to mention the vast array of food and drinks available at the buffet table, supplied by Beth's caterers of choice and our namesakes, Shaw's of Antrim. We had decided to host a celebration and screening of Unreported Ulster for our family and friends both as a memorial to Uncle Sean and his legacy in the form of an official opening of the new, Farset Investigations, and a marking of Patrick and Charlene's new lives, free of and from The Enlightenment, as well as what we hoped would be a successful expose of the evils of the organisation. We were also celebrating Ferguson's staying in Northern Ireland with us, which of course I was delighted about, but still couldn't quite get my head around since he broke the news a few weeks ago. Ferguson and I hoped that we could add a possible identity for Terror to our list of things to celebrate this evening, but as of yet, the results from the hair sample had not been returned.

Shortly before the programme was about to air, I took my place in front of the large screen that we had hired for the occasion, to say a few words. I've spoken publicly as part of my former job, hundreds if not thousands of times but as I looked at our friends and loved ones all dressed in their finery and enjoying each others company, I felt myself choked with emotion and tearing up. There was so much that I wanted to say but I just couldn't get the words out. Thankfully, before long I had my wife, best friend and novelist, who was not unaccustomed to a little public speaking herself, by my side.

In words that will remain with me until my dying day, she thanked those who had gathered with us to be part of our celebrations, paid a beautiful tribute to Uncle Sean, that was a mixture of respect, humour and grief, welcomed our new friends and colleagues into our lives, and finally named me as a worthy successor to Farset Investigations and Uncle Sean's legacy, before presenting me with a beautiful brass plaque for the outer building, which read:

Farset Investigations Est 1991, Proprietor - Mark Shaw, Licensed Investigator.

To the applause of those gathered, my emotions, which I had barely been able to control the entire time, finally gave way and I was able to give a tearful and brief word of thanks before Dana Boyd talked a little about her work with Uncle Sean and fittingly introduced the programme.

Although I had seen elements of the programme already, I was blown away by the final edit as it was aired live. I don't think we could have hoped for a more effective lifting of the lid on what Dana Boyd consistently referred to as ,The Enlightenment Cult, though at times I felt the viewing very uncomfortable, as I'm sure did Rodgers and Charlene. A cheer went up, followed by applause as the end credits began to roll and as I turned up the lights again, I noticed the sheer well of emotion that had been created. We had really achieved something great. Now it was time to celebrate. I walked toward and embraced my good friend and former colleague, Caitlin Price and was about to have a catch up with her when we were interrupted by an announcement from Charlene that really was the icing on the cake.

65.

The few days before and since the airing of The Enlightenment episode of Unreported Ulster had been harrowing for Drew Pinkerton. The media attention that followed created a pressure that none of the local Enlightenment Community had ever seen and it had all been connected through the use of his name, to him. The fallout for the Church and its members had been unparalleled in UK history. The contents of the programme had been picked up by nationwide media, resulting in intense Government Scrutiny of the organisation in how it runs its businesses and schools, as well as a review of its charitable status. Regional police constabularies had begun investigations into allegations of physical and sexual abuse, as well as reports of unlawful break up of families. UK wide, public and private sector customers of businesses linked to the Church, ended their contracts, taking their custom elsewhere. The expose was financially bringing the Church to it's knees. The cult branding had stuck and in some areas, particularly in Northern Ireland, people were showing unrest at having The Enlightenment live and work amongst them, with reaction ranging from windows broken and paint bombs thrown, to petitions to local councils to take action to remove them. The Enlightenment Spin Doctors and legal teams were in action 24/7 on damage limitation and thankfully they seemed to be turning a corner but that was of little consequence to Drew now.

Given the scale of the damage, The Prophet himself had become personally involved. His instructions to the UK faction of The Church had been clear on how they should proceed. Equally clear was his pronouncement of judgement on Drew. Today was the day that his sacrifice was to be made. With the exception of Drew and his nineteen year old son Daniel, the house had been empty for the last few days. The remainder of the family had been removed from the home after the pronouncement of, The Prophet, without the chance for any of them to say goodbye to one another. They would return to the family home later today and be allowed to continue their lives within The Church. That was of comfort to Drew and Daniel. They were soon to leave the house for the last time and it was highly unlikely they would see their family or friends ever again. Their final acts as members of The Enlightenment would be to avenge the damage caused to their Church and Community then face the consequences of Man's law as well as God's. Thousands of miles away, in Sydney, Drew's brother was also facing a similar fate. His crime was that he was relative to his brother and happened to reside in a place that strategically allowed for revenge for the attack upon The Enlightenment Church. He would do his duty gladly as he knew that if he were to be taken in the process, he would be assured a place in God's Kingdom. All three men had been drinking heavily in the final hours before they were to carry out the instructions they had been given. Now the time was close, they talked and prayed together for the last time before leaving their respective homes and lives behind.

66.

It had been frantic trying to restore the Farset bunker back to normality following the party but it was now looking business as usual as Ferguson and I waited for FBI Agents Ross and Curtis to arrive. We had offered to meet them at the airport since learning of their arrival time, though they had refused, opting to hire a car and make their own way. No doubt their first stop would be with the PSNI anyhow, so all we had to do was wait. I was anxious at the thought of the meeting, feeling a little intimidated by their status. As was customary I now realised, Ferguson remained unfazed. He had been at his workstation all morning, periodically moving between there and our profile board. I guessed that he was doing much the same as I was, preparing for our guests. We had both been working silently but it was a comfortable silence. That too had become normal for us, though on this occasion, it was broken by the ringtone of Ferguson's mobile. I heard him talk but because of the partition, couldn't make out what he was saying. After ending the call, he joined me.

'That was forensics. It was good news and bad news'.

'Get the bad news out of the way first'!

'They tested the hair sample for DNA but the hair had recently been bleached so most of the DNA had been destroyed'.

'And the good news'?

'There was a tiny bit of the hair near the root that had not been contaminated so they were able to get a DNA code from it'.
The lack of urgency in Ferguson's voice suggested that more bad news was to follow.
'And'?
'It was a female hair. They ran the code through the usual databases but no hits'.
'Great' I replied. 'So we're no further on'.
Charlene, or Gillian as I was struggling to get used to calling her, rang down to say that our guests had arrived. I asked her to show them down.
Momentarily we were greeting Agents Ross and Curtis. Ross with his close cut, salt and pepper hair looked to be in his late fifties, though his muscular frame suggested that he still liked to keep in shape. Despite his solid build, he was quite short in stature. Curtis on the other hand, was 6 feet plus, with a narrow frame and slight build. He looked to be early thirties and had short, dark hair, styled in a side shade and clearly kept in place with lots of product. After exchanging pleasantries and offering coffee, it was down to business. As we led them into the meeting room, it occurred to me that neither man seemed to have any reaction to our surroundings. I found this strange as it had not usually been the case for a first time visitor.
After we took our seats, Ferguson kicked things off by sharing the DNA results that we had just discovered.
'The National Database you mentioned DCI Ferguson…the NDNAD, where is the data compiled from'? Agent Curtis sat,

pen poised, waiting for Ferguson's response.
'From DNA taken from crime scenes and from criminal suspects' Ferguson replied.
'It only goes back as far as 1995 though' he added.
After writing a short note, Curtis fixed his gaze upon Ferguson again.
'Where is the sample now'?
'With the Forensic Science Agency in Crumlin'.
Agent Ross interjected.
'Why didn't you test it here? It would have been much quicker and you would have had access to a wider range of databases. I thought we had full inter-agency support on this'?
'We do but… I don't understand' I began, perplexed.
'What is there to understand? This place is fitted out to the same spec as an FBI field office. There was nothing to stop you processing the hair sample here' said Curtis.
Seeing the look upon my face, the penny dropped for the two agents.
'You didn't know did you'?
I leaned forward onto the table, covering my face with my hands. After sighing loudly, I sat back and explained the circumstances in which we had discovered what was now our base. On hearing what I had to say, Curtis wasted no time. Within minutes the DNA code had been e mailed to Ferguson after he had requested it. The code was now being processed by the FBI database and its associate databases and we would find out if any of them had matching records for it within a matter of hours.
'OK' said Agent Ross as we reconvened in the meeting room.

'Let's hear what else you got'.

I motioned toward the profile board and began to go through what we had compiled so far, when he interjected abruptly.

'I don't want to hear about the killer. I want to hear about the victims. They'll tell me what I need to know about the killer. Take me through your victim files'.

'Wouldn't you have been through those with DI Black already'?

'DI Black has his views on the case. I want to hear from you two'. Ross' tone remained blunt but I admired him for his directness and for his interest in our part in the investigation. We spent the next few hours going over each case whilst both Agents took notes, only stopping to seek clarity on occasion. Neither seemed shocked at our application of Rodgers mediumship talents to our investigation. When I tried to justify it unnecessarily, I was met with an explanation of the fact that although unusual, it was not unheard of within the realms of an FBI investigation. Both men were open to the notion, though indicated that DCI Black may have a more traditional view of policing. I got the distinct impression that their meeting with the PSNI did not go well. To my surprise, by the time we had talked through each of our victim files with Agent Ross and he talked us through the FBI interviews of the suspects in the US Murders, Agent Curtis was ready to give us a profile on Terror. As it turns out, one of the reasons that they had been assigned to the Terror case was because of Agent Curtis' strong profiling training and the high degree of arrests made as the result of his profiling ability.

'I'll type this up and email it to you later but for the moment

I'll just run through my notes' he began.
'Your killer is likely a male in his late thirties and is based locally. He would likely be physically attractive to both sexes and most likely heterosexual. He would struggle to form meaningful romantic relationships and would be unable to maintain any relationship for a significant time. He is most probably educated to a high standard and would be employed within the communications industry. He finds it easy to prey upon and manipulate others. His alter ego is a control mechanism which allows him to function within society whilst keeping his darker side in check until he chooses to unleash it. His hatred of celebrity and the credibility of celebrity probably stems from some sort of personal experience, yet through his publicising of the atrocities that he is responsible for and his need to have a following, it would suggest that he himself craves fame or some kind of recognition, possibly from a parent or parent figure. Certainly a figure of importance or authority in his life. His psychopathy has developed steadily most likely from his teens. He likely struggled to control his temper in his younger years and probably found some comfort in the study of notorious serial killings of the past'.
Ferguson and I looked at each other in a mixture of amazement and disbelief. Although we had gleaned some of what Curtis had shared with us from our own attempts at a profile, the amount of detail he was able to recover that we weren't was genius. Yet if we were to look at what he said, in line with the evidence, as I was now, every assumption made by him could be explained by the evidence that was there before us. Looking again at Ferguson, I concluded that his

thought processes in the last short time were similar to mine, in matching up deductions with evidence.
Shortly after the Agents left for their hotel. They had promised to contact us with the results from their DNA search on the hair found on Dowell's body as soon as they had anything. Ferguson and I decided to call it a night, though another full hour had passed before I actually left, as we were so amazed by the detail of the profile that we couldn't stop talking about it. It really looked like we were starting to make solid progress in unmasking Terror and who knows, we may even get a hit from the female DNA sample. I asked Ferguson to join us for dinner at home but he declined as he had arranged to be available for a Skype call from his family this evening. Making my way to the car, I was looking forward to filling Beth in on what we had learned from our visitors.

67.

Drew Pinkerton tried his best to focus as he waited for Mark Shaw to leave. At one time Shaw had been the closest thing to a friend that anyone inside The Enlightenment could have with someone outside of it. That didn't matter now. He was once a supporter of their Community and pawn of The Church and ironically and from Drew's point of view, from nowhere, had become a dangerous threat to that very institution. That wasn't really down to him was it? If it was he would put that right now, and who knows, perhaps in time, The Prophet might allow him to return. After all, there had been similar cases in the past. Thankfully it was dark now. Drew watched as little rivulets of rain ran down the newly waxed paintwork of Shaw's car as it sat parked under a streetlight facing Shaw's office building. Then at last, Shaw appeared in his field of vision. Drew put the VW in drive, then pulled out of the lay-by near the Divis Tower, at speed. Shaw was already in the middle of the left lane of the road and was exposed. Drew barely reacted as the vehicle slammed into Shaw, forcing him up onto the bonnet then over the roof of the Caravelle, only braking after the event. The impact had caused Drew to bump his head and there was a scratch on his right cheek but judging by the shattered windscreen and the blood spatter all over it, Shaw had fared much worse. Drew took a look in the rearview mirror, to see the shadowy outline of a figure lying still in the road. He realised that the engine was still running and his flight or fight instincts kicked in. He slammed the VW into drive again and launched it forward, but not before seeing Charlene McManus come racing out of the building towards Shaw.

Just a few miles down the road, Dana Boyd had just returned to the multi-storey car park on the Dublin Road, where she regularly parked for easy access to work. She had been to the gym at the Clayton Hotel and was feeling a post workout buzz when she opened the boot of her Mini Cooper and tossed in her gym bag. She got into the car and started it up before becoming aware of movement near the passenger side. It was just as she turned to look that it happened. The front passenger window exploded as it was hit by the crow bar being wielded by the young man at the side of the car. Instinctively she slammed the car into gear and it lurched forward. Struggling to remain in control of the vehicle she headed for the exit ramp. There was a deafening bang as the crowbar that the young man had been holding, hit the back of the car, having been launched toward the rear window. Shaking and still struggling to keep the car in check, she looked in the mirror, to see her assailant pursuing her on foot at a run. It was then that she noticed her dash cam positioned below the mirror and had the presence of mind to turn it so that the lens now faced to the rear and was recording the movements of her attacker. As the car neared the bottom of the exit ramp Dana became aware albeit, too late, of the sharp downward corner that led to the exit ramp of the level she was about to enter. She braked hard but not in time to stop the car from overshooting the corner and ploughing into a concrete support pillar at speed. Her pursuer stopped short of the vehicle before slowly walking toward it's mangled front end. There he saw the slumped body of Dana Boyd in the driver's seat, her face red with blood. Daniel Pinkerton stood ashen faced at the scene that lay before him. He was shaking uncontrollably and thought that he was going to be physically sick. At first he was oblivious to the shouts of the Security Guard who had appeared at the scene, though became all too aware of them as the man attempted to restrain him. Breaking free of the older man's grip, Daniel ran as fast as his weakened legs and alcohol addled brain allowed.

Approximately 10,600 miles away at the British Consulate in Sydney, Maria Ferguson was stood at her post under the marble arch just outside the main entrance. As the white Ute screeched to a halt parallel to the main gate, her senses heightened and her hand moved toward her weapon in its holster. She watched as a portly man in his fifties dressed in navy slacks and a plain, pale blue shirt, calmly exited the vehicle. He smiled in her direction as he moved to the canopy of the vehicle and reached inside before crouching down at the rear passenger wheel. Maria released her grip on the gun, surmising that the man must have had a blowout, which would explain the aggressive halt of the vehicle and his actions since. She continued to watch as he stood up straight again. She would have offered assistance but she was not allowed to leave her post. The man met her gaze again before she noticed the swift movement of his right arm. Before she could react, the glass bottle filled with petrol and plugged by a burning rag was flying through the air, arcing in her direction. On impact upon the stone path the bottle smashed, the resultant explosion engulfing the area around Maria in flames and trapping her in her position under the arch. The driver of the Ute watched the blaze for a few seconds until the height of the flames was such that he could no longer make out the form of Maria Ferguson. He calmly got into his vehicle and drove the short distance to the local police station before handing himself in.

68.

Beth Shaw brushed tears away from her cheeks with her left hand whilst clasping her husband's hand tightly with her right. He had survived the surgery to repair the perforated lung and ruptured spleen but he had lost a lot of blood and also suffered severe trauma at the base of his skull as well as other less serious injuries. At this point his chances of survival were sitting at around 60%. In a seat at the corner of the room, Tom Ferguson sat dumbstruck, still trying to comprehend what had happened. Thankfully Gillian had been quick to react and by the time she had called him to the scene, the ambulance and police were already on their way. Mark was still breathing at that point,and she had placed him into the recovery position and was trying to keep him warm. The emergency services had reacted quickly which greatly improved his chances of survival. For now though, in the early hours of the morning, he remained critical and Beth was inconsolable.

Outside in the waiting room Gillian was looking after Alecia. Both Beth and Mark's parents were on holiday in Spain though were urgently trying to book a return flight. Across the coffee table from where Gillian and Alecia were playing, Patrick Rodgers sat deep in meditation. He was sending healing to Mark and comfort to Beth when the ringing of his phone broke him from his concentration. The caller display indicated that the call was from his landlord. That was unusual he thought, as they rarely had any contact. He took the call but soon wished that he hadn't. After ending the call, Gillian, who had realised that there was something wrong, was waiting expectantly.

'The apartment… it's been gutted! Someone poured petrol through the letter box then put something to light it with through afterward. The whole place is destroyed. The police want to speak to us. They think that someone could have made an attempt on our lives'.

Gillian watched as her brother went into auto pilot, ignoring the murder attempt and rather focusing on what needed to be done practically at this moment in time.

He quietly opened the door to the room where Mark was being treated, and beckoned Ferguson out. Beth fearing that it was bad news about Mark also reacted and before Gillian knew it, the three of them were outside the door. As Patrick relayed the news, Ferguson's phone rang. It was DI Black.

'How is he? Any progress?'

'We're just waiting and praying at this stage' answered Ferguson.

'I thought you ought to know, we've just charged a Mr Drew Pinkerton with attempted murder and warned him that it could become a murder charge as well as a number of other driving offences, should we lose Mark'.

'You mean…'

'It was him driving the car. He handed himself in and confessed. We've already recovered the vehicle. That's not all though, we also have his son Daniel in custody'.

'What… why'?

'He also handed himself in, admitting to attempted murder. He has also been charged and warned that it may become a murder charge'.

'I don't understand'!

'He has admitted trying to kill Patrick Rodgers and his sister by setting fire to their apartment and also attacking Dana Boyd, causing her to have a life threatening car accident'.

'Dana, Oh No! Where is she, how is she'? The others looked at him in shock.

'She was taken to the RVH as well. She's probably somewhere near where you are now'.

'I'll check it out. I have Patrick and Gillian here with me. They've only just found out about the fire and have been asked to come make a statement. Do you still need them now'?

'That won't be necessary for the moment. I will still need to speak to them at some point but it's fine for now. They can contact me when they feel up to it'.

'Fine. What are the Pinkertons saying'? Again this drew a reaction of shock from all those standing beside Ferguson.

'That they are renegade from,The Enlightenment and that their actions are independent of, The Church. Their legal representative is on his way'.

'Bastards! I'll fill Patrick and Gillian in and get them to contact you. I'll see if I can find out what's happening with Dana too and stay in touch'.

'Thanks, and tell Mark's family I'm thinking of them'.

'Will do'.

Ferguson ended the call and was about to fill the others in when the crash alarm sounded outside Mark's room. Beth dashed back into the room shortly followed by the crash medical team. The heart rate monitor was showing a flat line and emitting a constant beep. Mark's heart had stopped and the scene descended into pandemonium.

69.

For a few moments Gillian Rodgers struggled to work out where she was when she first woke up. Hearing snoring coming from the next room though, brought her location back to her. She was in one of the apartments in the Farset bunker and the snoring was coming from her brother Patrick who was evidently still asleep on the sofa next door. The realisation that their home had been destroyed in a fire yesterday and that Mark Shaw and Dana Boyd were fighting for their lives waved over her and the reality of it bit hard. Even more so when she recalled who was responsible. They had almost lost Mark last night, though thankfully, the medical team were able to resuscitate him and stabilise his heart rate. She pictured Drew and Daniel Pinkerton in their holding cells. For the moment their faces represented the very thing that she hated with every fibre of her being,The Enlightenment. Again she silently vowed to make them pay. How she would ever truly get the vengeance that she craved, she did not know but it would happen, of that she was sure. She got up and pulled some clothes on, before checking her phone. Still nothing. She had tried calling Caleb several times yesterday evening and through the night but he hadn't called her back. He wasn't responding to any of her texts or voicemails either, which wasn't like him. She felt a brief pang of worry that perhaps The Enlightenment had somehow attacked him too, before dismissing it, thinking that they probably didn't even know who he was. She was still concerned for him though. Putting the phone into her pocket, she padded into the sitting room, where her brother was beginning to stir.

'Morning'.

Patrick sat up on the sofa that he had been sleeping on, his facial expression and tousled hair indicating that he had not quite fully woken up yet.

'Did I miss any news'?

'Not that I know of'.

'I hope they're OK. I still can't believe it. I thought the days of those Bastards wrecking our lives and hurting the people we love, were over'.

Gillian remained silent. She thought it best not to unleash the fury of her thoughts onto Patrick. He had enough to worry about. She moved to the side of the sofa to retrieve her shoes when the apartment door knocked. She opened it, to find Ferguson waiting.

'Hey neighbours'!

Before she could respond, Patrick called over her shoulder.

'Have you heard anything from the hospital'?

'No, not yet. I'm going to head up there shortly. I've made some breakfast. It's in the staffroom, so just come through when you're ready'.

After freshening up as best they could, they joined Ferguson at the table in the staffroom. At the centre of the table was a pot of coffee and a plate of croissants and pan au chocolat.

'I didn't sleep much so I went out to the all night garage and picked those up' said Ferguson.

'Great, thanks' replied Patrick. Gillian nodded in appreciation

before pouring coffee for them all and grabbing a croissant.
'Are you going to see DI Black today'? Ferguson asked.
'I need to cancel my clients for today first, then we'll go see him'. He looked toward Gillian. 'That OK with you'?
'Anything to make sure those Bastards pay for what they've done'. She replied, perhaps a little less controlled than she would have liked.
'We'll need to see the landlord too at some point and get some new clothes organised'. Patrick interjected, noticing that his sister had become embarrassed by her outburst in front of Ferguson.
'Whilst you are making your calls, I'll go up to the office for a little while. I'll need to set an auto reply on the email and forward calls to my mobile'. Gillian said.
Noticing how haggard that Ferguson looked, Patrick asked, 'Did you get any sleep at all last night?'
'None! I couldn't stop going over everything in my mind. I've been trying to get hold of my brother and sister in law as well but they haven't come back to me. We were supposed to be skyping each other last night but they didn't connect'.
Hearing that made Gillian's thoughts turn again to Caleb. She hoped he was ok and Ferguson's family too.
'I'll try calling again before I go to the hospital. I better get moving I suppose'. Ferguson drained the remainder of his coffee down before heading toward his apartment. Patrick called after him.
'We'll be there as soon as we can'.
'No worries'. He replied.
'I'll maybe collect Alecia and bring her back here for a while, if

her Grandparents still aren't back by the time we get there' Gillian added.
Ferguson nodded. 'Good idea! The poor kid must be in turmoil. It's no wonder she didn't want to leave her Mum last night'.
'I suppose we should make a move too' said Patrick, rising.
Gillian followed as he led the way to the upstairs building. They reached the door of his office first. Gillian continued down the corridor as he unlocked the door and unset the alarm. Upon reaching her office, she noticed the blinking light on the phone, indicating that there was a voicemail. Thinking it might be news from Caleb or news from the hospital, she lifted the receiver and dialled into the mailbox. As it turned out, there were several messages, all from the same person. Mr Paul Gibson, Senior Administrator at the British Consulate in Sydney had been trying to contact Ferguson. That didn't sound good she thought. She jotted down the contact number before calling Ferguson on his mobile and relaying the message. She had just booted up the iMac and was about to change the email settings on the Farset account when the door access buzzer rang. Looking at the security monitor she saw that it was the FBI agents from yesterday. She buzzed them in and before long, they were stood facing her at Reception.
'Good Morning Miss Rodgers' said Agent Curtis. She was impressed that he had remembered her name and felt her face flush. 'We'd like to see Mr Shaw and DCI Ferguson if possible'.
'I'm afraid it won't' said Gillian politely, before filling them in on Mark's attack. She also thought it best not to disturb

Ferguson either. It sounded like he might be on an important call if the message was anything to go by.

'I'm sorry to hear that' said Agent Curtis.

'Me too' added Agent Ross. Please, ask DCI Ferguson to keep us informed if he can. He has both our cards. I'd really hoped to catch up with him before we left. We've been called back to the US urgently. We're on our way to the airport now'.

'I'll ask him to call you as soon as he can. Is there anything I can help you with in the meantime'?

'No, if you could just ask him to call either of us when he can, and if you could, pass on our regards to Mrs Shaw'.

'Certainly, I will' replied Gillian.

'Actually' added Agent Curtis removing an envelope from his pocket and setting it on the counter of the Reception. 'Could you give this to him and ask him if the name, Charlene McManus means anything to him'?

Hearing the name sent Gillian's thoughts into whirlwind. She could barely get the words out to say goodbye to the Agents. She watched on the monitor as they left, trying not to implode at their unsuspecting revelation. Mark had been so excited by the meeting with the Agents yesterday and what came out of it, that when he called in to say goodbye to her before leaving yesterday, he told her about all about it. She was excited for him, knowing that he might now be one step closer to justice, one step closer to finding Terror. Now, she just felt sheer panic. If the hair found on Dowell's body was Charlene Mc Manus' hair, her hair, then that could only mean one thing. Caleb Doyle was Terror. He couldn't be, could he? The more she tried to dismiss the thought, the more it began to ring true. Overcome with anxiety, she just about made it to the toilet, before being violently sick.

Beneath her in the bunker Tom Ferguson's world was also about to change dramatically for the worst, as his call was put through to Paul Gibson.

'Ah, Mr Ferguson, I'm so glad to finally get to speak to you. I'm afraid I have some bad news'.

Ferguson braced himself. He'd had a feeling that there was something wrong but he hadn't bargained for what he heard next.

70. Part Four - Terror, Fear & Retribution

Nine days had passed since the attack, but it was only now that Beth Shaw was beginning to feel encouraged. Mark's condition had continued to show slow but sure improvement and the doctors had now moved him from the ICU into a High Dependency Unit. He still hadn't regained consciousness but the Consultant was confident that with ongoing care, he would make a full recovery. Beth was overjoyed at the news. The thought of losing Mark had been unbearable for her. How could she and Alecia ever cope without him in their lives? Thankfully now, that was a prospect they would no longer have to face. She stroked his cheek as she sat at the top of his bed side looking down at him. She wanted to create so many more memories with this man and to grow old with him. They had it all mapped out, including watching their beautiful daughter grow up and of course, there had to be grandchildren. The thought that they had come so close to losing all that pained her deeply. She surprised herself in that she hadn't felt anger yet. She knew that The Enlightenment were responsible but had been so concerned about Mark that nothing else had mattered, and now, their future and the future of their family and friends was the only thing that was important. She couldn't help however, but feel a pang of guilt at beginning to feel happier, whilst others were not faring so well. She looked down into the ICU part of the ward, where Dana Boyd lay. She too remained unconscious with her mother by her side. She had received a brain injury and although the surgery had gone well, she remained in a critical condition. Then of course there was Tom and his family. How they would ever get over the death of his Sister in law, she couldn't even begin to imagine. She wished that they could have been able to do more for them and hoped that they would get through the funeral service and burial today ok. Patrick and Gillian had not fared well either, losing their home and the majority of their possessions. At least she had been able to help there ,offering use of the spare apartment at Farset until they got something else sorted.

Engrossed in her thoughts, it was only when she felt a soft kiss on the hand that she had been stroking Mark's cheek with, that she noticed. Mark had regained consciousness. She was elated.

'Beth'?

'Yes' she just about managed, smiling and crying at the same time before waking Alecia who had been sleeping on a chair in the corner.

71.

Caleb Doyle switched his phone back on, having disembarked the plane in Dublin. His Father, his Ministerial colleagues and the other political hangers on had already been met by official vehicles and were in convoy on their way back to Belfast. They had just returned from a Business & Enterprise Summit in Washington DC. No doubt they were feeling pleased with themselves, particularly the First and Deputy Ministers, who had successfully negotiated inward investment of upward of £40 million for Northern Ireland in the next year. As Caleb Doyle, he doubted that any of the money would enrich his life. Still he got some good copy out of it and his Editor was pleased. As Terror, he had much more important things to think about. He checked the phone to see if he had network coverage yet. Seeing that he had, he immediately called Gillian. The time difference and his hectic work schedule had made it difficult for him to remain in contact over the last ten days or so, but the news she had relayed to him about the attacks perpetrated by The Enlightenment had made him feel infuriated. He needed to know more.

'Hey gorgeous'!

'Caleb! At last! It's so good to hear your voice. Where are you'?

'I'm in Dublin. I'm just on my way to the car park, then I'll be on my way home. I was hoping you would come over. I've missed you so much'.

'Of course I'll come over, I can't wait to see you' she replied excitedly. 'How long will you be'?
'Should be about two hours or so'.
'I'll meet you at the house. Have you eaten yet'?
'I'm starved, the in flight meal was gross'.
'OK, I'll get some food supplies and some beer and I'll see you soon'.
'You're a treasure! And Gillian…'
'Yeah'?
'I'm really sorry I had you worried and that I wasn't there for you. I'll make it up to you, I promise'.
'You bet you will Mr, now hurry home before I change my mind'. She laughed before ending the call.
Terror replaced the phone in his pocket and smiled to himself. Upon his arrival in Washington almost nine days ago, he turned on his phone only to find a number of frantic and worried messages from Gillian. In his return call, he managed to calm her worry, then eventually appease her anger. What he told her was true. It was only a last minute decision for his Editor to send him along to the Summit so he didn't get an opportunity to contact her. What he had neglected to mention however, was that the Editor's decision only came very early on what would have been the morning after the attacks. The night before had been spent in the bed of an attractive brunette member of his following and his phone had been switched off in order to allow him to get to know her a little better. Being a now celebrated serial killer with a cult following had brought with it some unexpected benefits.

72.

Having ended her call to Caleb, Gillian Rodgers felt herself begin to feel anxious again at how this evening was going to play out. She was determined that she would confront Caleb about his alter-ego, but was worried at how he would react.
Was she placing herself in danger? She was gambling that the answer would be no, but who knows? She wasn't even sure that the conclusion that she had reached was the right one, though the evidence and all her instincts were telling her overwhelmingly that she was right. Caleb had to be Terror and once she proved it, she had a proposition for him. After all, she had nothing to lose right. She'd already lied to the FBI, making the call supposedly on Tom Ferguson's behalf. She had told them of his family tragedy and that she had managed to ask him about Charlene McManus. His response had been no, there was no connection to the investigation that he knew of. She was possibly facing a prison sentence already, if the truth were to come out. She had lied and withheld information likely to be of use to police in the capture of a serial killer. If she was going to go to jail, it would be for something worthwhile she told herself. Vengeance! Steeling herself, she showered and changed before heading off to Sainsbury's at the Kennedy Centre en route to Terror's Malone Avenue lair. For better or worse, this evening will be one to remember.

73.

The steaming hot shower had powered away any fatigue that Terror had been feeling after his long flight and drive. Getting out of the shower, he grabbed a towel and quickly wrapped it around his waist, then lifted a smaller one from the rail and began drying his face and hair. He'd made good time on the drive home, so had decided to freshen up before Gillian arrived. Although he was yet to hear the full detail on,The Enlightenment attacks, he was pretty sure that he could use them to his advantage in bringing Gillian closer to the pseudonym he had created for her, Fear.

The doorbell rang whilst he was still drying off. He moved swiftly downstairs, opening the door whilst wrapped only in the towel, his head and torso still shimmering with the spray from the shower. He knew exactly the effect that this would have on Gillian, and that the long kiss that he pulled her into immediately, would increase that effect one hundred fold.

'Hey' he said after pulling his lips away from hers.

'Hey yourself' Gillian Rodgers replied before playfully pushing him away. ' Shouldn't you be putting some clothes on'.

'I guess I should he replied' feigning hurt. She laughed as he made his way back

upstairs and she headed out to the car to fetch their provisions.

Terror marvelled at the change in her. Charlene McManus would never had reacted so confidently to such an advance.

She would have been so timorous that she probably would have left in a fit of blushes. Not Gillian though! Her new name suited her and her new look was awesome. Probably Beth Shaw's influence he mused briefly. Whilst dressing, the thought came to him grudgingly, that it had probably taken the influence of the Shaw's, Patrick Rodgers and possibly even Tom Ferguson, as well as Terror, to help this young woman become what she had in the last months. He had been trying to suppress thoughts of these people since hearing of the attacks upon them and quickly tried to do so again, for fear that it might alter his mood. He had to remain in control at all costs tonight. He wanted to focus on helping Gillian in the next logical step in her evolution. What he was going to suggest may come at a cost, he thought, steeling himself. Depending on her reaction, he may have to end the life of Gillian Rodgers tonight. He didn't want to do that. He realised that he had come to love this young woman. For better or worse, this evening will be one to remember.

74.

As he stood in the Ellesmere Port office of Brigadier Nick Cruikshank, Tom Ferguson quietly wished he could erase the last few weeks. He felt riddled with guilt at choosing not to join his family in Australia. His mind flooded with what if's as he watched his older brother by one year, Michael, dressed in his full regalia, receive his honourable discharge from the Ministry of Defence in what formerly had been his Home base. Earlier today they had buried Michael's wife Maria, having repatriated her from where she had lost her life in Sydney, Australia. The service had been held in Liverpool Cathedral and her sacrifice had been honoured with a full, military funeral. It had been no less than she deserved, he had heard it said several times.With each time he heard it though, he wanted to scream, she didn't deserve it though. He knew what they had meant but in his mind, she didn't have to die. It was his fault she had been murdered. He was guilty by association with Farset. He had already tried to explain this to his brother Michael but he had refused to allow him to carry the burden of guilt that he felt.

'Maria was a soldier. I'm a soldier. We both knew what could happen as a result of our career and life choices, but we've always accepted that. That's what you must do also'.

How could he though? His Sister in Law, a woman that he had loved like a sister and admired for many years had been murdered. His brother had been robbed of his wife and their future together, and perhaps worst of all, little Emma had been robbed of her Mother.

He wished he had a fraction of Michael's bravery. He watched as his brother, with one hand placed on the shoulder of his young daughter as she stood in front of him, used his other hand to sign the discharge papers before receiving his wife's personal effects. They would spend the night in barracks before returning to Belfast with him tomorrow, to take stock and decide what the future holds for them. Michael had already decided though, that although it was where both he and his wife were born and bred and where she had been buried, Liverpool would hold no part in their future. The memories that the city holds would be too powerful to allow them to move on.

75.

Caleb Doyle took a long drink from the beer bottle as he heard Gillian outline each of the attacks and their severity. He listened intently as she moved on to the latest development that she had become aware of. Drew Pinkerton, his son and his brother were each claiming to have acted without the authority of The Enlightenment, a claim supported by a statement from the Church itself. They were also each claiming to have acted under the influence of strong anti-depressant medications, which had been backed up by blood tests and GP records, meaning that they could claim diminished responsibility on mental health grounds as a means of defence.

He watched as she became more and more riled as she spoke. He had played the part of psychiatrist to her so many times before, that it was something that they had both become quite comfortable with. He would usually listen attentively as she unburdened herself, showing empathy and occasionally prompting her with questions on how the events or experiences had affected her or made her feel. Tonight was no exception, except for the fact that tonight, whilst encouraging her to embrace her anger, he was struggling hard to suppress his own.

Although he knew it was far from the case, he took The Enlightenment attacks as a personal affront to him. If anyone was going to end the lives of Mark Shaw and Tom Ferguson, it would be Terror. They had also threatened the life of Gillian, the woman that now meant so much to him. ,The Enlightenment and its Prophet had just made a very powerful enemy in Terror and they would be held accountable to him for these attacks, of that he was sure.

'What has the police reaction been to these claims'? Caleb asked.

'Given the strength of the legal team, the blood evidence and the lack of evidence to the contrary of the Church statement and the Pinkerton's statements, they're concerned that a court may find in favour of diminished responsibility and sentence each of them to time in a secure hospital'. Her face flushed with anger and a hot tear ran from each eye, streaking down her face. 'They would be put under medical supervision and could be released back into society within two to three years. The Enlightenment as a Church would be unlikely to bear any responsibility'.

Caleb pulled her into a hug. 'I just don't know what to say. How can these people keep evading any proper justice? What would Fear do?'

He had asked the last question as a means of leading her into fantasising about her revenge, allowing him to suggest that she acted out on some or all of her responses. This is it, he thought, the pivotal moment. Her response sent him reeling.

'She would enlist the help of Terror, formulate a plan, then get the Bastards. So what do you think, will you help me'? She broke from his embrace, sat back and looked him squarely in the eye. 'Well… Terror, can you help me'?

Caleb Doyle's stomach sank and he began to feel nauseated.

For the second time his alter-ego had been discovered, and as with the last time, by someone one who he cared for deeply.
'What… How…'?
'How do I know? Is that what you were going to ask'? Gillian said calmly and without breaking eye contact. 'Why don't we go to the Glenvine Hotel for a drink and we can talk about it more there'? We have been there pretty recently haven't we? Except I didn't realise what it was called then. I would say that maybe I would feel safer there but based on recent events, I wouldn't be so sure'.
She could see the fear flicker momentarily in his eyes and realised that she needed to maintain control of the situation.
'Relax, no-one else knows' she said cooly. 'Just me, and that's the way I intend to keep it, so if you were thinking of killing me, you don't have to'. She paused momentarily. 'You haven't denied it I see'. Her gaze remained locked and her demeanour outwardly relaxed.
'What, being Terror or thinking about killing you'? Caleb replied.
'Both'.
'Don't worry Gillian, I have no intentions of killing you. I won't lie, there have been times that I've worried that I might have to. I wanted to encourage you to become Fear and was afraid at how you would react to my suggestion that you should commit murder. You see the thing is… I think I love you'.
Hearing what he had just said filled Gillian firstly with relief, then joy. True to form, she flushed.
'I think I love you too. He pulled her into his arms again. 'I

was so afraid coming here tonight to tell you what I had to say'.
'It was a very courageous thing to do but your courage is of no surprise to me. It's one of the things I love about you'.
'I'm ready' Gillian said, looking up into Caleb's eyes.
'For what'?
'To be Fear… really be Fear'.
'We have a lot to talk about' he replied. 'But first…' He leaned forward slightly, brushing his lips against hers before kissing her deeply.

76.

For the fourth time in as many minutes, I restarted the review I had been trying to read in the latest edition of Auto Express. On each of the other attempts to read it, I found my mind drifting. Over the last few days my memories of the night of the attack had been slowly returning. The vision of seeing Drew Pinkerton racing toward me as I tried to cross the road haunted my conscious and unconscious thoughts ever since. Still struggling to concentrate, I became aware of someone walking toward me in my peripheral vision. I looked up to see my former colleague and long time friend, Caitlin Price striding toward me in her usual purposeful manner. She smiled as she drew closer before entering the single room on the general ward that I had been moved to earlier today.

'I've been all over the place looking for you. How are you'?

'Yeah, they only moved me here this morning. I've been better'. I smiled, gesturing to the monitors and drip that I was hooked up to. 'Still, at least I've kept my good looks, right' I said, knowing that my face was a mass of swelling and bruising.

She set a carrier bag down on the end of the bed and removed a bottle of Coke Zero, a bag of party sized Mars bars and a packet of Haribo Wine Gums.

'I thought Barley Water and Grapes would be wasted on you' she said as she began to pack my treats into the locker beside me.

'You know me so well' I replied, grimacing in pain as I tried to sit up a little in the bed.

Perching on the empty seat at the side of the bed, she removed her handbag from her shoulder and set it on the ground beside her before sitting back.

'How've you been'? I asked, noticing that she looked a little haggard and for the first time, a little older than her 42 years. I remembered thinking much the same when I saw her at the party at Farset just before the Unreported Ulster airing.

'Fine' she replied, though her smile wasn't as convincing as she had probably hoped it would be.

'How's Martin and the family'? I continued.

'Yeah, everyone's fine. Mum and Dad are off on another Cruise soon'.

'Good for them. How's School'? She shifted uncomfortably.

'I've resigned' she said flatly . 'I can't work there anymore, not after what they did to you and the others'.

'But..'

'No buts, Mark. I'll find something new soon enough. I just wish I'd had the courage to do it years ago'.

I'd already known that I suppose. We'd certainly both discussed leaving the school often enough, particularly in light of what we had continued to learn about the practices of,The Enlightenment over the years and Caitlin had been a huge supporter of the expose´of those practices.

'How did they react'? I asked.

'Barely at all. They just told me that I would have to work out my contracted notice period. Things have been more strained than ever, since I told them'.

'What does your family think?'
'Mum and Dad are delighted. Mum has wanted me to leave for years now'.
'And what about Martin?'
'Actually, it was his suggestion. He knew I'd been thinking about it for a while and how I felt about what has happened to you and the others. He said it might give me an opportunity to find something closer to where he lives, then we can maybe think about getting married'.
'You mean'?
'Yes', she beamed. 'It's not official and we haven't picked a ring yet but I wanted you to be the first to know'.
'Caitlin, I'm so delighted for you. You deserve it, you both do. I would hug you but…' I leaned forward, again, grimacing in pain. Caitlin got up and leaned into me for a hug before retaking her seat.
'I still can't believe it' I said. 'Martin, certainly is a dark horse. Congratulations to you both! Beth and I will have to take you both out to celebrate whenever I get back on my feet… literally'.
'I spoke to Beth last night actually'.
'She didn't say'.
'No? You've been doing it again haven't you?'
'Doing what'? I asked, the tone of the conversation suddenly becoming less jubilant.
'You know, retreating inside yourself again. Not really talking to anyone about what's happened. Beth's worried about you, we all are'.
It's true, I do have a tendency to focus inwards at times of

stress or trauma. It's my way of dealing with it. I have to process and work things out for myself. It's always been my way and has always been a worry to those closest to me.

'There's nothing to worry about. I'll be fine' I said.

'Really! Mark, you were almost killed. We nearly lost you. Your colleagues were attacked, Dana Boyd may die, Tom Ferguson's Sister in Law was murdered and you'll be fine. You think'?

Caitlin always had a way of getting me to talk. Usually through her own straight talking and take no prisoners attitude. Today was no exception and my temper flared as a result.

'What's the point in talking about it, is it going to change anything?' I reacted angrily. 'You really want to know, how I feel? I'm angry! I'm pissed off. I nearly died, people did die and others lives are in tatters, and for what? What did any of it achieve? How can any of us move on from this?' I snarled.

Caitlin continued to push, her tone remaining calm and level.

'So what, you're going to just lie there and lick your wounds? What you did may have caused this devastation but you weren't acting alone. Everyone knew the risks and everyone played their part. A lot of good has come out of it whether you care to see it or not'.

'Did Ferguson know the risks, did his family, I don't think so?' I snapped.

'Everyone wanted justice Mark and that's what you delivered. Nobody could have expected,The Enlightenment to retaliate in the way that they have done. You need to deal with that'.

I knew that she was right but struggled to get past the fact that ever since I became involved with Farset, many people had lost their lives and my friends and loved ones were increasingly placed in grave danger.

'How'? I said dejectedly.

'Take the positives. Between you, you have severely, perhaps fatally wounded a cult movement. Think of the differences that would make to so many people's lives because of that. Think of the number of lives you've possibly saved, freed. That's a big achievement Mark! Besides the fact, you may have got justice for your Uncle Sean. What ,The Enlightenment have done lately proves beyond doubt that they are capable of murder'.

I nodded, before she continued.

'You know you still have a serial killer to catch. Terror is still out there and if The Enlightenment weren't guilty of killing Sean, it's a fair bet that he could be. You're work hasn't finished. It's only just beginning. You need to snap out of it Mark. Your family need you, your friends need you. You're the linchpin that holds everything together. You need to help everyone else to move on from this, lead those who are so loyal to you and care about you so much. But you can't do that unless you move on yourself. Your choice. Lecture over.'

She was right. There was no denying it. My body was healing rapidly and now, thanks to Caitlin, so was my mind. I smiled at her.

'Message received and understood' I said.

'Good' she said triumphantly. 'Cos I've got to go. Dinner won't make itself and it's my turn to cook'.

'You'd better get moving then, I know how grumpy Martin gets when he's hungry'.

We both laughed at the thought of it. She picked up her bag and put it over her shoulder before hugging me goodbye.
'I'll see you soon'.
'Definitely, and Caitlin… Thanks'!
'No worries. What are friends for'!
'Tell Martin Congratulations'.
'I will. Oh and Mark, talk to Beth'.
'Don't worry, I will' I said, before watching her stride as purposefully out of the ward, as she had into it. I smiled.

77.

The last few days had seen Caleb Doyle happier than he had been for a very long time and it was all down to Gillian. He watched her as she slept, thinking what a marvel that she was. Upon discovering the DNA found on James Dowell's body to be her own and realising who Terror was, she still had the presence of mind to cover for them both and mislead the FBI Agents.Through their recent conversations they had both realised that her actions only created a temporary solution though. There was still the distinct possibility that Mark Shaw or Tom Ferguson, or perhaps even DI Black, could have a conversation with Agents Ross or Curtis that could become the undoing of Gillian and Terror. Still, they had worked out a way to meet that eventuality. What was exciting him most however, was not only that Fear would shortly announce her presence to the world in spectacular style, but also that Terror's next and possibly penultimate victim had been chosen. The Prophet had for personal reasons, riled Terror, but had also earned himself the status of being #FamousForAllTheWrongReasons. With the insider knowledge and intelligence that Gillian was able to provide through her former existence as Charlene McManus, it was only a matter of time before The Prophet would be "taken". After that, his attention will turn to his final and perhaps most important victim, before retiring and allowing his followers to continue his legacy should they wish to, leaving him to continue a life of freedom as Caleb Doyle. He might perhaps even settle down with Gillian, have a family, further climb the ranks at, The Chron. Who knows?

Gillian stirred, breaking his train of thought.

'Morning sleepyhead, you want some coffee'? He asked.

'I'd love some' she said sleepily before turning around, curling up and pulling the duvet more tightly around her. 'Wake me when it's ready'. She closed her eyes.

'I'll need you to move your car in a while. I need to go out soon' he told her.

'But it's Saturday! I thought we could just have a lazy day around the house, then maybe go out this evening'.

'We still can, but there's something I've got to do first'.

'What is it'? She asked.

'I'm going to visit Mark Shaw in hospital'.

'What'? Her eyes sprang open. She was awake now ok.

'I've been thinking, I haven't really spoken to him since the day I met you in his office. He's a smart man and he knows my reputation. I'm sure he has wondered why I would seemingly have just given up in helping find Terror, especially if it would advance my career if I did. I don't want him or Ferguson getting suspicious about my absence for any reason, especially if it means they make the connection about our relationship'.

'Why would they?'

'I disappear off the scene and suddenly you have a mysterious new boyfriend who nobody has met yet'.

'Fair point I suppose, but why don't you just visit him at home, he should be getting out of hospital in a few days'.

‘I know, but it’s complicated. Mark, Beth and I go back a long way. I’d rather not go to the house. I’ll get us some coffee’.

78.

After moving her car out from behind Caleb's in the driveway, Gillian returned to the hallway and waved him off with a smile. He should be gone for a while so that would give her some time to do what she needed to. After fishing her phone out of her handbag, she took a seat on the sofa and opened the voice recorder app on it. She had made quite a few recordings of Caleb over the last few days, unbeknownst to him, beginning with her accusation that he was in fact Terror and his subsequent admissions. This would be the first time that she had any opportunity to play them back, to ensure that what was being said was clearly audible and reasonable sound quality. What she had said was true, she did love him and she did want to be Fear, but still, she felt like she needed some kind of insurance policy against Caleb, just in case, hence the recordings.

She scanned through each of the recordings in turn, looking specifically for particular parts of conversations, including the admission of killing Sean Brady, the identity of some of the, Terrorists and how he came to manipulate them so easily to murder.

'Largely, they choose the victims, not me. It's easy to identify some whack job who has an unhealthy resentment for particular famous people, or the world of celebrity in general. Then it's just about honing that resentment into one single focus. "Murder" she heard Caleb/Terror say clearly on the recording. The irony that he had probably used the same or similar techniques to prey on her resentments and insecurities was not lost on her. Still, she loved him nonetheless. What she was doing was just for her own security and peace of mind… right?

Satisfied with the content and quality of the recordings, she uploaded them to her cloud before emailing copies of the sound files to both her work and personal email accounts. She then deleted the recordings from her phone, for fear that Caleb may come across them. When she had finished, she began the more enjoyable task of browsing properties online. Since the fire, she and Patrick had agreed that they should maybe look at buying a place together. Maybe an apartment or a small house. After compiling a list, she emailed a list of the links to Patrick for him to have a look at. Hopefully when she returned back to the apartment at Farset where they were staying temporarily, tomorrow, they could decide which ones might be worth viewing. Setting the phone down on the arm of the sofa beside her, she sat back and curled her feet up underneath her, making herself comfortable. As she relaxed, she contemplated her future. She loved the fact that she was free from The Enlightenment and had created a life that allowed her to be happy. She had embraced her renewed family relationship with Patrick and her newly formed relationships within the Farset family. Then there was Caleb. Through him she had found love and the ability to embrace the darkness within her. She just hoped that she could continue to find ways to balance all the aspects of her life, particularly since her life was so complicated at the best of times. She reminded herself of a quote she saw somewhere recently, "Life is to be lived in all situations, whatever they be".

79.

Using my newly acquired walking stick to steady myself, I stooped a little to look into the hospital locker at the head of the bed, checking to make sure that I hadn't left anything behind. Beth had already taken the majority of my stuff out of it last night, leaving me with only the bare essentials that I would need for today. Apart from the clothes I was wearing, my wash bag and dirty clothes were all I had left, and I'd already put those into my sports bag.

'Hey Stranger'!

I tried to turn around, momentarily forgetting that I needed the stick to balance, and almost toppled over. I managed to steady myself by grabbing the edge of the bed, though lost my grip on the walking stick, which made a loud clattering noise as it hit the floor. Looking up from where my line of sight had followed the stick as it fell, I was faced with the sight of Caleb Doyle, as his frame filled the doorway.

'Sorry Mark, I didn't mean to startle you. You OK?'

'I am now' I said, seating myself at the edge of the bed. 'I'm still trying to get used to that thing'. I nodded at the stick on the ground. Caleb moved forward and lifted it, leaning it against the bed beside me.

'Sorry I haven't been able to be around. I've been thinking of you though, how are you doing now'?

'No worries, I'm well on the mend now, though things were pretty grim for a while. I've seen through, The Chron, that

your Editor has been keeping you busy, even a US trip no less' I replied. 'Take a seat'.
'Yeah, he's been pushing me more in the direction of the Politics stories. The Chron's political correspondent is due to retire in a few years, so I think I might be in mind to fill his shoes'.
'That would be quite an achievement for you, given your age'.
'Yeah, but I doubt he's doing it for the benefit of my career. I think, he thinks that having the Deputy First Minister's son take a lead in this direction, might give the paper an inside track and boost sales'.
'You don't sound too enamoured' I said.
'No, the job itself is fine, I quite enjoy it. It's having to spend so much time around him that bothers me. I've tried to avoid him at the best of times for years and now I see him practically every day'.
'Things still that strained between you and your Dad'?
'That's the understatement of the century, still, I came here to talk about you, not him'. He nodded toward my bag. 'I take it you're getting out today'.
'Yes. The doctors initially thought I might have to stay for a bit longer, but thankfully, I'm healing well so there's no point in my taking up a space that could be used by someone more in need of it'.
'That's very noble of you' he smiled.
'It has less to do with nobility than it does with stir craziness' I replied.
'I don't blame you. I can imagine' said Caleb as he looked around the room. 'Still, your Uncle Sean wouldn't be happy.

What was it he used to say? A Saturday flit is…'
'A short sit'. I finished the sentence for him before we both started to laugh. Sean was a firm believer in this old superstition, that if you were discharged from hospital on a Saturday, it would not be long before you would find yourself back in hospital again. 'I hope not. I've enough to de dealing with at the moment'.
It was nice to share an old memory of Sean with Caleb, I thought to myself. It reminded me of how close we once were when we were younger. Before the distance crept in and definitely before his relationship with Beth. He wasn't to know that Beth and I were together at that stage. Still, we would never have that closeness again I thought, but he wasn't necessarily a bad person, although Beth and Ferguson may beg to differ.
'Yeah, I've been following The Enlightenment stuff. I hear the guys that attacked you are going down the diminished responsibility route'.
'What?' I couldn't believe what I was hearing.
'You didn't know'?
'No' I sighed and lowering my head, shook it in disbelief.
'Sorry mate, I thought you knew'.
I began to laugh in spite of myself and soon found that the absurdity of the situation had me in creases.
'What? What's so funny'? Caleb asked in a mixture of self consciousness and questioning.
Through bursts of laughter I said, 'You are! You come in here, nearly knock me off my feet, then tell me that the people who did this to us are pleading diminished responsibility. With

friends like you, who needs enemies'? I asked before creasing with laughter again.

'Sorry… again' he replied awkwardly before bursting into laughter himself.

In truth, I knew that the situation wasn't funny at all, but the laughter helped me to release some of my pent up anger and for that I was grateful to Caleb. We laughed considerably more in the next short time, as conversation turned to reminiscence about our younger days, growing up together and times spent with Uncle Sean.

'You know, I still miss him every day' I said, the memories of good times, making me suddenly melancholic.

'Me too! You were lucky though. You got to spend much more time with him than I did. I'd already lost him years before that' Caleb replied.

'The argument'? I asked.

'Yeah. I still feel so guilty'.

'I don't really know anything about what happened Caleb, but I'm guessing that you were caught in the crossfire between Sean and your Dad. You were only a teenager' I offered in comfort.

'But I didn't stay a teenager. There have been plenty of times I could've reached out to Sean over the years but I didn't. Instead, I just let resentment build up because he hadn't reached out to me. At times I hated him for that. It's too late now though ,a lot of water has gone under the bridge since then'.

'Caleb, I don't know what to say. I know he cared deeply for you if that's any consolation, and I know that he struggled with what happened and that he lost his relationship to you as a result'.

'Thanks Mark, I appreciate that' he said softly, trying to regain his composure.

'Hey, I better leave you to it. I came here to see you and maybe cheer you up. I doubt I've done either' he added, before standing up again.

'Don't be daft! Good friends laugh together and cry together. You've helped me today more than you know' I replied. He nodded.

'Good, and you know, The Pinkertons and The Enlightenment will get what's owing to them, I guarantee it'. He smiled. 'And I know I haven't been able to help much lately, but if there's anything I can do on the Terror thing, let me know'.

'Will do. We may have a bit of a break on that, but everyone has been out of commission lately, so we haven't been able to follow up on it. I'll let you know if it comes to anything' I replied.

'I look forward to it' he said. 'Speak to you soon'. He waved before taking his leave and just as my phone alerted me to a text. It was Beth. Car will be outside main entrance in 10 minutes, it read.

80.

Terror reflected on his visit with Mark Shaw as he made his way back to the car. He had surprised himself with the level of warmth that he had felt toward his former friend, and with his own revelations of his feelings about Sean Brady to Shaw. He had come to a realisation during their short time together today. In many ways, their background and personal connections made them each a side of the same coin, one reflecting what's good about humanity, the other, what was bad. Which of them was which, he also had formed an opinion on, but he wasn't going to dwell on that now! He had reached a much more profound conclusion. He needed Mark Shaw, just as good needs evil and darkness needs light. For that reason he pledged to himself that Mark Shaw would not die at Terror's hand. He also reaffirmed in his mind that, The Prophet could have taken the Yin from what was his Yang in ordering the attack on Mark Shaw. For that he would pay the ultimate price.

81.

The short journey from the ward to the main entrance of the hospital via the lift, made me realise that I still had quite a bit of recovering to do. The pain in my right leg was almost unbearable, despite the fact that the only damage sustained was to muscles and ligaments. Miraculously, I had survived the attack without breaking any bones, other than ribs. It was a miracle that I'd survived at all, I supposed. I was a bit annoyed with Beth last night, when she said that she would just meet me outside, but figured that maybe she was trying to encourage me move independently. I saw the back of the car a short way off in the distance, as it sat in a pick up bay just outside the doors. I continued to hobble feebly towards it, wondering what I must've looked like going along with my Lonsdale bag hanging across my body and my stick in hand. I watched as the drivers door swung open and waited for Beth to emerge. Instead I saw Tom Ferguson get out of the car. He smiled at me and began to walk toward me. I smiled back but suddenly found my stomach churn. All at once, I was delighted to see him but dreading the prospect of having to face him at the same time. I readied myself as best I could in the short time that I had. When Ferguson reached me, he carefully embraced me before saying anything. His action reduced me to tears and I soon found myself sobbing into his shoulder.

'I thought you would never want to set eyes on me again. I'm

so sorry about Maria' I managed to say between sobs.
'It's fine, Mark. You've nothing to apologise for, none of us have. We weren't to know what would happen. I realise that now'. He stepped back from the embrace but placed one hand firmly on each of my shoulders, looking me in the eyes. 'We need to be strong Mark. We need to heal. We need to be there for those around us and we need to make sure that justice is done properly. I need you to do what I'm doing. Channel all the bad feeling, the guilt, the anger, into something positive. Our families and friends are relying on us. We need to be strong for them and for each other'.
Like Caitlin Price before him, he was right and I was much more ready to move on now that I knew that I still had him by my side and on my side.
'I'm ready' I said simply.
'Good, because it starts now'. He smiled and supported me as I walked to the passenger side door of the car. 'The Welcome Home Committee awaits. Beth said to tell you that she knew it would probably be the last thing you wanted, but Alecia had her heart set on a Welcome Home Party for Daddy and she hadn't the heart to say no'.
I smiled, 'Beth's right but it's probably just what I need'.
'It'll do you good, besides there are some people I want you to meet'.
On our journey toward Antrim, Ferguson filled me in on how well that his brother, Michael and niece, Emma had been coping since Maria's death. They were both devastated at her loss and both missed her deeply, but both knew that she would want them to be positive and move on. I was surprised

to hear that they had chosen to settle in Belfast and were looking for a house to rent, but was glad for Ferguson, that they would be around him. He was thinking about sharing the house with them too, which would also be good for him I thought.

As we turned into the driveway, I saw that the front door had a Welcome Home banner pinned across it. I had barely opened the car door before the front door was flung open and Alecia came running out, followed shortly by Beth.

'Welcome Home Daddy' said Alecia excitedly as she reached me, still trying to manoeuvre myself out of the car. She leaned against me, trying to hug me but afraid of hurting me also. I bent forward a little and kissed her on the head.

'Its great to be home, Wee Chicken. I've missed you too'.

'Yeah, we've missed you Daddy' Beth smiled, before taking my hand and helping me out of the car. When I was finally on my feet, she kissed me before whispering, 'Sorry, she was so intent on it, I couldn't say no'.

'Actually, I'm looking forward to it' I replied before she and my now faithful walking stick, helped me into the house.

There was quite the crowd there to greet me when I went in. Obviously, both my parents and Beth's parents were there. They were also joined by Beth's friend Susan and her daughter Jo, Gillian and Patrick, Caitlin and Martin and finally Ferguson's brother Michael and his daughter Emma. They all cheered as we entered, making me feel very humbled and very grateful. It struck me that there was someone missing, though. My thoughts turned to Dana Boyd, still unconscious in the ICU. In the short time we had been able to get to know her, she had very much become part of our ever expanding team. I had visited her several times when I too was in hospital, and each time she had shown no signs of improvement. I hoped that that would soon change.

Ferguson brought his brother and niece over to introduce them.

'Mark, this is Michael and Emma'. I reached out and shook Michael's hand.

'It's nice to meet you' I said. 'I've heard a lot about you and I'm so sorry to be meeting you in such sad circumstances'.

'Thank you. It's nice to finally meet you too. We've heard a lot about you, haven't we Emma'. Emma nodded and smiled before I took her tiny hand and shook it too.

'I'm very glad to meet you Emma. Your Uncle Mark has told us lots about you'.

'Can Emma come play with us again now'? Alecia piped up.

'Of course she can' said Michael. 'You'd like that wouldn't you Emma'? With that, she smiled again, before running off to join Alecia and Jo.

Before long, the conversation flowed, as did the tea and coffee, as we consumed the sandwiches, cakes and nibbles that Beth, Susan and Gillian had prepared. Throughout, we began to get to know Michael, who seemed to be every bit as decent and charming as his brother and I couldn't help but think, slightly taller and better looking. I laughed to myself at the thought that Susan had probably noticed that long before any of the rest of us. I turned my gaze toward her just in time to see her brush a strand of brunette hair away from her eye, as she remained engrossed in conversation with my Mum.

Perhaps not, I thought, then noticed that Patrick, who had been his usual gregarious self up until now, had suddenly gone quiet. I wondered why and decided to check on him whenever I got the opportunity.

Unbeknownst to me until minutes later, Patrick's consciousness was less with us at that moment, than it was with Dana Boyd. It became apparent when he suddenly blurted out, 'That's it, she should be fine now' bringing the conversation to a complete stand still and turning every head in the room toward him.

He laughed self consciously before explaining that he had become aware that Dana was about to pass away and that his Spirit Guide had indicated to him that it was not yet her time. He had then been working with his Spirit Guide to ensure that she did not cross over, which now thankfully, he had been assured, she would not.

As he was explaining this to us, approximately twenty miles away in the Royal Victoria Hospital, Dana remained unconscious in the ICU. Her Mother was holding her hand when she felt it. She doubted herself at first but then it came again, the slightest, almost imperceptible movement of Dana's hand. Her prayers had been answered, she thought as she lifted her daughter's hand to her mouth and kissed it softly.

82.

This is it. Today was the day, I thought to myself. A little over two weeks after returning from hospital and calling a halt to all things Farset for everyone involved until today, I was ready to return to work. My words to Ferguson when he picked me up a few weeks ago still echoing in my mind, I repeated them to myself as I faced the mirror. 'I'm Ready' I said aloud, noting that my recent ordeal had aged me, and hoping to myself that I was indeed ready.

At least the stick was gone now and although I still had pain and walked with a little bit of a limp, I could drive again. Whilst I had undergone a regime combining physiotherapy with rest and recuperation over the last few weeks, The Fergusons had rented a house in the same development as ours in Antrim. It made sense for lots of reasons, not least of which was that Emma, although a little older than Alecia, had become firm friends with her, so having her close by would help her adjust. The Rodgers family had also rented a new place, a deceptively large apartment in Ridgeway Street, practically on the doorstep of the Lyric Theatre. Between both families, The Ikea Staff and Farset Vito Van had been kept busy in this last while.

I came down the stairs slowly, the pain of doing so bringing me out in a sweat. Beth met me in the hall at the bottom of the stairs.

'You sure you're up to this? You could take a few more days

you know'.
'I'll be fine' I replied.
'You have your meds'?
'Yes, they're in my inside pocket'.
'OK, Good Luck'! She kissed me before calling to Alecia, 'Daddy's off to work now, come give him a kiss'.
She ran out to me and I leaned down and scooped her into a hug and kissed the top of her head. 'Be good for Mum, especially when you are getting ready for school' I said.
'I will' she replied before disappearing off again, leaving me to make my way to the car.
The journey tired me more than I had expected it to and I was glad to finally find myself pulling up into the underground garage at Farset. I had decided to avoid the front entrance, trying not to relive the attack any more than I needed to for the moment. There was nobody around when I got into the bunker so I went directly to my office, powered up the iMac and used the intercom to see if Gillian was around yet. After a few short rings she answered with,
'Morning Boss! Welcome Back'.
'Thanks, Gillian. Its great to be back' I said. 'You sound very chirpy this morning'.
'That's one of the things you pay me for' she laughed.
'And another is making coffee' I quipped.
'Which is why, if you look in the canteen, you'll find some brewing'.
'You're good' I said.
'I know' she retorted. 'I was just about to forward you an email that has come in from a Mr Michael Dean. He was

hoping to set up a meeting with you. He is planning to fly in from Washington on Thursday evening and meet with you on Friday morning first thing if possible'.

'Good. Can you reply to him and set up the meeting for 08:30' I asked.

'No worries, I'll put it in your online diary and make Beth and Tom aware as well. Will they be joining you'?

'Most likely but I'll get them to confirm with you'.

'No problem! Speak to you later'.

So I was finally going to meet Farset's mysterious benefactor. I was looking forward to it, I had a lot of questions that I wanted to ask. I lifted the phone again to call Beth. I wanted to make sure that she would be free for the meeting. Surprisingly, she answered almost instantly.

'Hello'.

'Hi Beth, it's me'.

'Mark. I literally had the phone in my hand, I was just about to call you'.

'Is everything OK'? I asked.

'Yes everything's fine, but the Postman has just been. There's an important looking letter addressed to you. The franking stamp says it's from the PPSNI'.

The Public Prosecution Service of Northern Ireland, that could only mean one thing. I instructed Beth to open the letter, to confirm that my suspicions were correct and they were. It was a summons. I was due to appear as a witness for the prosecution in the trial for attempted murder, that Drew Pinkerton was to face in three weeks time. That was a lot quicker than I'd anticipated. Again the words of Caitlin Price and Tom Ferguson echoed in my mind and for the second time today, I heard myself utter aloud, 'I'm ready'.

After finishing the call with Beth and confirming her attendance on Friday, my attention turned back to my iMac, which had gone into sleep mode. I booted it up again and began to sign in to Sean's cloud, as per my now normal routine. I had only typed a few characters when I realised that I was actually in the process of typing in the wrong details. I had absentmindedly began to type the details of my own personal cloud account, probably owing to the medication, I figured. I was about to delete and start over when for some reason, again perhaps habit, I looked up from the keyboard to the monitor. That's when I got my second shock of the day. Right there in the space allocated to type in the username, the iMac had used autofill to complete another account frequently accessed from this machine. By sheer fluke, I was now reading the e mail address, maureentaylor@msn.com. Unfortunately the autofill had not completed the password and I had absolutely no idea who Maureen Taylor was. I noted down the e mail address, then signed in to Sean's cloud and began a search through his files, to see if I could place her. The document search returned a negative. I was about to do a web search when Ferguson and his brother Michael appeared in the bunker. I went out to meet them.

'Morning Guys'! I greeted them.

'Good Morning' they replied in unison. Ferguson added 'Sorry we're late, we ended up on a Skype call to Australia this morning. Then the postman arrived with a summons for me'.

'I know. I got one too' I said.

'And us', I heard from behind the Fergusons, as Gillian and Patrick came in. 'I've just opened my post there now' said Gillian. 'Ours is still being redirected to here. I haven't gotten around to giving them the new address yet and there were identical letters for us. I presume Dana has received one too'.

'We thought you should know Mark and it looks like the trial is pretty soon' added Patrick.

'I know. Three weeks time' I answered grimly.

'The PPSNI team will likely want to meet with us soon, to prep us' said Ferguson, likely speaking from experience.

'We need to make sure we do everything we can to debunk the diminished responsibility idea' I said, more authoritatively than I'd intended.

'Absolutely' said Patrick. 'Between You, Gillian and I, we should be able to provide a fair amount of evidence to the contrary, having known the Pinkertons pretty well'.

'I wish there was something that we could do to tie,The Enlightenment Church to their charges too' I added.

'We could talk to the PPSNI I suppose, see if they have anything beyond the circumstantial' said Patrick.

'You won't have to' interrupted Michael Ferguson. 'That's what my Skype call was about this morning. An e mail sent by a senior member of the Church in Sydney to both the Pinkerton brothers, has been leaked to the police there. It appears to suggest that the attacks were ordered by The Prophet. They've started an investigation'.

His revelation was met with several air punches and exclamations of Yes and Brilliant, from the assembled company.

'The Police in Sydney will likely make contact with the PPSNI, if they haven't already' said Ferguson, smiling, probably for the first time in a while I imagined.

'Looks like we could be on our way to seeing justice served' said Michael with a slight tremble in his voice.

I nodded slowly but part of me was thinking that,The Enlightenment have always found ways to evade justice and when I turned my gaze to Patrick, I sensed that he was thinking much the same. I turned to Gillian.

'When the PPSNI make contact could you put a schedule in place for any meeting or meetings that they want to have. I presume they might want to meet us as a group then have some individual meetings'.

'Will do' she replied.

'I'd better get back upstairs, I have a client due soon' said Patrick.

'I'll walk up with you' said Gillian.

'Gillian, before you go, did the FBI come back with the DNA results from the hair that was found on Dowell'? Ferguson asked.

'Oh… Yes they came in the morning after the attack. Sorry, with everything else going on, it slipped my mind. It was a false lead. It looks like you may have contaminated the crime scene when you went over to the Glenvine. The hair was actually mine or at least Charlene McManus' anyway. It must have been transferred from me to you, then from you to the body somehow. I've emailed Agent Curtis on your behalf to let him and Agent Ross know already. Sorry, I should've mentioned it earlier'.

Ferguson looked wrapt in thought for a few seconds before growling, 'Shit, I'm usually so careful'.
'Looks like it's back to the drawing board' I said.
Gillian and Patrick left, heading back to the offices upstairs.
'Michael was at a bit of a loose end' said Ferguson. 'I thought I'd show him around the place. He might be able to help us out in some way'.
'Sure that's fine. Glad to have you around Michael'. I turned my attention to Ferguson again.
'I may have come across something this morning. I'm still working on it but I'll catch up with you later when I've hopefully made a bit more progress'.
OK, let me know if you need anything in the meantime' he replied before leading Michael through to the staff area and apartments.

83.

Within seconds my net search for Maureen Taylor began in earnest. After looking through several possibilities, I came to the conclusion that the only one that might even remotely connect with Sean, was a woman advertising her occupation as a US based Photo Detective. I began to dig a little deeper but the more that I learned about this Maureen Taylor, the more that I doubted that she was who I was looking for. Deciding to move my search a little closer to home, I opened up, The Belfast Chronicle web page and began to search the online archive of Births, Deaths and Marriages Notices. Within minutes, I was reading the death notice of Maureen Doyle nee´Taylor, Wife of our now Deputy First Minister and Mother of Caleb Doyle.

I could have kicked myself for not making the connection myself from memory. Still, I only ever knew her as Mrs Doyle. The solving of this mystery begged two further questions. Why would Uncle Sean have a cloud set up in this name and how could I get the password for it? I had a feeling that I probably already knew the answer to the first question. The second was going to prove more difficult. I was determined however, not to let it beat me, so relied on my knowledge of Uncle Sean to help me. Clicking on the "Forgot Password" tab, I was faced with two security questions. The first was, simple enough, First Car? I knew that Sean's first car was his much loved, Vauxhall Viva, finished in gold metallic paint, he would often boast over the years. I typed the answer and saw a green tick appear beside it.

The second question, Name of First Pet, was more problematic. I knew he had a Springer Spaniel in his younger years and I can vaguely remember it as a child. The problem was, I couldn't remember its name and didn't know whether or not it was his first pet. I racked my brain trying to remember the name, before realising that Mum or Dad would likely know. One quick phone call later, I was typing the name, Brandy into the answer field for the second question. I waited for what seemed like an age before to my surprise and relief, another green tick appeared, indicating that it was the correct answer.

I was now faced with the message that a link that would allow me to reset my password had been sent to my recovery email address. I had gambled that this would have been Sean's own and thankfully, I was correct. I reset the password, taking note of what I had changed it to, then used the new password to open the cloud. The first folder of two folders I came across was labelled "The Ghost". I opened it and began to scan through the contents. From cursory inspection, it looked like the file related to paramilitary attacks, including crime scene pictures. I figured that this folder harked back to Sean's days as an investigative journalist during the troubles. I decided to go through it in detail later, to see if it yielded any clues to who may have murdered him, opting to look at the second folder, which was labelled "Good Times".

I opened the folder and was bombarded with a litany of photographs. They looked to have been scanned from old

snaps, converting them into digital format and appeared to have been arranged chronologically. Their contents confirmed something that I had always suspected, Sean had been having an affair with Maureen Doyle and it looked like they were very much in love. The earlier photographs were mainly of one or both of the couple at various events and places. There were others later that included Michael Doyle and later, Caleb as a child. The ones with Caleb, spanned his childhood into his mid-teens. Looking at them I noticed something that I had never seen before, probably because I wasn't looking. There was a considerable resemblance between Caleb and Uncle Sean. He couldn't be, I thought, but I had to wonder if I was looking at Uncle Sean's son, my cousin. I scanned further down the page. The photographs here were of Caleb, taken from the web, showing his graduation and charting his career development. Now I realised why Sean had always been so fond of him. Yet another of Sean's secrets had been uncovered from the grave. I scanned on down to the bottom until my eyes fell upon the last picture, a Selfie. I stared in horror as I saw the smiling face of Caleb Doyle, with his arm draped around Owen Grant, in what I recognised from the Crime Scene Photographs, as the Majestic Hotel. I could feel the hairs rise on the back of my neck. I hovered the cursor over the picture. The time and date stamp correlated with that of Grant's murder. If I'm correct and I'm pretty sure that I am, Caleb Doyle, was not only my cousin, he was Terror also.
'Knock, knock'. I looked up to see Ferguson. 'Anything yet'?
'No, not yet'!
'Anything I can do'?

'I don't think so ,not yet anyway. Where's Michael'?
'He's just left. He didn't want to disturb you'.
'You OK'? Ferguson asked.
I knew I should tell him what I had just discovered and hated lying to him but I had decided that my family had the right to know first. I would speak to them tonight and tell him tomorrow, then we could take the next steps to catch Terror.
'Yeah, I'm fine! You'? I replied.
'Yeah' he hesitated. 'You know, the hair thing has been bugging me all morning. I'm always so careful at crime scenes and I put on the full CSI protective clothing kit as soon as I arrived and before I entered the crime scene. I just don't get it'.
'We probably need to bring DI Black and his CSI team up to speed on it. I don't want them to think that we're withholding anything from them. They probably still think that no identity could be found from the sample'.
'I'll call them now'
'Thanks'.
He left, closing the door behind him. I watched as he walked to and took a seat at, what had become, his desk. As he lifted the phone to call Black, I picked up my mobile and called Beth for the second time that day.
'I can't explain now but could you arrange for us to meet with Mum and Dad at their house after work. There's something that I want to talk to you all about. It's nothing to worry about but I can't explain at the moment. I'll see you all there later'.

84.

I knew that what I had to tell my family was going to be hard on them but I hadn't reckoned on the reaction that I got when I broke the news. My Mum just seemed to implode, then crumble into a mixture of grief and shock. It was bad enough hearing that Sean most likely had a grown up son, without having to process the fact that this person was a prolific serial murderer who had incited others to follow his path.

My Dad went immediately into crisis management mode, as would be typical of him. His initial reaction appeared to be one of shock also, then he immediately went to comfort Mum. I'm not sure how, but I got the impression that he maybe knew Sean's secret and that his shock was merely that it had been uncovered.

Beth was surprised at the news that Sean had a son but her surprise turned to anger and disgust when she heard who he was and what he had done. She later told me that a lot of that anger had been directed toward herself for her involvement with him. Knowing her so well though, I had already reached that conclusion.

Regardless of our individual reactions, we did all agree on one thing. Caleb Doyle had to be brought to justice. Now we just needed to work out how. I texted Gillian and asked her to contact the others and set up a meeting for everyone, including Michael Ferguson if possible, for first thing tomorrow morning. When I'd gathered everyone together I would let them know what I had found and we could work out how to catch our killer.

85.

Gillian Rodgers looked at the clock beside the bed. It read 04:58. Reaching for her iPhone, she unset the alarm which had been due to go off at 05:00. In truth she could've done without setting any alarm at all, as she had not slept a wink. Her test was this morning and she had lain awake all night due to nerves, a mixture of fear and anticipation. If she passes this, she will be ready. Caleb was awake too.

'You OK'?

'Yes, I think' Gillian replied before rising and getting dressed.

'Here goes' she said as she leaned down and kissed him before making her way out of the bedroom.

'Good luck, I'll be thinking of you' Caleb called after her as she made her way downstairs. She went into the kitchen and poured herself a glass of water, drinking it quickly in a bid to cool herself down. Her body temperature had begun to rise already, just like it always does when she is stressed.

Within forty-five minutes, she was driving down the Co.Londonderry Lane that was home to Causeway Academy. She had taken many tests here but none of them were ever like this. She drove on past the school building and parked her car in the lane alongside a derelict cottage beside the stream. She had made good time she thought as she opened the boot of her car. She lifted out the leather gloves and donned them, before lifting out the length of heavy lead pipe that Caleb had supplied, before closing the boot again. She left the car unlocked so that the flashing lights of the alarm arming would not draw any attention from anyone. Not that it was likely to in this truly rural location in the darkness of the hour. She walked the short distance back up toward the school, being careful to stay out of sight of the CCTV cameras around it. She was well aware of their range and had factored it into her planning. She waited in the hedges on the apex of the bend in the road just beside the main gates. Now all she had to do was be patient, which was easier said than done in her current state of mind. Within five minutes she could see the headlight beams of an approaching vehicle making its way down the lane. Just like clockwork she thought to herself as the vehicle came to a standstill outside the main gate and its sole occupant turned off the ignition and made his way toward the gate before she could make out his identity. The monthly School Management Meeting was obviously being held according to its usual predictable schedule and as usual, one of,The Enlightenment Priests was fulfilling his duty to volunteer to set up for the meeting. Not today! Gillian allowed herself to be consumed by every negative and vengeful thought that she had ever had about her former Church as she sprang upon her victim. Surprising him from behind, she had struck him hard on the back of his head with the lead pipe. He fell hard too, though had made little sound. Still holding the pipe and still blinded by rage and cloaked by darkness Gillian began to kick the prone figure hard and continuously as he lay there unable to defend himself. She used her foot to shove the man down the slight slope where the footpath was lowered to accommodate vehicles coming and going through the main gates. Now lying face-up,the man remained motionless as Gillian Rodgers crouched over him. She raised the copper pipe in her left hand one final time before bringing it down hard on the man's face with a sickening crunch.

As she walked away from the body, back down the lane towards her car, the rage had completely left Gillian Rodgers, having being replaced by a sense of calmness and peace. She'd done it she thought to herself. She was Fear now. She had passed the test. Now all she had to do was follow Terror's instructions in what she was to do next. As she neared the car she threw the length of copper pipe into the stream. On reaching the car and opening the boot again, she took out the black plastic bin bag that was sitting in the boot well, removed her gloves and trainers and placed them into the bag. Next she lifted out the navy overalls and put them on over her clothes, being careful to ensure that they were buttoned up completely. Finally she put on a pair of cargo shoes, wiped the blood spatter from her face with some wet wipes, before depositing them in the black bag and topping off her new outfit with a black baseball cap. Tying up the bag tightly, she placed it back into the boot before closing it and returning to the driver's seat. So far, she had followed Terror's plan to the letter. Gunning the engine of the 1 series, she drove quickly up the dark lane without the use of headlights. She knew the terrain well, she thought and wanted to remain unnoticed as she drove the rural back roads that eventually led onto the main road back to Belfast. Reaching the end of the lane more quickly than she had anticipated, she braked too late, overshooting the junction and stopping just short of the hedgerow that it faced. Just as she reached down to shift gear into reverse, she heard a loud tyre screech before the car was filled by the light from the headlights of the oncoming car that was desperately trying to avoid plummeting into her vehicle side on.

86.

Caitlin Price normally enjoyed being up with the birds but not this early and definitely not today. Although rarely asked to attend School Management Meetings held by The Enlightenment Governors, she hated it when she was. The meeting this morning was probably going to be the worst though, it would be the first time she would face the entire compliment of her employers since resigning her post. Nearing the School building she tried to comfort herself with the thought that in a few hours the meeting would be over and it would be her last. Slowing slightly to make the turn as she approached the lane, she was suddenly confronted with a vehicle sitting side on in the road, blocking her path. Her foot already covering the brake pedal, she pressed down hard on it, trying to avoid collision. The tyres screeched loudly before the ABS system on the car kicked in. In the milliseconds that had taken to happen, Caitlin was already sure that she wouldn't make it. Taking her foot off the brakes, she swerved around the other vehicle, narrowly missing it, before managing to make the turn into the lane. Braking hard again as she attempted to correct her steering, she overcompensated and the front passenger side of the car crumpled into the bush covered fence that served as a barrier to the adjacent field, before the whole passenger side scraped along the fence for several feet and the car at long last came to a halt.

Instinctively, Caitlin got out of the car and ran back up toward the junction, only to be caught in the glare of the reverse lights of the other vehicle. Within a few short seconds the reverse lights went out and the car sped off in the opposite direction to that which Caitlin had been travelling. Through a combination of the darkness and having been dazzled by the reverse lights, she had been unable to see the number plate, nor was she sure of the type of car that it was. The only thing that she could remember from the instant that her headlights lit the car up, was that it was small and red in colour.

Cursing to herself, she began to walk back down the lane. It remained too dark to inspect the damage to her car she thought. It would be better to drive it into the school grounds if it is still running, so that it's not a danger to others ,then she could call the police. Just as she put her hand on the driver's door handle, she heard a loud click and the area around her was bathed in harsh white light, as the timer for the external lights of the school building and grounds, activated them. Blinking to adjust her eyes to the light, Caitlin saw the Skoda Octavia sitting in the lay by just beside the gate. The car looked empty and there didn't seem to be anyone around. She could see that the gates remained secured with their heavy lock. She opened her car door and leaned across into the passenger footwell. Lifting her bag up onto the driving seat, she retrieved her keys and phone from it before making her way toward the gate. As she reached the front of the Skoda, she was faced with a sight that she would never forget. On the footpath before her lay the battered and bloodied remains of Robin Mercer, the newest member of the Board of Governors. Despite the horrific nature of the scene before her, Caitlin's first aid instincts kicked in and she tried to determine whether there were any signs of life. There were not. Trying to maintain her composure, she made two phone calls. The first was to the PSNI, the second, to Mark Shaw.

87.

The roads on my journey toward Causeway Academy were eerily too familiar, I thought to myself as I hurriedly travelled to the site of my former employment. Caitlin had been so composed when she had called me a short time ago but it did not take long before the trauma of the accident that she'd had, and the discovery of the body, started to impact upon her emotions. It was for that reason, and the fact that I feared for her safety, that I knew I had to go to her. Beth, worried for my safety, had text Ferguson, who in the short time it had taken me to get dressed, and get downstairs, had readied himself and was waiting at the front passenger side of the car when I opened the front door. It was still pretty early and we were making good time due to the relative absence of the traffic that would gridlock these roads in the next few hours. Ferguson had been fairly quiet throughout the journey so far, as had I, both of us likely strategising as to how we would meet the situation that was about to unfold in front of us.

As it turned out, the PSNI were already at the scene when we arrived. The area around the main gateway into the building had been tented and cordoned off. It was currently under the guard of two PSNI officers, as they no doubt waited for a CSI team and the arrival of the Investigating Officer, who given the links to the other Enlightenment attacks, I'd surmised would be DI Black.

A secondary set of gates further down on the boundary of the

School Grounds and known to me as an Emergency Exit, was open and was being manned by two further officers. I noticed that in addition to the car that looked to be part of the crime scene, there were a further five cars in the school car park. Three of them were Police vehicles and the other two I recognised. One as Catlin Price's Audi, which looked to be fairly banged up, the other, a Land Rover Discovery, owned by Governor in charge of Finance, Sam Mortimer. I pulled up to the gates and introduced myself and Ferguson as being with Farset Investigations. The young officer made us wait momentarily while he radioed inside. A moment later, we had been cleared to be on the premises and were being waved inside. Instinctively I drove to what used to be my dedicated parking space before parking up. When we got out of the car, the officer who had waved us in, was waiting for us. Ferguson asked the name of the Officer In Charge, who as it happened was Sergeant Joe Kendal.

When he led us inside the building I was surprised at how my return made me feel. It had only been a relatively short time since I'd left, so the place retained a familiarity for me. What was different though, was that whilst I used to feel comfortable here in what was my domain, I now felt repulsed and when sighted by Sam Mortimer, made to feel distinctly unwelcome.

'Get out, you have no right to be here' he bellowed at me as he charged up the corridor as fast as his portly physique would allow.

I was about to respond to him when I heard Ferguson's voice boom down the corridor.

'We have every right to be here. What has happened here this morning could be linked to one if not several aspects of an ongoing investigation of ours'.

'Besides which' I added, somewhat weakly by comparison to Ferguson, 'we have PSNI clearance to be here'.

I looked sideways at our escorting officer, who nodded confidently in the direction of Mortimer. He looked like he was going to explode. Just then, the door of what had once been my office opened and Caitlin was led out by a man who I had presumed was Sergeant Kendal.

'Caitlin' I called out and tried to walk to her as quickly as my injuries would let me. Ferguson matched my movement step for step, careful I noticed, not to overtake me. I respected him for that.

Caitlin rushed toward me and had already began to break down before I hugged her.

'You OK'?

'I will be. I think I'm just in shock'.

'Where's everyone else? Surely the other Governors should be here by now and some of the staff would be arriving soon'.

'No. No-one else is coming. The police asked me to give them a list of who would be due to arrive this morning and they took my phone. I presume they have kept everyone else away'.

Sergeant Kendal was now deep in conversation with Ferguson a short distance away from us. I led Caitlin back over to them.

'Sergeant Kendal, I'm Mark Shaw' I said extending my hand which he shook in greeting. 'I just wanted to check if you were finished with Miss Price. I'd let to get her to a hospital and get her checked out'.

'No, Mark, I'm fine' Caitlin interjected.
Ignoring her remark, Sergeant Kendal replied, 'I think that's a good idea Mr Shaw. Miss Price has already given us her statement'.
'I'm going to stay here and work the scene with the CSI' said Ferguson. I nodded, 'I'll come back for you once Caitlin has been checked out'.
'No worries'. He looked to Caitlin. 'You should get checked out, just to be safe'.
She was about to protest when I interrupted, 'No arguments, otherwise I'll call Martin'. She had told me in our earlier telephone conversation that Martin was in London to close a pretty important business deal and that she didn't want to tell him what happened until later, as she knew he would worry and likely return home prematurely.
'Fine' she replied as I linked her arm and we walked up the corridor toward the exit, a walk we had made together thousands of times before, though not quite like this.
'What are we like'? I laughed at the thought of me slowly limping along, supposedly leading her to get medical attention. Caitlin laughed too, some comic relief likely being exactly what she needed at the moment.

88.

Gillian Rodgers, although shaken by her near miss, remained controlled as she continued to carry out her instructions from Caleb. Once she had reached the main Belfast Road, she turned on her headlights and made her way back to Caleb's house, making sure that she drove carefully and was mindful of speed limits all the way. She couldn't afford to attract any unwanted attention. As soon as she arrived back, she retrieved the bag from the boot of the car before walking on down the driveway past the front door and around to the back of the house where Caleb was waiting for her. Silently in the darkness, she stripped off everything she had been wearing before making her way inside and straight to the shower, where she remained under the hot stream for the next fifteen minutes. Gloved himself, Caleb lifted the bag,then the discarded clothes and shoes. Walking a short way down through the garden and out the gate into the entry that ran parallel to all the houses in the street, he dropped everything into the old fashioned metal dustbin that had long since been left behind following the refurbishment of one of the neighbouring houses. He removed the petrol can that he had stowed beside it earlier and doused the contents of the bin with petrol, before stepping back slightly, removing the book of matches from his back pocket. He struck a match and let the flame take hold for a few seconds, before tossing it into the bin and watching for a moment as the bin struggled to contain the fireball that it now housed. Finally, he tossed the remainder of the book of matches into the bin and removed the polythene gloves before throwing them in too. With that, he made his way back through the darkness into the house and made his way upstairs with thoughts of joining the newly incarnate Fear in the shower. A short distance away in Ridgeway Street, Patrick Rodgers awoke with a sickness unlike any other he had ever experienced before. Having been physically sick several times in quick succession he was now being shown images of darkness by his Spirit Guide. Images that he had been warned of before and through fear, had chosen to suppress. Now he suspected, it was too late.

89.

Having been given a clean bill of health by a doctor in the casualty department of Antrim Area Hospital, I had dropped Caitlin off to Beth at our house before heading back up to collect Ferguson. We'd had to sit quite a few hours for Caitlin to be seen, so I was pretty sure that the crime scene would have been processed by now and was keen to hear what Ferguson had to say.

I arrived to find him chatting to DI Black at the gate, as the officers manning it, waved me in. I stopped just inside the gate, beside the two men and wound down the window.

'Mark, nice to see you up and about again. You had us worried for a while there'. DI Black's tone was much more friendly than it had been in our last few meetings and I detected a note of genuine warmth in it.

'Thanks, though I doubt that many here lost much sleep worrying about me' I said nodding toward the school building.

'You might be surprised. Not least because it could have made the difference between a murder charge and an attempted murder charge' he replied.

Feeling uncomfortable at the reminder of how close to death I had come, I changed the subject.

'Anything to report from here'?

'Yes' Ferguson replied, 'We'll know more after the autopsy but it looks like our victim, Mr Mercer was struck hard on firstly on the back and later front of his head with a blunt instrument, as well as being repeatedly kicked judging by the marks on one side of the body and scuff marks on the ground beneath it'.

'A single perpetrator? I mean if the marks were only on one side of the body' I surmised. DI Black nodded.

'Anything on the murder weapon'?

'We haven't found anything as yet. It has either been dumped somewhere around here or the killer has taken it with them' said Ferguson.

'We've also got a partial footprint from beside the body and it looks like it matches some other footprints in the mud along the grass verge leading up from an old derelict cottage just round the bend. There was a tyre track there too. We're tracing both the tyre and footprints for make and model of tyre and trainer' DI Black added.

'Interestingly, the footprints look to be fairly small for a man, so it's possible that our killer could be female or perhaps fairly young' stated Ferguson.

'So any theories yet'?

'From what we got from our interview with Mr Mortimer, our victim was quite a big deal in the local Enlightenment Community. He could have been involved in orchestrating the attacks on you and the others. Maybe some of the Pinkerton's family or friends decided to take revenge.The level of violence would certainly suggest a personal connection to the victim. I'm about to go interview the family' said Black.

'Sounds plausible' I answered. 'We better leave you to it'.

Ferguson motioned toward the car when I remembered about the mix up with the evidence transfer on Dowell's body.

'Did you manage to catch up with DI Black about the hair'? Ferguson nodded before getting into the car.
As soon as we were clear of the PSNI I said to Ferguson 'There's something I need to tell you about'.
'There's something I need to tell you about too' he replied. His face had turned ashen.
'You first' I said.
'The CSI guys processing the scene today, were the same crew that were at, The Glenvine. I hadn't been able to get hold of them when I called yesterday, so I asked them about the hair today'.
'And'?
'And they confirmed that I had definitely followed procedure correctly and had suited up before entering the crime scene'. He paused. 'They also told me that they had noted the hair on the body before I even arrived'.
I was horrified. What he was saying could only mean one thing.
'That means that Gillian has a connection to Terror' I said.
'Or is Terror' Ferguson surmised aloud.
'She's not Terror' I said flatly.
'How do you know? We can't rule anything out at this stage'.
'Yes, we can'.
'How can we'? Ferguson said, mildly irritated.
'That's what I wanted to talk to you about. Because I know who Terror is'.
Ferguson's jaw dropped as I named Caleb Doyle as Terror, my cousin and the likely perpetrator of Uncle Sean's murder.

90.

Ferguson had been understanding of my reasons for keeping him in the dark and I was relieved that he now knew. As we travelled, we continued to make connections from our profile and what we knew about Caleb Doyle. The more we talked about it, the more obvious that it had become that he was our killer. What was also a major concern now though, was that he was clearly the mystery man in Gillian's life. If her hair had been found on James Dowell's body, then was she complicit in the murder? Was she involved in any of the other killings? We couldn't be sure of the level of her involvement but her connection to Caleb Doyle was a worrying one nonetheless.

'We're going to have to be careful how we play this' I said. 'We need to start building a case against Doyle and we can't take the chance of Gillian warning him off. We'll need to keep her in the dark'.

'I agree' said Ferguson. 'We can't do anything to jeopardise getting Terror. We can't know either way if Gillian is involved yet but I think it would be safest for all if she is frozen out for now'.

Ferguson pulled his phone from his pocket. 'I'm going to e mail Black and the FBI Agents. We'll set up a video conference at Farset for later tonight, UK time, so we can brief everyone and come up with an action plan. The fact that it's out of hours also means that Gillian need not know about

it'.
'Sounds like a plan' I answered.
'I'll copy you in on the email too' he said as he began to type, 'I'll ask everyone to confirm their attendance with me only, just in case anyone would call Gillian or e mail the office'.
'Thanks for that' I replied. I glanced across at him as he continued to work his iPhone. 'Can I ask you something'?
'Course' he replied.
'What's your gut feeling on Gillian? Is she involved or is Doyle just mocking us'?
'Let's just say that I'm worried about her and leave it at that for now'.
His answer, although noncommittal, confirmed my own thoughts. I didn't want to believe ill of Gillian, but since learning of her connection to Doyle, I'd had a bad feeling that I couldn't shake.
'In that case we have another problem' I said.
Ferguson looked at me, puzzled.
'Patrick! He is our friend and he is worried about her. We owe it to him to say something but I know that if we say anything to him, he may feel the need to confront her, which could lead to her tipping off Terror'.
'We can't take that chance' Ferguson replied emphatically, 'and let's stop calling that little prick Terror. It's Doyle from now on'.
I knew he was right but if Gillian wasn't involved, we could be compromising her safety and not making Patrick aware of that did not sit well with me. As it turned out, I would find out soon that I needn't have worried.

91.

Gillian Rodgers still felt electrified. She couldn't remember ever feeling this alive before. If she was being honest with herself, that scared her more than a little but she was determined not to allow herself to dwell on that. Things had been very quiet since she arrived at the office and she wondered if the reason that this morning's meeting had been cancelled, had anything to do with her visit to Causeway Academy this morning. She reasoned that it likely was, since there had been no sign of Mark or Tom since she had arrived this morning. She worried a little that she may have left incriminating evidence behind but consoled herself with the fact that she had followed Caleb's instructions to the letter. She hadn't seen anything of Patrick today either, it had occurred to her. It wasn't like him not to check in with her, she thought. She decided to make her way up the corridor to his office. The door was open, though the small waiting area was empty. She moved close to the door of his consultation room and was about to knock, when she heard him in conversation with a woman. Deciding that he was with a client, she decided to leave again and catch up with him later. She had barely moved away from the door however, when it opened suddenly and she was confronted by the woman who her brother had been deep in conversation with.
'Charlene' she said, startled.

'I go by Gillian now' Gillian replied. 'Didn't Patrick tell you'?
Sonja Williams, close friend of Patrick Rodgers and fellow Medium appeared flustered at being face to face with Gillian despite having met her a few times before.
'Yes, he did' she replied, 'Sorry, it slipped my mind. It's good to see you'. She turned her attention back toward Patrick. 'I'd best be off. I'll catch up with you soon'.
'Great, and thanks for your help this morning. I would've been lost without you' Gillian heard Patrick reply before Miss Williams mumbled her goodbyes and left. She stuck her head around the door, to find her brother sitting at his usual seat. His appearance shocked her though.
'Hey there, just checking in on you, I didn't see you come in this morning. You OK, you don't look well'?
Patrick waved her in without speaking and then looked straight into her eyes for a time longer than she felt comfortable with, before uttering shakily, 'Gillian, what have you done'?

92.

Patrick Rodgers was sitting waiting for us in the Farset bunker when we arrived back. He looked like death warmed over I thought to myself on first noticing him.

'Hey, hope you don't mind' he said by way of greeting, before nodding at Gillian's keys, which lay on the desk before him, 'I let myself in'.

'Sure, no worries' I replied. 'You OK? Where is Gillian anyway, there's no sign of anyone upstairs at the office'?

'No, That's why I'm here. You two should sit down. I think we need to have a chat'.

With that Patrick began his story of how he awoke feeling ill this morning and how his Spirit Guide had revealed to him, images of a murder that he feared that his sister had carried out. His description of the scene at Causeway Academy was so detailed it was almost like he had been there. After taking counsel from a good friend and gifted Medium, as to the type of evil that he could be about to encounter, he had confronted Gillian in his office. He could tell from her energies that she had done something heinous and what was worse, it was of her own volition and not that of an evil entity that he had expected. Ferguson and I were dumbfounded. Not only was Gillian associated with Caleb Doyle, she was also a killer in her own right.

'Where is she now'?

'She's gone. I tried to stop her but she ran off. I've been trying to call her ever since but she won't answer her phone. I didn't know what to do next. That's why I came down here'.

I looked at Ferguson, who sensing what I had been thinking, nodded his agreement. I began to tell Patrick what we had learned about Caleb Doyle and his association with Gillian. He was stunned, we all were. It was a lot to take in but it looked like it was true. I tried calling Gillian but it went straight to voicemail.

'The phone' I said, 'I've just realised. The phone that Gillian got. It must have been Caleb who gave it to her. Remember Patrick, the night you came to…'

'The night I collapsed. It was the energy from the phone that must have caused it to happen the second time. The phone must have been at the scene of the murder' Patrick said.

'So it was either Caleb's own phone, or more than likely, Gillian is using Sean's stolen phone' Ferguson finished the thought.

My iPhone began to ring again. Glancing at the screen, I saw that it was DI Black.

'DI Black, any news'?

'Mark, we got a match for the tyre imprint. It's from a BMW 1 Series, Sport. That model sounded like it may be a match for the car that Miss Price almost hit this morning, so based on the direction that she said it sped off in, we checked the traffic cameras on the main road and got a hit, so we ran the plate. Mark, you're not going to like this, but the vehicle was registered to Farset Investigations'.

As soon as he had matched the tyre to the vehicle, I'd had a feeling that I knew where he was going with this, but it didn't

stop my heart from sinking as a further piece of evidence of Gillian's guilt was uncovered.
'Have you got anyone looking for the vehicle'?
'No, not yet, I wanted to speak to you first' he replied.
'Good, hang fire on that if you can, at least until after our meeting later' I said, before filling him in on Gillian's involvement with Terror.
When I had finished the call with DI Black, it occurred to me that if Patrick had Gillian's keys, then the car might still be here at Farset. A quick look in the underground garage confirmed that. Within thirty minutes, it was being examined by a team of forensic technicians. A further three hours later, it was confirmed that traces of mud on the paintwork and tyres, matched that which the tyre track had been found in. There were also minor traces of blood in the boot well and on the driver's seat belt, which were being traced to see if they matched the victim. Although mostly circumstantial at the moment, the evidence of Gillian's guilt was stacking up. We all tried several times more, to contact her, but it was no use, she had dropped off the grid for now and was most likely being harboured by Caleb Doyle. This raised serious concerns for her safety, concerns that meant that the time until our tactics meeting, could not pass quickly enough for any of us, but for Patrick most of all.

93.

We were due to connect with the FBI Field Office in Quantico, Virginia to have our Videoconference with Agents Ross and Curtis at 23:00 UK time but by 22:15 we had already assembled in the Farset Conference Room. In addition to Ferguson, Patrick, DI Black and I, we were also joined by Beth and Michael Ferguson. At this stage, there had still been no word from Gillian and all of us were becoming increasingly concerned for her wellbeing. We spent the next hour sharing the information we had on this mornings murder and possible links between Gillian and Caleb Doyle. Around 23:20, Beth left momentarily, then returned with a fresh pot of coffee, which we each refilled our cups from before our Videoconference started. Personally, I was already wired from a combination of caffeine and adrenaline, but in an attempt to remain sharp and focused, drank the coffee regardless.I was glad that Ferguson had suggested that his brother Michael join us. Ferguson had felt that his skills in intelligence gathering from his Army Career, amongst other skills sets he would have as an accomplished soldier may have been of use to us. I agreed, as so far, he was proving insightful, especially in some of the information that he had been able to glean from Patrick on Gillian's comings and goings, and moods and habits of late. Luckily, Beth's friend, Susan had agreed to look after the kids, who as a trio were becoming firm friends and were relishing the thought of a sleepover.

At 23:30 precisely, our conference screen was filled with the sight of Agents Ross and Curtis, who looked like they too had had a difficult day.

After I introduced those members of our panel who they hadn't met, they asked me about the attack from,The Enlightenment, which they had heard about from Gillian the morning after it had happened. Clearly they were interested and had questions, so as tactfully as I could, bearing in mind the grief of the Ferguson brothers and the thoughts that haunted the rest of us, I filled them in on the scale of the attack and the upcoming legal proceedings. Talk of Dana Boyd made me feel guilty that I had become so engrossed in our own investigations of late, that I had not visited her in a while. I decided to rectify that at the earliest opportunity.

Horrified, they pledged their support to us and offered to help in any way they could, offering access to the entire platform of resources available to them as Special Agents. I felt humbled by their offer and its generosity and warmth. A quick glance around the table showed that I was not alone in what I was feeling. Sensing the emotional charge in the room on our side of the screen, DI Black quickly neutralised it by calling us to order. He then briefed the agents on the suspected identity of Terror, how the conclusion had been reached, and the newly developing situation with Gillian Rodgers. As they had when they were in the office at Farset, they listened intently and took notes before responding. Agent Curtis spoke first and cut straight to the chase.

'In the murders of Tyrell Jones, Neil McCarron and Dave Tohill, we've managed to identify persons of interest. Jones' ex-wife in his case, and a member of their Entourage, as far as the other two go. We have quite a bit of circumstantial evidence in both cases, but nothing concrete yet, and certainly nothing that would identify either as followers of our guy, Terror. We'll have our IT people check out any possible link to Caleb Doyle and we'll do a bit more digging him too'.

'He's spent a bit of time in the US recently' I interjected, 'He works for our local Newspaper here and his Dad is our Deputy First Minister. They were both in Washington for an Enterprise Summit'. Curtis nodded vigorously as he noted what I was saying.

Agent Ross, who had been reasonably quiet thus far, addressed Patrick.

'Mr Rodgers, the phone that your Sister has been using, it's an iPhone, isn't that correct'?

'Yes' replied Patrick nervously, 'We think it may have possibly belonged to Sean Brady before being given to Gillian by Doyle'.

'Does Miss Rodgers have an iCloud linked to the phone, do you know'?

'She does have an iCloud account but I don't know if it's linked to the phone. I actually set the account up for her. I still pay for it from my bank account' Patrick answered, still trying to control his nerves.

'Would you know the login details of the account?'

'Yes… I think, unless she has changed them'.

Sensing where Agent Ross was going with his questioning, I took out my own phone, disconnected my own Cloud account and waited. Agent Ross asked Patrick for the details and as he recounted them, I scrawled them on my notepad, before entering them into my phone. Within seconds, it was connected to Gillian's Cloud. Then it was a simple matter of using the Find My Phone feature and within a few minutes, the location of the phone had been pinpointed to the Ramada Hotel, Portrush. What we couldn't be sure of yet, was whether Gillian was ok, or whether she was even the one currently in possession of the phone. My revelation of the location set DI Black in motion.

'We won't have much time before she gets an email to alert her that we have logged into her Cloud. If she or Doyle are tech savvy, which at least one of them is likely to be, they'll know that we've found them. I'll get some officers from the Portrush Division over there now'. DI Black left the room to make the contact that he needed to.

'I need to go there. I need to be with her. Mark, can you take me'? Patrick was almost trembling in fear.

'Of course' I said, 'Tom, could you and Michael take another car and follow us up? We may need you'.

'Meet you out front' said Ferguson before he and Michael headed for the garage.

After apologising for the abrupt ending to our meeting, I thanked Agents Ross and Curtis and promised to keep them in the loop of any developments, before ending the teleconference call. I looked at Beth.

'I suppose there isn't even any point in asking you to stay here or telling you that it could be dangerous'?

'You suppose right, smart guy so let's move'. Whilst DI Black returned to Grosvenor Road Station to direct the operations of the PSNI in Portrush, our convoy was swiftly journeying toward the popular seaside resort, each of us concerned at what we might find there.

94.

The email alert had thrown Gillian Rodgers into a state of panic. She desperately wanted to call Caleb but he had told her that she must not contact anyone in any circumstances, especially him. He had been so strong earlier and had known exactly what to do when she rang him and told him about her encounter with her brother. She had been on the verge of losing it when he came to pick her up, she had been so frightened that she may have been caught. Gillian didn't doubt her brother's gift, even if Caleb had. Still, he had managed to calm her. The next stage of their plan was to be enacted soon and after that neither of them would need worry about the suspicions of others. She had bought into what he had said and even remained relatively calm when he dropped her at the hotel, told her to book in and wait for him to contact her. That was before she realised that she had been compromised. That was before she thought she was about to be hunted down. That was before she was thrown into blind trepidation. Pacing up and down the hotel room floor, she began to feel more and more trapped. Memories of the Shut Up House returned to haunt her. Not to mention the memory of her trying to end her own life. It was Patrick who had been there for her then. Without his gift and psychic connection she could well be dead now. He had helped her. Perhaps that's what he had been trying to do at his office today. She began to feel angry with herself for having panicked and running. She stopped pacing, sat down on the bed and lifted her phone. Staring at it, she wondered should she call Patrick. What could he do for her now? Would he even still want to help her, knowing what he now knows? Maybe he has alerted the police? Perhaps it's them who tracked her down? He certainly would have alerted Mark. Maybe it was him who was likely coming to track her down.

As she continued to hold the phone, the screen lit up and it began to ring. The caller display indicated that it was Beth Shaw calling. Deciding to bite the bullet, Gillian ignored Caleb's advice and answered.

'Hello Beth' Gillian said, finding herself sobbing uncontrollably as soon as the words had left her mouth.

'Gillian, Thank Goodness, are you ok'?

Gillian tried to answer but the words wouldn't come.

'Look Gillian, we're on our way. Patrick, Mark and I will be there soon. Are you hurt? Are you alone'?

Gillian managed to find her voice, albeit shaky. 'I'm ok. I'm alone'.

'Good, can you tell me your room number'?

'301' she responded, her voice quivering.

'We'll be there in about 5 minutes. Try to stay calm, we'll see you soon'.

'OK, Beth' Gillian replied, meekly.

Gillian put the phone back down on the bed. Part of her was relieved, part of her terrified. Caleb would be furious and she knew exactly what he was capable of. For a brief moment, she thought she should contact him but then decided to wait it out and see what the others had to say.

No matter what happens next, she can't change what she did this morning, she thought. She needs to live with the consequences now regardless, but she was fine with that. To say that she was afraid of what will happen to her was an understatement, but did she regret the murder? The answer in her mind was no, an emphatic no!

95.

When we pulled up on Main Street facing the hotel, we were already aware of the Police presence in nearby Kerr Street and Causeway Street. DI Black, who had been in continued contact with Ferguson who had just pulled in behind us, had told the two units stationed, to await further instruction. It was past midnight when we got to the front entrance of the hotel, so the main door was locked. Patrick rang the bell and we were soon met by the Night Porter, who after we gave him a brief explanation as to why we were there, let us in. After confirming with Gillian that she was expecting us, he allowed Patrick, Beth and I to make our way to room 301. Walking along the corridor toward the room reminded me of the murders of Owen Grant and James Dowell. I hoped that we weren't walking into a trap. I didn't think that we were, but if today had proven anything, it was that none of us knew Gillian Rodgers as well as we thought we did.

Patrick reached the door first and knocked softly. Gillian answered almost immediately, opening the door widely for us to enter. She had stayed silent at first, regarding each of us nervously. Finally Patrick embraced her and Beth and I watched on as the two of them disintegrated into tears. I had been struggling to fathom what was going to happen next, so I couldn't imagine what must be going on in their minds. After a few moments, they broke from their embrace and I motioned them to sit down on the bed, which they did. Beth took a seat at the table beside the window and I pulled the seat from under the dressing table and turned it around so that I was facing everyone.

Addressing Gillian, I spoke calmly and evenly.

'Gillian, first of all, we're all so glad you are safe. I'm so relieved to see you'.

'Me too' said Patrick, wiping a tear away. 'Me three' echoed Beth.

Gillian nodded and smiled nervously, wiping tears away from her own eyes.

'Gillian, we know about what happened at Causeway Academy this morning and we know about Caleb but we need you to tell us everything' I said.

She met my gaze before looking sidelong toward her brother, who nodded.

'We just want to help you Gillian' added Beth, 'but we need to know what's been going on'.

I opened a bottle of Spring Water that sat on the dressing table beside me and poured some into a glass. I handed the glass to Gillian. Her hand shook as she took it, spilling some water over her. She took a drink from the glass before setting it on the bedside table. We all watched intently as she took a deep breath, then began to speak.

'I'm sorry for dragging you all into this, I really am' she began, 'but the first thing that I need to tell you is that I don't regret a moment of what I did this morning'.

On hearing that, it took every ounce of willpower that I had, not to react. I tried to avoid eye contact with the others, not wanting to appear judgemental, rather encouraging her to continue, but I knew that they too were at war with themselves in the attempt to hold their tongues.

Gillian who now seemed strangely calm, then continued to tell us about her relationship with Caleb, how it had developed, how she had found out that he was Terror and about her own inner demons of anger and desire for revenge, before finally talking us through the lead up to, act and aftermath of the murder that she had committed in the early hours of what was now yesterday morning.

Beth, who I later realised had been recording the conversation on her phone, waited until Gillian had finished speaking before asking.

'What was the plan now then? Did he just abandon you here or is there something more that we should know'?

Gillian's face flushed and she began to look uncomfortable. 'He told me that he would speak to me soon, then we could move to the next level'.

'The next level'? Patrick looked at her intently.

It was Beth, who the penny dropped with first. 'Fear' she said accusingly, 'You were…there were going to be more victims'.

Gillian returned Beth's accusing look, with a mixture of scorn and horror. Patrick got up and silently walked past me into the en suite bathroom. I heard him begin to break down, but no-one moved to comfort him. Gillian continued to stare down Beth, as I looked on, struggling with what to say or do next.

In a second of clarity, I called Ferguson and asked him to join us. I then used the phone in the room to contact Reception,

to ask the Night Porter to allow Ferguson entry. I waited in the hallway for him, just outside the room. When he arrived, I filled him in on everything that we had learned since arriving, before leading him into the room. When I returned, Patrick was still in the bathroom and sounded inconsolable. Beth was staring silently out into the darkness of the coast and Gillian stared straight ahead of her, a scowl upon her face. She didn't even flicker an interest at the arrival of Ferguson.
'We need to talk before we contact DI Black again' I said. Ferguson nodded.
'I'll go speak to Patrick. We need to stay strong on this'.
I went into the bathroom to find that Patrick was now sitting on the floor with his back against the bath. He had stopped crying, though the rims of his now heavily bloodshot eyes burned red and he too stared ahead of him. 'I heard' he said, before standing up and walking toward me. I backed out into the room, allowing him to pass. Beth's gaze remained fixed on the view from the window. Something wasn't right. The atmosphere when I'd returned with Ferguson had been much heavier when it was when I had left, if that was possible.
'You OK'? I asked Beth.
She turned to look at me and nodded. Gillian interjected, her tone dripping with sarcasm, 'Yes she's fine. The truth hurts is all, isn't that right Beth'?
Beth sighed heavily. 'Look Gillian, I was only trying to help you. Caleb is not a good person. Just look at the situation that you're in now. He doesn't love you, you're kidding yourself'.
Gillian sprang to her feet and swooped toward Beth, stopping just short of her. She leaned her head in menacingly close to

Beth's face before spitting, 'Me. I'm the one kidding myself. You're pathetic'!

Beth leaned back a little, regaining some personal space. She was made of strong stuff and I knew that she would not be intimidated by Gillian. She spoke softly but firmly to Gillian, 'Gillian, you need to back off. You don't know what you're talking about'.

'Oh, but I do Beth. I know exactly what I'm talking about. You see, Caleb told me all about your pitiful little affair. You were quite the besotted little puppy dog by all accounts'. Gillian turned toward me, leering, 'I'm sorry Mark. I hope I haven't shattered your illusion of your perfect little wife. Still, maybe I'm doing you a favour'.

I was seething. I didn't recognise this person stood in front of me. It certainly wasn't the Gillan I knew. It was like someone had flicked a switch in her head. I was about to react to her snide remarks when Beth spoke to her from behind, masking her anger as best she could.

'So did the amazing Caleb tell you who broke off our relationship'? Gillian again focused her attention toward Beth, but didn't answer.

'No, I thought not'. She certainly had Gillian's attention now… and everyone else's. 'Yes, I did have an affair with Caleb' she continued, 'It was years ago, when we were at University. It's not something that I planned on and it's definitely not something that I'm proud of, but I learned from it. I learned just what a good man that my husband is and how much I loved him. Still do. I also learned what a sick, psychotic excuse for a man Caleb Doyle is, so if you think I'm jealous of your relationship with the great Terror, you're so far wrong you wouldn't believe. You know, I came here tonight to help you, to save you, because I cared about you. I should never have wasted my time'.

Gillian was about to react when suddenly Patrick grabbed her. Gripping the tops of her arms so that they would be pinned by her sides. Their heads almost level he screamed, 'Enough' right into her face before shoving her hard onto the bed. She locked shocked as he towered above her. It seemed that this was a side of him that she had never seen before. None of us had.

'Now I'm going to talk and you're going to listen. Clear?' he growled.

She nodded before pulling her legs up and moving to a seated position at the top of the bed. She was visibly trembling now.

Patrick continued gruffly. 'Let's get one thing straight, Caleb Doyle doesn't love you. He doesn't give a damn about you. Where is he now, eh? Didn't you wonder why he brought you here,why he left you here alone? He didn't want to be near you in case you got caught. He didn't want anyone making a connection between you and him, for fear Terror would be caught. You're disposable to him Gillian. If you were caught here, which you have been, then you would be left to face what you've done on your own. And what about the test, I mean, challenging someone to commit murder, I don't know what was worse, him for suggesting it or you for going through with it. You were just his sick little puppet. You don't realise it do you? He controlled you just as much as,The Enlightenment did, more, and yeah you might hate them, we all do, but they never asked you to kill, and certainly none of us ever had the notion to kill any of them. You're sick Gillian, psychotic. It's unimaginable that you could be so evil as to commit one murder, but to plan more, a serial murderer, Fear, I can't even begin to fathom how lost your soul must be'. He paused momentarily to let her process what he had said, before finally spitting out the words, 'You disgust me' before turning his back on her and returning to where he had been sitting in the bathroom.

Gillian sat on the bed dumbfounded. She began to shake her head from side to side as she came to the realisation that although Patrick's words had been harsh, they had also been true. Ironically, it was she who was now realising that the truth hurts. She was visibly crushed and began to sob hard again. Beth got up from her seat near the window, and took a seat on the bed beside Gillian. Cradling Gillian's head in her arms, Beth comforted her, consoling her with the fact that we would all do what we could to help her.

Ferguson turned to me. 'I think I might have a plan but we're going to need DI Black's agreement and we're definitely going to need a good solicitor'.

'Let's do it' I replied, 'At this stage anything's worth a shot'.

96.

'You OK'? I asked Patrick as I looked at him sitting in the backseat through the rearview mirror of the car. He hadn't spoken since we left Gillian at the hotel, almost half an hour ago.

'Yeah, I just wish that I hadn't been so hard on her. I've already lost her once and no matter what she's done, I don't want to lose her again'.

'You won't lose her. You said what she needed to hear and the way you said it shows how much you care for her, she knows that' I replied.

'I hope so. I just hope we can get her through this ok'.

'Are you still OK with the plan'? I asked. 'I mean, we're all worried, but you're happy that it's the best option right'? At this stage I wasn't sure if I was trying to persuade Patrick or myself that our chosen course of action was the correct one.

'Yeah, I just hope that it all works out the way it's supposed to'.

'She's a smart girl Patrick. She knows what to do. She'll be back with us within a few days at most' I replied, hoping that I sounded more convinced than I actually felt.

Ferguson's plan was not without its dangers but it was a good one nonetheless. From weighing up the evidence that the PSNI had, he felt convinced that we could persuade DI Black to be sympathetic to a plea of diminished responsibility in Gillian's case at a later date, rather than pushing to build a case for murder one, provided that she worked as an informant for all agencies in the apprehension and capture of Terror. This of course meant everyone involved pretending that our finding and meeting Gillian had not happened. What's more it also meant, leaving her in Doyle's clutches, when he deemed it appropriate to contact her again. Thankfully, DI Black was supportive and the decision was rubber stamped by the FBI also. As a precaution, we managed to check Michael Ferguson into the room next to Gillian. Doyle would not have seen him before, so would not realise that Gillian was covertly under his protection. His experience more than qualified him for the job. Gillian was happy with the arrangement too, grateful of the opportunity to continue to have some form of normal life beyond what she had done. She had even given us access to conversations she had secretly recorded, where Caleb Doyle admitted to being Terror and discussed how he groomed his followers. Now all we had to do was wait.

I glanced sidelong at Beth. She too had been fairly quiet.

'What about you , you ok'? I asked.

She nodded.

'You know, I was really proud of you back there' I said, smiling.

She turned her head toward me and returned the smile, weakly.

'So you should be, that's one heck of a wife you've got there. I'm glad she's on our team' said Patrick, leaning forward and placing his hand on Beth's right shoulder.

She turned her head toward him and covered his hand with

hers, her smile now shining a bit more brightly. 'Thanks Patrick' she said.
'OK, enough with the mushy stuff' he replied before turning his attention to me, 'Is Ferguson still behind us'?
I quickly checked the mirror. 'Yes' I replied.
'Good, I'm starving'. He pulled his phone out of his pocket and dialled Ferguson.
'Hey Ferguson, there's a 24hr KFC in Ballymena. Last one there pays'. He ended the call and looked up at me. 'I think you know what to do' he said.
'I certainly do' I replied, before planting my right foot more than a tad more firmly toward the floor, causing us all to explode with much needed laughter.

97.

Caleb Doyle stifled a yawn as he finished writing the article that he had been working on. He had been covering the story of a fire that had been accidentally started at a Recycling Plant on Kennedy Way in West Belfast yesterday. He'd heard about it just after he dropped Gillian off and had made his way directly to the scene, before continuing to work the story from the Newsroom since. In truth, it wasn't necessarily the type of thing that he would necessarily follow up, but as soon as he'd heard about it, he knew that it would take hours, even days to bring the fire under control, giving him the perfect excuse to spend a lot of time in the Newsroom. The Newsroom was the perfect place to keep on top of any breaking news, particularly that of the violent murder of a member of The Enlightenment Church at one of the Group's NI Schools. So far there had been no mention of it. He knew that the murder had been committed more than thirty hours ago, and still nothing. He was relieved but also wondered why not? If the PSNI were involved, he doubted that they would have any reason for a media blackout. If anything, the public feeling toward,The Enlightenment was so negative at present, that they would not be put under any public pressure to catch the perpetrator. Another option that he had mulled over was that,The Enlightenment perhaps opted not to report what had happened, choosing instead to cover it up for their own sake.

If the body had been discovered by a member of their Church, it would have been relatively easy for it to have been swiftly removed from the scene and the death not reported. Especially, since the Group manage their own undertaking and burial arrangements. It would have been strange but certainly plausible. Regardless, he was now pretty sure that Gillian was not in the frame for anything. He decided that the time was now right to make contact. He rose from his desk, put on his jacket and made his way outside into the bustle of Belfast's Cathedral Quarter, where he could make the call as he walked, without fear of anyone overhearing his conversation. She answered on the second ring.

'Caleb, at last, I've been going out of my mind here' she said anxiously 'Where are you'?

'Relax Gillian, everything is fine. You can come home now'.

'What… how'?

'I've been keeping check on the PSNI links with The Chron, nothing's been reported. Whatever Patrick thinks that you've done, I'm sure he can be persuaded otherwise'.

'I don't know Caleb. You don't understand his gift, I do, I've seen it for myself, and what about Mark, I mean, I just took off from work, what do I tell him'?

'That you had a fallout with your brother and you were so upset you had to take off for a while, to clear your head. Mark Shaw won't be a problem. As long as you can smooth things over with Patrick, that's the main thing. Has anyone tried contacting you'?

'Just Patrick, but I didn't answer… just like you said' Gillian lied.

'Good Girl, I'm sure you can deal with him when you get back, I mean, you're smart right'?

'I'll try to come up with something. I hope I can work things out with him. Caleb, I've been thinking…about Fear, the next stage' Gillian continued, 'I…'

'Don't worry. Look, we can talk about it later, you just concentrate on getting safely back to Ridgeway Street'.

'Aren't you coming to pick me up'?

'Sorry hon, I'm caught up in the middle of a story, I can't get away'.

'But I'll see you later, right'? Gillian asked.

'I don't think it's wise. I think you should spend a few days making things up with Patrick and making amends with Mark. Maybe we should cool things off for a day or two. I'll call you later'.

'But… Caleb'?

'It's for the best Gillian. Look, I'll call you later, I have to go. Love you'.

'Love you too' said Gillian, dejectedly, before Caleb ended the call.

As she placed the phone into her handbag, Michael Ferguson, who had been sitting at the table near the window in the hotel room, applauded softly.

'Well if things don't work out at Farset, you could always take up acting' he said.

'I'm a nervous wreck' replied Gillian, holding up her trembling hand for him to see.

'You were great, now let's go get some breakfast before we get the train. Mark highly recommends the breakfast here'.

'He would' said Gillian, rolling her eyes.

98.

Although practically every muscle in my body felt like it was on fire, I felt good as Patrick and I finished our relatively short run through Ormeau Park. I was finally at the stage of my rehabilitation where I could start to improve my fitness levels and mobility again and this evening was the beginning of that process. Patrick also had new fitness goals in mind, having just given up smoking for the third time in as many weeks, so we were glad of each other's company. I was also glad of the park bench that we were now sitting on and the bottle of cold mineral water in my hand. When we had both finally gotten our breath back, we were able to get to the other reason we had met up this evening, Gillian. She had been back for three days now, both to home and work, much to our relief, but neither Patrick nor I had been able to get the whole picture as to how well she was coping, both with the prospect of spending time in a secure unit, and her working as an undercover operative, to all intents and purposes, in the apprehension of a serial killer.

'Where is she this evening'? I asked.

'At home. Apart from a trip to Sainsbury's at Forestside with me yesterday evening, the only time she has left the house is to go to work. Doyle has told her that they should cool things off for a while and that they shouldn't see each other for at least a few days'.

'Has she had any contact from him'?

'Yes, she had a call on Tuesday night after she had returned home. He wanted to find out what she had told me and what my reaction was. We had agreed before he contacted her, that her story was that she thought that she was pregnant and that I had picked up on that energy and disapproved of what she had done. She had fled to gather her thoughts and take a test and after finding out that she wasn't pregnant, decided to stay out all night to punish me for my judgement'.

I pursed my lips and nodded, 'Sounds plausible, did he buy it'?

'He seems to have done. He told her that she should spend time building bridges with me and that he would contact her again in a few days. She hasn't heard from him since, not that I know of anyway'.

'How is she in herself do you think'? I asked.

'It's hard to tell. I mean on the face of it she seems OK but I'm still getting mixed messages from her aura. There's a lot of darkness there still'.

'How are you coping'?

'Well enough… I think. Part of me wants to protect her and make sure that she's OK, part of me is worried sick that she might give in to her inner demons again, and part of me despises her for what she has already become, but like I said before, she's my sister and I love her. I already lost her once, I don't want to lose her again'.

'I can understand that' I replied. 'I'm abhorred at what she has done, despite her choice of target but she's become like family to me too, just like you and Ferguson have and I want to make sure she's OK'.

'Thanks Mark, I appreciate that. How's she been at work'?

'OK, I would say her usual self, but you know what I mean'.

'What about Beth, how has she been since the other night? Gillian feels really bad about what she said'.

'Beth has been fine. She's OK. In fact, she asked me to invite you and Gillian up for dinner tomorrow evening, to clear the air. She thinks of you all like family too. Families fall out sometimes, and that's OK, but they're always there for each other when it counts'.

'We're lucky to have you both. Tell her we'd love to come to dinner tomorrow. I'll bring the wine and Gillian will bring the dessert'.

'Sounds good to me'.

'How've you been'? Patrick asked.

'Yeah, I'm fine, I'm getting a bit stronger every day and I'm starting to feel like my old self, before the attack again'.

'And what about the whole Terror thing? It can't have been easy discovering his identity, then finding out that you're likely related'?

'Actually, I'm just relieved to have found Sean's killer. Any closeness I had with Caleb vanished years ago. Mum and Dad are taking it pretty badly though, I'm worried about them more. Dad and Sean were more like brothers than brothers in law. They were best friends all their lives, and Mum and Sean were always close. They were both struggling to deal with his death already, without finding out that he died at his own son's hand, a son that whether we like it or not, is family'.

'You'll all get through it. You're strong'.

'We will, provided justice is served' I said.

'It will be' replied Patrick, 'It will be'. He stood up and began to stretch again. 'You see that coffee shop just there at the corner of Deramore Avenue'?

I nodded. 'First one there buys the coffee' he said before sprinting off and leaving me in his wake.

'You're getting too accustomed to pulling that trick', I panted as I finally caught up to him outside the coffee shop.

'Snooze you lose, my friend. I'm just kidding, I'll get the coffee, you grab a table outside'. He pulled at the front of his sweat soaked t-shirt, 'I think we'd be better for business outside than we would in'.

I agreed. Within a few moments Patrick had returned to the table that I'd commandeered, with a tray holding two Americano's and a huge slice of Victoria Sponge cake.

'I thought we'd share this' he said as he cut the cake into two pieces and placed one of them onto a side plate for me.

'So much for our fitness regime' I said.

'It was either this or a cigarette'.

'Fair enough'.

'And misery loves company right'?

'You've twisted my arm'.

'I know, it was a piece of cake' he joked. 'You all set for our big day tomorrow'?

'About as set as I can be I suppose'.

'It's 11:30 she's coming at isn't it'?

'Yeah' I replied, 'She wants to meet us all as a group first, then see us individually after. Stick close to Gillian'.

'I was thinking that already. Mind you, it'll do her no harm to see how a Prosecution Lawyer prepares a case. It might make her appreciate the deal that Ferguson managed to cut her, all the more. You've another meeting first haven't you'?

It had been just my luck, that our meeting with the Solicitor assigned to the prosecution in the case against the Pinkertons, had been scheduled to take place on the same day as my meeting with the elusive Michael Dean.

'That should be an interesting meeting as well' Patrick said.

I nodded.

'You look at bit apprehensive, you worried about it'?

'Not worried… more dreading' I replied.

'I thought you'd been looking forward to it'.

'I was, but now that it's coming near the time, I feel like I'm getting a visit from the Headmaster'.

'Well, speaking from personal experience, that's no picnic' he laughed.

'You're just too funny' I mocked, 'Just eat your cake'.

99.

If this morning so far had been anything to go by, today was not going to be my day, I thought to myself as I finally managed to get into the car. It was already 08:11 and I hadn't left yet, meaning that I had approximately 18 minutes to travel the 20 miles to work through morning rush hour traffic. There was no way I was even going to be close to arriving on time for my 08:30 meeting with Michael Dean.

As I frantically tried to negotiate the steady stream of traffic blocking my being able to cross the Dunsilly Roundabout, I called Gillian.

'Hey, it's me, I'm running late' I said as she answered my call.

'How late Mark, he's already here'?

'I was worried that might happen. Just bring him down to the staff area and get him some coffee, I'll be there as soon as I can'.

'Will do. What happened, it's not like you to be late'?

'I know, I was just about to leave earlier, when Alecia was sick all over me… and my new wool suit, so I had to change'.

'Yuck. She OK'?

'Yeah, it's just a bug I think, it's been making its way through her class'.

'Poor little chick. You'd better get here fast, he didn't seem all that impressed that you weren't here when he arrived'.

'I'm working on it, what's he like'?

'You'll see soon enough' she said, the giggled a little before

cutting me off.
Having finally arrived, more than half an hour late and feeling a lot more flustered than I'd planned for, I finally came face to face with Michael Dean. He was not at all how I expected. In my mind's eye he was a lot like Uncle Sean had been in looks, though perhaps a little fatter and certainly more tanned. In reality he was very different.
'Good Morning, Mr Shaw'! He rose from his seat and extended his hand in introduction. 'I'm Michael Dean'.
'Very nice to meet you at last Mr Dean, please, call me Mark' I managed to say as I shook his hand while he towered over me. At around six feet four in comparison to my five nine, Dean was an impressive figure. Dressed in a navy blue business suit, crisp white shirt and claret coloured silk tie, his outfit was topped off with a pair of dark brown brogue shoes and accessorised with a pair of gold cufflinks and matching tie clip. It was clear that his appearance was important to the tall, toned African-American. He appeared to be around fifty years old judging by his features, though his neatly styled hair and dress sense made him look a fair bit younger.
'Apologies for being late'.
'That's quite alright, Mr Shaw, your assistant told me about your daughter. I hope she gets well soon' Dean replied.
'Thank you, I appreciate that'. I led Dean to my office, whilst all the while trying unsuccessfully to pin down which State his dialect hailed him from.
'I hear from Agents Ross and Curtis that I'm somewhat of a mystery to you' he began as he took a seat in my office.
'Yes' I said, looking at him surprisingly. 'You know Agents

Ross and Curtis'?

'Yes, they're associates of our Agency, they've been keeping me up to date on your investigation. Two fine Agents, it wasn't by coincidence that they were assigned to the Terror investigation'.

'They've been invaluable to us. Two really nice guys too. Your Agency'?

He nodded and smiled. 'Straight to the point, your Uncle said you were sharp. Another fine man, much missed'.

Now it was my turn to nod, 'Unbearably' I answered.

'He was an important member of our Agency, one of our founder members in fact'.

I listened as yet another secret of a man I thought I knew inside out, was revealed.

'I have known Sean Brady for many years and in recent times, worked with him as a fellow member and CEO of the Philanthropic Patriots Foundation(PPF). We represent the interests of a group of wealthy and influential American Businesspeople who are either emigrants from the UK and Ireland, or are descended from emigrants from this part of the world'.

I was intrigued to say the least.

'We fund and work with many agencies, such as Farset Investigations and have associates within many related organisations, to allow us to fulfil our raison d'être'.

'Which is?' I asked.

'To use our wealth and influence to ensure justice and fight criminality on behalf of our compatriots'.

'A very noble cause, I'm impressed' I said, 'but there's one thing that I don't understand, why private agencies like Farset, why not provide extra resource for the PSNI for example?'

I expected that I already knew the answer but he confirmed it for me anyway.

'Simple. Private agencies are not subject to the same amount of regulation and accountability. It removes a significant amount of the red tape that can often hamper an investigation'. I nodded Yes in recognition of the fact, before he continued.

'You will already know that we fund Farset as per our agreement with Sean and that will continue regardless. However, I'm here today to offer you the opportunity to take your Uncle's seat on our board of Trustees. Agents Ross and Curtis have been impressed with the team that you have assembled and with your attitude and approach to the Terror Investigation. I know that it's not yet concluded but the Board Members feel that you have exceeded their expectations and in finding your Uncle's killer, have earned your right to succeed him'.

'I'm flattered at the commendation, though my primary focus has always been about getting justice for Sean' I said.

'As it should have been. Another reason why you have proven yourself to the Board'.

'How would it work'?

'Farset will continue to run under your chosen directorship and will find and choose its own cases. However, when requested by the Board, Farset will take on cases that the PPF feel that you would be in a position to help with. As a PPF Board Member, you will attend meetings either by

Videoconference or in person. Your role will be to help provide guidance in the work of the PPF and to develop multi-agency relationships with other private agencies and associates. You don't have to give me an answer today, but I would like you to give my offer due consideration'.

'I will' I replied. 'I give you my word on that'.

'Oh, and another thing, as I've already alluded to, the PPF have close links to the FBI, particularly the Agents Training Centre in Quantico. We'd like to send some of your team for training there and you yourself eventually. There is little point in having a state of the art operations base and not having the expertise in using the equipment that it contains'.

'I agree. I'll think about that too'. Remembering my next meeting, I looked at the clock on the wall behind Dean. Despite my lateness I still had a bit of time to spare before my next meeting. I decided to ask him a little more about his relationship with Sean.

'Sean and I first met in the late 1980s and had been firm friends ever since' he opened, the smile in his eyes indicating the closeness and warmth of their friendship. 'My Father emigrated to the US from East London. He settled in Dorchester, Boston where he met and married my Mom, before eventually becoming a magnate in the Restaurant Industry. He was disappointed that I chose not to enter the family business, opting for a career in law enforcement which eventually saw my recruitment to the FBI. That's where I first came across Sean. I was part of a team investigating the US funding of terrorist activity in Ireland and found myself on placement in Belfast trying to gain intelligence on the supply of weapons to the Republican Movement. He was amongst the first people I made contact with. He was an investigative journalist at the time so it made sense that he would have his ear to the ground and that to be able to be successful in doing his job, would have no obvious political affiliations. We worked closely for a while and although we were unable to uncover any irrefutable evidence on the supply of weapons, we did make a possible connection to someone outside the system. I thought that I had noticed a pattern in the methodology and timings of many unclaimed murders in both the Loyalist and Republican factions, though was ordered back to the US before I could investigate further. Sean continued the investigation on my behalf and found that we may have been looking for an assassin for hire. We coined the name, The Ghost for our would be assassin and early investigations proved promising, before Sean felt that the trail had gone cold and ceased the investigation'.

'Or did he' I thought, as my mind whirred back to Sean's hidden Cloud drive and the folder marked, The Ghost. I hadn't looked at the file in any great detail yet but now suspected that it revealed the identity of The Ghost. If true, then the only reason that Sean would have concealed the identity is if doing otherwise would harm the people he loved, in this case, I suspected, Maureen and Caleb. This meant that The Ghost must be none other than our Deputy First Minister, Michael Doyle. I decided quickly that I had no desire to afford any further protection to any member of the Doyle family.

'Mr Dean, I have another meeting scheduled in a few minutes

time but I would really like it if you could stick around. I've got something that I haven't been able to look at in any great detail as yet, but I think you might be interested in it'.

'By all means. I have a flight to London this evening and had planned to spend the time in between now and then being a tourist in Belfast. I gather things have changed dramatically since my last visit, but I'm happy to have a look at what you've got'.

I logged into the Cloud account and brought up the file whilst quickly explaining about Sean's hidden folder. I then invited Dean to take my seat at the desk before I called Gillian, asking her to bring some lunch for Dean from the buffet that she had arranged for the attendees of our next meeting. I then left the office en route to the Boardroom but not before catching a glimpse of Dean's jaw dropping as he realised what he was looking at.

100.

With the exception of Gillian, I was the last to arrive at our meeting with PPSNI Representative, Sam Lynas. Dressed in a cement-grey trouser suit, black blouse and black court shoes, she removed a leather bound notebook from her briefcase, before introducing herself to me. I shook her hand and was surprised at the firmness of her grip despite her petite stature. As soon as she spoke I felt at ease that she would be our representative. There was something about her tone that was authoritative yet empathetic. I got the distinct sense that she could handle herself in a courtroom.

I took my seat at the table and took a drink from the unopened bottle of water on the table. Gillian had set the room up well I thought as I looked around. In front of each delegate was a bottle of water, a file pad and a pen, whilst over in the corner stood the buffet table, laden with sandwiches, cakes and pastries. Alongside it stood a hot drinks station. Very corporate, I thought. Gillian scurried in, having served Dean his lunch and took the remaining empty seat at the table. Taking that as her cue to begin, Miss Lynas stood up, brushed a stray black hair from the shoulder of her jacket and started to speak.

After reintroducing herself to the group, she thanked us for our attendance and Farset for hosting the meetings before running through her schedule for us. After our initial meeting here, we were requested to fill in victim impact statements which would be submitted as evidence to the trial. She would remain available until late afternoon to assist anyone who needed it, in producing their statement. Assessing the determined looks on the faces of those around me, I felt that putting their feelings down on paper was not going to be a bother to them.

'I cannot emphasise enough, the importance of the victim impact statements' she said. 'As you know, the defendants are likely to plead diminished responsibility at their pre-trial hearing next week. I'm sure I can argue a strong case to ensure that they both progress to a criminal trial, however, strong statements from you all will help make the Judge's decision all the more clear cut'.

'We'll certainly make sure that you're not short of ammunition' said Beth, 'and I think I can speak for everyone here in saying that we're disgusted that they have managed to avoid their case going straight to trial'. Everyone nodded their agreement.

'Their current locale doesn't help matters for us though I'm afraid' Miss Lynas said.

'What do you mean'? I asked, perplexed, 'They're still in custody aren't they'?

'You mean, you haven't been informed? They're still in custody in a manner of speaking, in that they are under guard at all times, but their defence was able to make a case that they were in need of immediate treatment. They were moved to a private healthcare facility in South Belfast a few days ago'.

This revelation was met with audible gasps of shock from around the room and as I took in everyone's reactions I

noticed that Diane Boyd, Dana's Mum was fighting back tears. I had visited Dana yesterday afternoon. She remained comatose and her mother who had barely left her bedside since she was brought into hospital, remained distraught.
Michael Ferguson, who had been seated beside Mrs Boyd at the table, offered her a handkerchief. I heard him whisper lowly to her, ensuring her that justice would be served on the Pinkertons at the outcome of the trial. The old woman nodded in hope. Little did any of us realise that an extraordinary turn of events would mean that there would never be a trial.

101.

Like everyone else around the table in the Boardroom yesterday Gillian Rodgers was seething at the disclosure of the now whereabouts of the Pinkertons. It was a clear ploy by the defence to sidestep any criminal trial or in the event that a criminal trial did take place, gain the sympathies of the jury. The subject had been much talked about around the table at dinner last night when she and Patrick had joined the Shaws and as it turned out, the Fergusons. Like the others, Gillian was worried that their tactics might work and like the others, she was angry at the audacity of what they were doing. She, Patrick and Mark knew best of all that,The Enlightenment had a reputation for being able to evade justice and in this case, she had a gut feeling that that was exactly what was going to happen. It wasn't though was it, not now that she had decided to ensure that it wasn't. That decision was chief amongst the reasons that she now stood in the home of Caleb Doyle.

She was glad that she had ultimately enjoyed her evening with Patrick and what she had dubbed her Farset family. She had made things up with Beth, which she was grateful for. Beth had been a good friend to her and she had only struck out against her in anger. At least now it had been resolved. Everyone had been so nice to her last night. They were clearly worried about her, the choice to be an informant against Terror and the potential danger that it would put her in. She wasn't going to be able to carry out that role now though. Of course, they didn't know that. Caleb had unwittingly helped her with that choice in their call late last night, where he encouraged her to take vengeance on the Pinkertons. As always, he had an idea of just how to do it, which was why she now stood alongside him over his kitchen table as he was in the final stages of synthesising some castor oil beans, into a homemade Ricin powder. Soon she would play her part.

102.

Fear gazed at her reflection in wonder as she was faced with the full length mirror reflection of her guise. She thought briefly about how she had been similarly awed by her transformation from Charlene McManus into Gillian Rodgers. Not in her wildest imaginings of what her Fear persona would look like, did she ever think that she would have come full circle. She was glad to have kept an outfit of Charlene's as a reminder of how far she had come, as now she was dressed in a long denim skirt, a high necked blue and white striped sweatshirt, thick flesh coloured tights and navy leather sandals. Her hair had been washed and allowed to dry naturally, accounting for what was now an unkempt, unstyled frizz. With it's now lighter colour, she bore a striking resemblance to Drew Pinkerton's daughter, and what was all the more important, looked every inch the young Enlightenment female.

Downstairs, Terror had carefully attached the Ricin powder filled bags to the inside of the envelopes, securing them in position so that as the envelopes were opened, the bags would be pulled apart, causing a lethal cloud of dust to rise into the face of the person holding the envelope. The envelopes had been clearly addressed. He had to stifle a laugh when he first saw Fear, now dressed for her mission. As he handed her the envelopes, she could see from his eyes that his adrenalin levels were high. Hers were too. She was reminded of how alive she had felt when carrying out the attack at Causeway Academy. Those same feelings were coursing through her now. She kissed Terror then made her way out the door. She would be more careful this time. Her car remained in the driveway as she now cycled the short distance to the clinic, where she left the envelopes with the Receptionist with the request that they be passed on to her Father and Brother as soon as possible as they contained messages of good luck for them from their family and friends.

Within minutes she was back at Caleb Doyle's house changing her outfit, applying her make up and straightening her hair. Celebrations were in order they thought, so walked the short distance across to the Malone Lodge Hotel, where they drank Prosecco in Macklin's Bar before enjoying an early dinner of Grilled Salmon in the Knife and Fork Restaurant. They had set in motion a chain of events that would lead to a painful and prolonged death for Drew and Daniel Pinkerton over the next few days. They would not evade justice this time.

103.

Ferguson held little Emma in his arms, hugging her tightly as they stood near the escalator leading to the Departures area of Belfast International Airport.

'You look after Daddy for me won't you, Princess?' he whispered to her.

She nodded and smiled at him before he set her down again, turning his attention to his brother Michael.

'You take care, you hear, and I want to speak to you both every day'.

'We will, but we'll only be gone for a few months Mark, we'll be back before you know it. Come September, Emma will start at Antrim Primary and I will start at Farset as planned'.

Ferguson nodded and smiled. 'I know, I'm just going to miss you that's all'.

Michael hugged his brother. 'Take care bro, we'll speak soon, I promise'.

'Have a safe trip, both of you' said Ferguson as he watched them ascend the metal staircase that would deliver them to airport security, then through to Departures.

Things had moved quickly in the last few days since Mark's meeting with Michael Dean. It had since been agreed that Farset would become officially affiliated to the PPF, with Mark taking a seat on the Board. Michael Ferguson had been offered an employment role with Farset and was about to embark on three months intensive training at the FBI Field

Office in Quantico. Not to mention, the fact that the file on The Ghost provided proof enough to take down Michael Doyle. His days as Deputy First Minister would end soon, with his arrest, though not before he is unwittingly used to help end the reign of Terror.

With a final wave to his family as they reached the top of the escalator, Ferguson turned toward the exit. He was glad that arrangements had been made to allow Emma to accompany her Father. It would be good for them both. He also knew that he was probably being overly emotional at their leaving. He couldn't help it though. Last time he had said goodbye to them at an airport, Maria had been with them and they had been a complete and happy family. He still missed her greatly himself, so couldn't even begin to imagine how they must be feeling without her. He had always looked up to his brother but how he has coped and the way that he has been with Emma, made him nothing short of a hero in Ferguson's eyes now.

Making his way back to the car, he became lost in memories of happier times with his family and thoughts that though things would never be the same again, that maybe this fresh start might mean that in sometime in the future, they might know true happiness again. After all, he himself, was beginning to feel at home as part of the Farset family.

He had just pulled out of the carpark when the screen on the dashboard of the car indicated an incoming call. It was Mark.

'Hey, Mark'.

'Ferguson, hey. They get away OK'?

'Yeah, I've just dropped them off. I'm on my way back'.

'That's why I'm calling. I need you to go somewhere else instead. I've just got word that Drew and Daniel Picton are in intensive care at the Royal Hospital with suspected Ricin poisoning. Can you get over there and try to find out what's going on'?

'Will do, Ricin'?

'Apparently. Patrick and I are on our way to meet DI Black at the Private Medical Facility they had been in. Apparently, there's some CCTV that he wants us to look at. I'll check in with you again as soon as I find out anything'.

'Likewise, speak to you soon'.

104.

As Patrick and I made our way through the perpetually heavy South Belfast traffic, I remembered that I was supposed to meet Caitlin for lunch. As soon as we were stationary again I sent her a text, explaining where I was headed anyway.

'Is she finished already'? Patrick asked, 'I thought they were making her work her notice'.

'They were' I replied. 'That was before they got word that The Prophet has deigned Northern Ireland worthy of a visit and decided it would be best that she wasn't around when they were preparing for it'.

'I'm surprised. I don't ever remember The Prophet ever coming to Northern Ireland. He usually flew into England and made us flock to him'.

'I wondered about that too when I heard. Have you ever met him'? I asked.

'Me? No. I've never met him personally. I was never worthy enough. I did attend some of the conference visits he held though and I did endure having the ugly bastard's big piggy face staring down at me from his framed picture on the chimney breast of our sitting room every day. That was more than enough'.

'I wonder if we've had something to do with his visit' I mused.

'I wouldn't doubt it. It'll certainly cost the local Church though. I'm sure there'll be many an envelope being stuffed with cash in every household, as a "gift" between now and his arrival. His visits generally create quite a spectacle you know, even in security alone'.

'Really'? Despite all that I knew, I was still surprised at this.

'Oh yeah, very Presidential, security entourage, a convoy of identical SUV's with tinted windows, covered walkways between the vehicle stop point and entrance to the Church, the works'.

'Sounds a bit over the top, is it vanity or paranoia'?

'I would say a mixture of both, though you can bet since recent events, the security will be stepped up further still'.

Our conversation was interrupted by our arrival. After finding a spot in the cramped underground car park, we made our way to Reception, where DI Black was waiting. He led us into a private consultation room.

'What happened'? I asked. He gestured for us to sit.

'Apparently, they had both gotten sick over the last few days. It was initially thought they'd had a reaction to their medication but when they both began to deteriorate rapidly, the connection was made to an incident a few days ago. It seems that a visitor left a package each for them. When they received the packages and opened them, they contained what was thought at the time to be some sort of flour bomb. Thinking that they had been pranked, they cleaned up the mess, then cleaned themselves up. No-one thought any more about it until earlier today. The Practice Manager, realising that they were not in a position to treat them here, arranged ambulance transportation and then called us'.

'And they have footage of who dropped off the packages'? I

asked.
'Yes, I spoke to the Receptionist who was on duty at the time. She said that a young woman dropped them off. She looked to be a member of,The Enlightenment by how she was dressed, so she thought nothing of passing the packages on. The young woman had said that the packages contained well wishes from family and friends for her father and brother'.
'Have you seen the footage'? Patrick asked.
'Yes, it certainly looks like a member of,The Enlightenment alright. That's why I wanted you two to look at it. I thought maybe you could help me ID the woman, verify that she is indeed Drew Pinkerton's daughter'.
'Sure' said Patrick.
DI Black brought up the footage on the laptop. To be such a high end and costly facility, it appeared that little money had been invested in their security system judging by the picture quality. It didn't help that the camera angle made it difficult to make a 100% identification.
'I can't be definite but I'm pretty sure that it's the Pinkerton girl' I said.
'It is her, it's definitely her, she even walks the same way, look' said Patrick.
As the recording was played back to show her physically walking into the Reception Area, I had to agree with Patrick. It definitely was Imdela Pinkerton.
'Looks like, The Prophet has another problem to deal with when he arrives' said Patrick with a smirk.
'He and I both' said Black. With that, Ferguson called. After speaking to him briefly I returned to the conversation with

Black and Patrick.
'That was Ferguson. Drew Pinkerton went into cardiac arrest a few minutes ago. He's dead'. They were stunned into silence.
'It seems that Daniel has been bleeding heavily internally also. The medical team are trying all they can at the moment but it looks like they're going to lose him too' I added.
Before they could react, the door knocked and a young PSNI officer addressed Black.
'Sorry to interrupt Sir. I just wanted to let you know that the CSI have managed to find trace amounts of the powder in one of the two patients rooms. It's being taken away for analysis. The bin had been emptied into the main bin, which has since been collected. Should I contact the Refuse Department'?
'Yes, if it does turn out to be Ricin, then they need to be informed, though I would imagine that if the powder was spread around the volume a refuse lorry would contain, it's unlikely to be of any threat. Still, let them make that judgement.'
'Will do Sir'.
'Thanks'.
'What makes you suspect Ricin'? I asked.
'I didn't, at least not initially, but it seems that one of the staff here is a Breaking Bad fan. Apparently it had been used in a similar way in the show and he made the connection between the powder and the symptoms that appeared in the Pinkertons. Apparently its very difficult to trace post mortem and can be fatal when administered as a powder and inhaled'.
'Sounds like Drew didn't stand much of a chance' I said.
'Nor does Daniel if you apply the same logic' Black replied,

'I'll arrange for Imelda Pinkerton to be brought in'.
'Why would she have wanted to kill them'? Patrick thought aloud. It didn't make sense to me either, but I guess that it was Black's intention to get to the bottom of that when she was brought in for questioning.

105.

When we got back to the office, Ferguson was in Reception with Gillian.

'Any more news'? I asked.

'They couldn't save Daniel. He passed just after I last spoke to you. His remains and those of his Dad's are being held for post-mortem'.

I wanted to feel sorry that they were dead but the truth was, that I wasn't.

'Looks like we won't be getting our day in court after all' I sighed.

'Someone needs to contact Sam Lynas, oh and Dana's Mum, she'll be devastated' said Patrick.

'I'll do it' I said, 'since it was me who got her daughter involved in this whole mess anyway'.

'That's not strictly true Mark, and anyway, I wouldn't be surprised that she'll be glad to hear the news. She might feel that they got what they deserved' said Gillian.

As it turned out, she was right about that. When I phoned Diana Boyd, to giver her the news, she received it with great joy, before cursing the Pinkertons to hell. She had some news for me as well. Dana had regained consciousness this morning and was talking. I was ecstatic with the news and rushed back to Reception to tell the others, just in time to hear the end of Patrick's recount of our trip to the clinic.

'I can't believe Imelda could do such a thing. We were really close friends at one time, I wouldn't have thought she was capable' Gillian was saying as I came in. I couldn't help but think that only a short time ago, we were all saying something similar about her.

106. Part Five- Fear and Redemption

The vast expanse looked exactly as Gillian had described it Terror thought as he looked around the interior of the Church, or Meeting Room, as she said The Enlightenment preferred to call it. Tomorrow this room will be packed with hundreds of his faithful flock, waiting to be awed with the presence of The Prophet and the weight of his words. What they will witness instead however, would be his spectacular demise. Terror couldn't help but smile at the prospect.

Having informed the Council of a scheduled large gathering to be taking place tomorrow, it was not unheard of for The Enlightenment to receive a visit from a Health & Safety Compliance Officer prior to the event. This afternoon they were receiving such a visit, or at least that's what they thought. Having led the young man who had met him here around the exterior of the building and its grounds as part of his Inspection, Terror continued inside. After cursory looks at Fire Exit signs, he deliberately began to show outward signs that there may be a problem, before sending the young man scurrying off in search of a Risk Assessments folder. Now was his chance. Terror removed the small device from his pocket and concealed it securely under the pulpit, before arming it. When the young man returned, Terror perused the folder before asking him to sign what looked to be an authentic audit form and leaving. The young man looked relieved Terror thought to himself as he left. Little did he realise that he had been duped and that come tomorrow, he may find himself being blamed for the death of The Prophet, presuming of course that he himself had survived the blast.

Gillian awaited him when he returned.

'It's done' he said simply. He took a seat opposite her, noting that she had barely reacted to what he had said. 'Aren't you pleased'?

She smiled weakly. A markedly underwhelming response to the one he had hoped for, he thought to himself. He was surprised, after all, it was she who had practically masterminded the entire setup when she learned that The Prophet was to be the next victim #FamousForAllTheWrongReasons. She was the one who told him of the security around The Prophet and of the extreme lengths that were gone to, to ensure that his sermons were not recorded. Without her he wouldn't have known that when The Prophet arrives, the doors of the Meeting Room are locked and an electronic scanner is used to detect potential recording devices such as mobile phones. They had both been amused by the irony that in trying to trace electromagnetic frequency, the scanner itself would emit a frequency that would detonate the bomb that would be placed directly in front of The Prophet.

'What is it Gillian? What's wrong? You look like you're having second thoughts'. She could barely look at him now. 'Are you'? He asked, his tone becoming more exasperated.

She nodded and her eyes began to tear up. She tried to wipe the tears away.

'The people of the local area have informed the PSNI of their intention to have a peaceful protest outside the Meeting Room. There could be thousands of them there' she said. He listened as she continued to fight back tears.
'We can't risk innocent lives Caleb' she managed to blurt out before descending into breathless sobs.
He stared through her, the psychopathy of Terror still very much at the fore of his consciousness. He felt the anger rise in him as he took in her pitiful appearance.
He tried to remain calm, for her sake more than his. 'Innocent lives, how will innocent lives be a risk? The bomb was only designed to ensure the death of The Prophet. You already know that, the blast radius is minimal'.
'We don't know that for sure' she snapped, 'and anyway, think of the smoke from the blast,the flying debris, the possible fire, think of all those people trying to escape a locked building. That's all before you even consider all those gathered outside and the risks to them. It's madness'.
Terror moved off his seat and knelt in front of Gillian imploringly.
'What has happened to you'? He asked. 'Where is Fear? You want The Prophet to die don't you? You want those who tormented you all your life to have to watch as their Leader meets his violent end don't you'? He took her jaw in his hand, gently rubbing her skin. She nodded compliantly. 'Then what's the problem'?
A large tear ran from each of her eyes, streaking down over her cheekbones and onto Terror's thumb and forefinger.
'You know that's what I want Caleb but there has to be

another way' She said pleadingly.
'This is the way Gillian and that's it, that's how it's going to be'. Terror growled.
'But… they'll be there, at the protest. We can't risk harming them Caleb, we can't'. She pleaded.
'Who… what are you talking about'? He demanded.
Realising that she couldn't avoid it any longer, she murmured, 'The Shaws, Tom and Patrick, DI Black has asked them to attend. He thinks they will be a calming influence on the protestors'. Her voice trailed off and she searched his eyes for a reaction. Finding none she continued, her voice rising and tone deepening in sheer desperation, 'You can't do this Caleb, I won't let you, please'.
He removed his hand from her face and stared hard at her. In one swift movement, he struck her hard across the face with the back of the same hand, causing her head to whip violently to the right and a streak of blood to escape from between her lips. For a few seconds she struggled to comprehend what had happened, before being hit by realisation and the fireball of pain that accompanied it.
As she tried to regain focus, she saw Terror rise to his feet and stare down at her. His face was taut with anger as were the sinews of his neck. The rapid pulsating of his jugular vein transfixed her. She had never seen him like this before and immediately feared for her life. He reached forward and pulled her hard to her feet, before slamming her against an adjacent wall with a force that pushed all the air out of her lungs. She felt the back of her head crash against the wall, though by the time that her body slid down it onto the floor, she was no

longer conscious.
Terror towered above her, surveying the damage. At first he saw no movement but then bending down for closer inspection, noticed that she was still breathing…just.
Becoming aware that his body was enveloped in a cold, clammy sweat, he sat down in the armchair again. For a long time he just sat there, still, watching Gillian's breaths becoming increasingly shallow and further apart.
He hadn't wanted any of this. He loved her. He thought she would be pleased at what he had done. She'd made her choice though and it was the wrong one. Nothing could stand in the path of Terror, not even Fear, not now, not ever. If the Shaws and her brother were more important to her than the fulfilment of his destiny, then she must deal with the consequences. Terror rose to his feet again. He knew exactly what he must do next, and with a heavy heart, he did just that.

107.

To say that I was worried about attending the protest outside The Enlightenment Church this morning would be an understatement to say the least. I was determined to carry it through though, determined to be strong, especially since I had been asked specifically to escort a very special guest to the rally, a special guest by the name of Dana Boyd. She was met with a round of applause from Beth, Ferguson and I as she entered the Farset building, linking the arm of her Mother on one side and holding a walking stick in the other. Despite being a little unsteady, there was no other indication that just a few short days ago she had been unconscious in the High Dependency Unit of the Royal Victoria Hospital. In all likelihood, she should still be in hospital, or at least at home resting, but there was no keeping her away from the protest today.

Today was going to be yet another angst ridden one, as we not only had the protest to contend with, but our folder of evidence on The Ghost, Deputy First Minister Doyle had been passed onto the PPSNI. They had deemed the evidence sufficient for charges to be brought and had requested that the PSNI bring him in for further questioning. The PPF had used the full weight of its contacts to ensure that instead of being interviewed at a Police Station, the interview was to be held at Farset. The rouse was that it would spare undue media attention and security issues, though in reality it was more

about baiting Caleb into capture.
Still, first things first I thought, we need to go.
'Let's move' I said to the others, before noticing that Gillian wasn't with Patrick.
Noting my look, he said, 'She was supposed to meet me here this morning, first thing but she's not here yet. I've tried calling a few minutes ago but nothing'.
As soon as he had started to speak, I got the feeling that something could be wrong.
'She may just be running late… but I've got a bad feeling about this' I replied.
'I haven't picked up on any negative feeling, but I'm not always able to, less so when I'm feeling anxious myself'.
'You guys go on to the protest' said Ferguson, 'I'll see if I can catch up with her and we'll meet you there'.
'I'll come with you' said Patrick.
'No, I'll be fine' Ferguson protested. 'You go ahead with the others, we won't be far behind'.
I placed the palm of my hand on Patrick's back, ushering him forward before he could object any further. Like I'd said, I was getting a bad feeling about Gillian's absence, whatever the reason and was pretty sure that wherever she was, it would be best for Ferguson to find her alone.
When we arrived, the crowds of protesters were much smaller than had been anticipated. I was thankful for that at least. We took our place at an empty area of the footpath, just opposite the main gate. The PSNI had secured the place for us for it's strategic location, should we need to address the crowd. Given the numbers, I now doubted there would be a need for

that. I unfolded the camping chair that I had been carrying before helping Dana into it. The car park of,The Enlightenment Hall was already full so I was sure that the Prophet's cavalcade would be here soon. I looked around the small crowds while we waited. They were assembled in little pockets of around six or seven, along the footpaths parallel to the road that led to the Hall. They were lost in muffled conversation until the moment when the cavalcade arrived. Patrick was right, I thought, very Presidential. Like clockwork the gates opened and the vehicles swept into the grounds. The car in the middle of the group stopped level with a covered walkway that had been erected at the entrance, wherein it was immediately surrounded by security. After some brief commotion, only a few security people remained outside. The crowds, including us, watched on silently. Whether anyone cared to admit it or not, we were temporarily awed. We waited patiently for the meeting to end and The Prophet and his followers to leave. For us each minute felt like an hour. Not just because we were waiting to stand in protest at,The Enlightenment and all that they stood for. That was only part of it. The more important reason why time seemed to be passing so slowly, was that we were all now sick with worry, as Ferguson and Gillian were yet to arrive.

108.

After trying unsuccessfully to reach Gillian on her phone several more times, Ferguson was now on the road, en route to Caleb Doyle's, Malone Avenue Home. He had initially intended to go to Gillian's apartment in Ridgeway Street but figured it that since Doyle's house was the last place she was known to have been, it should be his first port of call. On arrival, he noticed that Doyle's car was gone but Gillian's was still there. He carefully made his way up the path and rang the doorbell, his other hand never venturing far away from the weapon he now sported, courtesy of the PPF. He waited a few moments before ringing the doorbell again. He moved to the front window, looking through to see if there was any sign of Gillian. There wasn't, though Ferguson himself shared Mark's feelings that something wasn't right. He tracked around to the back of the house and looked through the patio doors. Still nothing. He tried the door handle. It didn't budge. He returned to the front of the house and studied the front door. Although the rest of the house was fully double glazed, the front door was wooden, in keeping with the character of the other houses in the street. The lock appeared to be a straightforward mortice from what he could see. He toyed with the idea of forcing the door open. He'd done it many times before in his days on the force. He wasn't on the force now though, and this would be breaking and entering, he thought to himself. Still, he did work for the PPF now and was afforded its protection, besides, Gillian could be hurt or in danger… or worse.

The door blasted open with a bang, having felt the full measure of the force exerted by Ferguson against it. He moved through the downstairs of the house quickly, weapon drawn just in case. Still nothing, though the sitting room smelt strongly of cleaning product, most likely bleach based judging by the odour. He moved upstairs and through each of the bedrooms, continuing his anxious search. They were empty. Finally, he came to the door of what he presumed was the bathroom. It was closed, so he knocked and called out for Gillian. There was no response. He tried the door. It was locked. His heart was racing with anxiety at the prospect of what might be on the other side of it. Again he called out and again there was silence. Putting his shoulder to the door with all the force he could muster, he managed to force it open. The image he was met with when he entered the bathroom, was heartbreaking. There Gillian Rodgers lay in the bath. She was fully clothed, though the bath was half filled with water, pink with blood. Only one of her arms was visible and it bore a slash mark across her wrist. A small, bloodied knife lay on the floor beside the bath. She was dead, of that he was in no doubt. He was also in no doubt of the circumstances, he'd spent enough time as a DCI in the homicide division to be sure. The scene may have been staged to look like a suicide but he was without question that Gillian Rodgers had been murdered.

He may have been experienced he thought to himself, but no amount of experience can prepare someone to find a young girl who they cared about, in such desperately tragic circumstances. He left the room, allowing himself a luxury not often afforded to an officer finding a victim. He cried for the loss of Gillian, before composing himself and making the necessary calls he now needed to make. Firstly to the PSNI, and secondly to Mark.

109.

Terror was beginning to feel anxious as he waited amongst a small number of journalists stationed near the perimeter of The Enlightenment Meeting Hall. He looked at his watch again, he was sure at this stage that there must have been a problem with the bomb. It should have detonated by now he thought. He decided to give it a few more minutes before, if necessary, taking matters into his own hands. For now he was content to watch Mark shaw and his team from his vantage point further up the road. He was sure that neither Shaw or the others had spotted him, or at least if they had, there had been no sign of it. He was content to keep it that way. He noted Ferguson's absence from the gathering and made the assumption that he may be trying to locate Gillian. Poor Gillian, he had loved her so and wondered how he was going to be able to function without her now that she had forced him to do what he had done. He would cope for now though, after all his mission was still to be completed. The Prophet will be killed and shortly after, the man that he remembered more as The Ghost than as his Father, would too meet his long fated demise. Terror had planned to settle with Gillian after that but that was never going to be now. He was devastated by that notion.

He continued to watch Shaw from the distance, his interest peaking as Shaw received a phone call which appeared to distress him. It couldn't be Gillian, he questioned himself.

They couldn't have found her, they didn't even know where she was.
Shaw was speaking to Patrick Rodgers now. He too looked agitated, then all at once distraught and overwhelmed with what he had been told. It had to be about Gillian he thought and if that's the case, then they know about him, Caleb Doyle, probably Terror also.
Terror's head was swimming. This can't be happening, he thought. Had Gillian betrayed him? Was she playing him for a fool? He couldn't think straight. He needed to get out of here he thought. He can't afford to hang around any longer. He took his phone from his pocket and dialled the number that he had stored earlier. Within the first ring, the call connected and a bang, similar to that of a gunshot was heard from inside the Meeting Room, shortly followed by a cacophony of screaming and wailing from inside the building. He had planned to savour this kill, but now it was only a means of distraction, to facilitate his escape. He made his way quickly to his car, which had been parked up on the footpath a few yards further up the road. Wasting no time, he gunned the engine and was soon streaking past the confused onlookers who were unsure whether to turn their attention toward him or what appeared to be unfolding within The Enlightenment Assembly.
He had definitely caught the attention of Mark Shaw though, which at this stage, was the last thing that he wanted. He checked the rearview mirror and saw Shaw moving towards his own vehicle at a speed that looked much quicker than someone who had sustained the recent injuries that he had,

should be able to reach. Still, Terror was confident that there was no way that Shaw would catch him, especially since he was now at the final junction that would lead him to the beginning of the motorway. He hadn't been prepared for this, he thought. He should've had more time to work things out. He needed to think and he needed to stay out of sight until he had time to think, but where? Then it came to him, he knew just the place.

110.

I felt like my world was imploding around me in those few moments since I took Ferguson's call. Learning of the death of Gillian was devastating enough in itself, but then having to tell Patrick and the others the news was possibly one of the hardest things that I've ever had to do. I hadn't even had time to gather my own thoughts before being struck with shock again at the apparent attack inside the Meeting Hall. Then there he was, out of nowhere, trying to flee the scene, Terror.

'Stay here' I shouted to the others before running toward my car as fast as I could.

I needn't have bothered though. He'd had too much of a head start and we were in such close proximity to the motorway, that there was no way I would be able to catch him. I joined the motorway anyway, all the while trying to work out where he was going and what he would do next. I hit the telephone button on the steering wheel and scrolled down until I had Ferguson's number. I pushed the button again and the dialling tone could be heard loudly through the car speakers via the bluetooth system.

'Mark'. He answered simply, sounding dejected.

I quickly filled him in on what had happened and warned him that although unlikely, he may have Terror headed in his direction. My next call was to Beth. I needed her to get the others back to Farset safely. She answered on the first ring.

'Mark, are you OK'?

'I'm fine but I've lost him. I'm on the motorway trying to work out where he might be headed. I've warned Ferguson that he might go back there. Are you three OK'?

'Yes, we're with the PSNI officers, they're asking for your location, they're going to send a car after you'.

'Beth, I think I might have just worked out where Caleb's going to. Tell the one of the officers to contact DI Black and have him station some plainclothes police around the perimeter of the City Cemetery. I'll be in contact with him again soon. You need to get the others away from there, back to Farset'.

'I'll call Dad'.

'Good, what's it like there, does anyone know what happened'?

'The police are still trying to get access but they think that what we heard was an explosion. Most of the protesters have started to leave, probably afraid that they could be danger, others are waiting it out to see what happens'.

'Better to be safe than sorry Beth, you all need to leave as soon as you can'.

'Mark, when you get to the cemetery, wait for the police and if he's there, let them handle him. I've almost lost you once already, I don't want to face that prospect again'.

'I will, don't worry. Love you'.

'I love you too, I also know you, so please be careful'.

Taking the exit at the Park Centre, I left the motorway and drove up the Donegal Road before rejoining the Falls Road, near the Rock Bar. From there I struggled in traffic for a short distance before finally crossing the bottom of the Whiterock

Road and driving up the steep hill at the entrance of Belfast City Cemetery. If my hunch was correct, Caleb Doyle, Terror would be here. From seeing him leave abruptly, shortly after I broke the news to Patrick, I had concluded that he had realised that Gillian's body had been found and made the connection that we must be on to him. This would have thrown him, I thought. After all, we knew from his profile that he likes to plan everything meticulously, to be in control. He wasn't in control now though, so he would've needed somewhere to lie low, plan his next move. Here would be an obvious choice to do that, at least that's what I would have done in his shoes.

Uncle Sean was buried at the new part of the cemetery, where it was fairly open and views of the Whiterock Road, the Leisure Centre and Falls Park could be seen. I decided to leave the car parked up beside a monument in the older part of the cemetery before continuing up the hill on foot. I patted the side of my jacket, to ensure that my newly issued weapon from the PPF was there, though I hadn't completed any firearms training yet, making it little more than a prop. In the distance, sure enough, Caleb's car was parked near Sean's grave, whilst he stood at the grave side. If I continued straight up the hill, he was sure to spot me in the distance, so I turned left, tracking around the perimeter of the fence acting as a boundary to the Falls Park. I was then able to cut across a smaller path and approach Caleb from behind without his noticing. I quickly checked my phone. Black had text, the message alerting me that the plainclothes officers were now in place. It was only when I was almost beside him, that he registered me. He turned toward me and realising who I was, he scowled and reached toward his pocket, presumably for a weapon.

'Caleb, wait'! I put my hands up, 'You don't have to do that. I just want to talk to you, that's all'.

He sought reassurance in my eyes before scanning around him.

'No-one else knows I'm here Caleb, I promise' I lied.

He let his hand fall away from the weapon, though continued to regard me with suspicion. I lowered my hands again.

'How did you know to look here'?

'It's where I would've come to if I'd been in your position' I answered.

'And what position is that exactly Mark'? He scoffed.

'Oh. Come on Caleb, you don't have to keep up the pretence, we found her… we found Gillian'. I felt my voice begin to tremble in the mention of her name.

'Is she OK? We rowed last night, and, and I hit her'. He said, lowly.

'She's dead, Caleb' I spat, 'She's dead because you killed her'.

'No' he replied, appearing shocked, 'She can't be dead, she can't'.

'Give it up, Caleb' I growled, 'You killed her then tried to stage a suicide. What were you going to do, just leave her there, pretend to find the body when it suited you? Or was that going to be one last, sick surprise for the police to find when they searched your house on your capture? Did you really think anyone would have believed it was suicide? I would've thought that the great Terror would have known better. From what I've heard, there was very little bleeding. Strange since she was supposed to have slit her wrists. That can only mean one thing. She was already dead before the cuts were made'. I was surprised at the effect that my words had on him. He dropped to his knees, then moved to a seating position with his back against the base of the headstone. He eyes were glazed over and he looked dazed.

'I didn't want to do it Mark. I didn't want to kill her. I loved her'.

'We all did, Caleb. Why did you do it'?

'She was trying to stop me going after The Prophet, she was trying to protect you all, I guess I snapped'.

All the while he spoke, his eyes remained fixed straight ahead of him, staring blankly at another headstone at the other side of the plot.

'Why Terror, Caleb, why all those murders'?

He turned his head toward me, looking directly into my eyes.

'You wouldn't understand'.

'Try me' I countered.

'He made me what I am, he created Terror, the blood's on his hands. He has to pay, I'll make him pay'. Caleb was becoming more enraged with every word he spoke. I should try to calm him down I thought, for my own safety at least. I didn't want to though. Something inside me wanted to keep pushing.

'Who, your Dad? The Ghost'? The shock at the mention of that name was clearly visible in his expression.

'Yeah, Caleb we know all about it. Your Dad will get what he deserves soon enough, but you can't hold him responsible for all this. All this was your doing .You could easily have just killed your Father without any of the Terror stuff but that wasn't enough for you was it? You wanted to be better than him. You created Terror in response to The Ghost because of some twisted inferiority complex. He treated you with cruelty and contempt all your life and yet you still yearn for his approval'.

'You could be right in some of what you say' He said calmly, 'but the only thing I truly yearn for now, is to kill my Father. That was always going to be Terror's endgame. He began to look straight ahead of him again, as if addressing the owner of the headstone which he faced.

'He killed my Mother you know. I can't prove it but I know he did. I wasn't there when she died but there was something about how he acted when I got back that made me sure of it. His later revelation of being The Ghost confirmed it for me. He found murder easy'.

'Like Father like son, eh?' I said sarcastically.

Caleb jumped to his feet and screamed, 'How dare you compare me to my Father, I'm nothing like that man'.

I looked around Caleb where he stood, directing my full attention to Uncle Sean's headstone while I spoke.

'You're certainly right Caleb, you're nothing like your Father, nothing like him at all'. I kept my gaze fixed on the headstone and just let the statement hang in the air.

'You… you mean?'

'Yes, Caleb, that's right, you've already murdered your Father' I said with a sneer.

It felt good breaking him down like this, it was no less than what he deserved. I wasn't prepared for his next action, however, as he lunged at me, propelling me backwards toward the side of his car. We began to struggle as I tried to get free from his grip. We grappled for what was probably seconds, though it felt like minutes. He was much stronger than me and I was tiring rapidly. It was then that I saw the knife and then that I realised that I was fighting for my life. The struggle intensified as I put every bit of energy I could muster into freeing myself. It was no use though, I was fading fast. I felt the knife tear at the skin between my chest and left forearm as he caught me with it. The pain from it paled into insignificance though when compared to the ache felt by every muscle in my body as lactic acid began to build up in my system. I felt like I was about to lose consciousness when I heard the crack of a gunshot. Terror stumbled back off me and I slid down the side of the car, to the ground. He was holding the side of his thigh, which was bleeding heavily from the bullet now lodged therein. He looked in the direction that the shot had come from, whilst trying to steady himself. I followed his gaze, only to find Ferguson, in firing position, behind the relative cover of a headstone. His gun remained fixed on Terror. Terror dropped the bloodied knife and appeared to reach behind him, presumably for a weapon. Ferguson's gun rang out again and Terror toppled backwards to the ground. The dot of crimson on his chest bloomed quickly as he bled, spreading down and across his shirt.

Ferguson rushed toward me. He took off his jacket, rolled it up and placed it against my knife wound.

'Keep this pressed tight against it' he barked, before calling in the plain clothes officers and requesting an ambulance. 'Can you walk to the car, we can patch you up a bit better from the first aid kit, until the ambulance comes'? I nodded before looking down at the jacket, which was now drenched in blood. I had stupidly thought that the ambulance was for Terror and that I had only been grazed. I looked from the jacket, back toward Ferguson, who now had his arm around my waist and one of my arms around his shoulder as he tried to support me to the car.

'I thought the ambulance…' I tried to say, my breathing suddenly becoming laboured.

'…was for him. No, he won't be needing one, not now.'

111. Epilogue

Ferguson, Beth, Alecia and I stood behind Patrick as he continued to climb down over the last few stones, leading to the water's edge. Once in place, I handed him down the urn containing the ashes of his sister, our beloved Gillian. He carefully removed the lid before allowing the wind to take her around the coast of Rathlin Island and beyond. This place had seemed most fitting as a choice for Gillian's final resting place. Here she would achieve peace and freedom and perhaps finally, the closure that her spirit had craved so. Although we continued to mourn the tragic loss of a young life, Patrick although not yet able to communicate with the spirit of his sister, felt a sense of her content having released the ashes. Strangely enough, we all did.

As we walked the short distance back to the Manor House Hotel, to continue with our self imposed retreat, I again contemplated the events of this last week. We had all felt the loss of Gillian keenly, then there was the news that had been leaked regarding The Prophet, who had somehow survived the bombing, but now would only ever be a shadow of his former self. I'd guessed that this would've presented, The Enlightenment with more of a problem than that they would've had, if he had died. He was in no position to lead them now, in his vegetative state, yet while he lived, a new leader could not be elected. Although I shouldn't have, I took some delight in their quandary. I couldn't help but wonder would he soon meet his end courtesy of a close aide with beatific ambition. A likely scenario, though hopefully one that I would only ever read about.

'Lost in thought again I see, Mr Shaw' Ferguson brought me back to the moment. Beth and Patrick each had Alecia by the hand, allowing her to count to three before each swinging her off her feet in front of them. The loss of Gillian had been hard on her too, so it was nice to hear her laugh, nice to hear the three of them laugh. I looked at Ferguson as he walked by my side.

'Sorry, I've been doing that a lot this week haven't I'.

'We've all had our moments, but then you more than most' he smiled, 'still, who can blame you, after all, you did come close to losing your life, for the second time within a few months'.

The mention of Terror's stabbing me made me subconsciously look down toward the direction of my wound and sent my mind whirring into the replay of my abiding memory of that day. I was in the back of the ambulance, my wound being dressed by a paramedic. My consciousness was wavering due to the amount of blood loss but I heard it distinctly when the officer asked the question of Ferguson, 'you sure you hit him the second time?'

'Yes, definitely, I could see him starting to bleed out as I lifted Mark'.

'Well he's not there now, there's no sign of him'. I realised that I was lost in thought again and snapped myself out of it.

'Do you think they'll ever find him'? I asked Ferguson, knowing that the cemetery and it's surrounding areas had been meticulously searched by the PSNI and that they were continuing to do so.

'There's no way he could have survived his injuries. Even if he had for a while and tried to make a break for it, he would have lost consciousness before long. They'll find him'.

The newspapers were already reporting the death of Terror, Caleb Doyle, as well as the arrest and subsequent multiple murder charges that his Father and Deputy First Minister, Michael Doyle was now facing. On the advice of the PPF, we had come to Rathlin to avoid the media glare and to allow us time to grieve and time for me to recuperate.

Ferguson nodded toward Patrick, who with Beth and Alecia, had now gained considerable ground on us.

'Do you think he'll be OK'? He asked.

'In time, he will, I think'.

'I need to tell you something Mark' said Ferguson, his expression becoming much more serious, 'That day, I found her…Gillian, I stayed while the CSI processed the scene. I saw something in the bedroom. I wasn't sure at first but I checked out the security footage later'.

'What was it?' I asked, with concern and intrigue.

'An outfit… the same outfit worn by the girl who delivered the packages to the Pinkertons. It was her Mark, Gillian delivered those packages'.

'Does anyone else know what you found'? I asked.

'The whole house has been processed for evidence now, but I think the focus was more on finding evidence against Doyle, so I would doubt it'.

Now I nodded in Patrick's direction.

'He's been through enough, we all have, let's just leave it at that'.

'That's exactly what I thought, I just needed to share it with someone'.

'I'm glad you did' I nodded.

Trying not to dwell on what I had just heard, I changed the subject.

'I wish we could stay here for a few more days'.

'I know, but we can only hide away here for so long I suppose. Anyway, you have your flight to catch tomorrow afternoon, bossman'.

Tomorrow I was headed for New York, to attend my first PPF meeting as a member of the Board. The first item on the agenda was a debrief on the Terror case, something that I was in no way comfortable about leading on.

'Time enough to worry about that tomorrow' I said, 'for now my main priority is to have a drink to the life and memory of Gillian Rodgers'. A short time later we all did just that.

112.

The house was in complete darkness as the #Terrorist made her way from the kitchen, knife in hand, through the open planned dining room-come sitting room,into the hallway and up the stairs. The darkness didn't bother her at all, in fact, in some ways she embraced it. It didn't hamper her movement either, after all she had been in this house, Mark Shaw's house thousands of times before so she was well used with the layout.

Having reached the landing, she looked in the direction of Alecia Shaw's bedroom. A soft snoring could be heard emanating from the little girl's room. The #Terrorist moved further along the landing and crept into the room where Beth Shaw slept. She felt an element of pain at what she was about to do but Mark Shaw would pay for taking Terror away from her, they all would. She had lost her lover and her leader at the hand of Ferguson and Shaw and she was determined that they would suffer they way she has, ache with grief the way she has. Moving closer to the bed she stood over Beth Shaw as she slept. Tears brimmed in her eyes as she raised the knife and held it above head height. She gave a low whimper as she prepared to bring the knife down, a whimper which made Beth wake with a start. She saw the fear flicker in Beth's eyes with the realisation that she was about to die, die at the hands of her best friend and unbeknownst to her #Terrorist, Susan Blake. In one swift movement the knife came down hard, ending a relationship which began in the playground over thirty years earlier.

A Note From The Author

This book would not have been possible without the help and support of my family and friends, particularly Heather, Bella, Patsy, John, Ellie and June. For each of you and the things that you have done to help and support me throughout this project and throughout my life, I will be forever grateful.

A further note of thanks to My Wonderful Wife Heather and our Beautiful Daughter Bella for putting up with the long hours that I have spent in my Study, researching and writing.

Finally, thanks to Sean, for pushing me on this project on each of my visits.

About The Author

A visit to a medium and a well-timed word from his wife led west Belfast man, James Murphy, the confidence to get writing. And, he's never looked back since...

With his début novel, The Rise of Terror, now in its second print run his second book is nearing publication.

Based around the primary school building James attended the 'Terror' is a trilogy of novels based around a fictional private detective agency, Farset Investigations.

But unlike many tried and repetitive crime fiction yarns James has created an intricate web, including amongst the principal characters a medium.

When a family friend persuaded James to visit a medium he received a message telling him to knuckle down to writing.

That happened around the same time when an off-hand comment to his wife, Heather, about being able to write better than the book he was reading had her tell him plain and straight to stop talking about it and do it!

The 41-year-old saw The Rise of Terror published as he turned 40, a welcome birthday present and the motivation to keep working at his writing.

The Queen's University graduate went on after gaining his degree in English to qualify as a teacher of English at the Institute of Education, London.

With a family and a career that has seen James take on roles such as Head of Department and School Principal getting the time to write hasn't always been easy – especially when inspiration, in his own words, can pop into your head at four in the morning and you just have to open the computer.

A firm believer in researching his work James is set to release 'I Am Terror' in December 2017.

11477802R00200

Printed in Great Britain
by Amazon